maybe one day

Books by
MELISSA KANTOR

Confessions of a Not It Girl

If I Have a Wicked Stepmother,
Where's My Prince?

The Breakup Bible

Girlfriend Material

The Darlings Are Forever

The Darlings in Love

Better Than Perfect

MELISSA KANTOR

maybe

one

day

HARPER TEEN
An Imprint of HarperCollinsPublishers

HarperTeen is an imprint of HarperCollins Publishers.

Maybe One Day
Copyright © 2014 by Melissa Kantor
All rights reserved. Printed in the United States of America.
No part of this book may be used or reproduced in any manner whatsoever without written permission except in the case of brief quotations embodied in critical articles and reviews. For information address HarperCollins Children's Books, a division of HarperCollins Publishers, 195 Broadway, New York, NY 10007.
www.epicreads.com

Library of Congress Cataloging-in-Publication Data
Kantor, Melissa.
Maybe one day / Melissa Kantor. — First edition.
      pages   cm
      Summary: "Zoe thought that being cut from her ballet program was the worst thing that could happen, but when her best friend, Olivia, is diagnosed with a life-threatening disease, Zoe quickly learns that not being able to dance is the least of her problems"—Provided by publisher.
      ISBN 978-0-06-227921-7
      [1. Best friends—Fiction.   2. Friendship—Fiction.   3. Leukemia—Fiction.   4. Sick—Fiction.   5. Ballet dancing—Fiction.   6. High schools—Fiction.   7. Schools—Fiction.   8. Family life—New Jersey—Fiction.   9. New Jersey—Fiction.]   I. Title.
PZ7.K12823May   2014   2013008064
[Fic]—dc23   CIP
                                                                          AC

Typography by Andrea Vandergrift
14 15 16 17 18   CG/RRDH   10 9 8 7 6 5 4 3 2 1
❖
First paperback edition, 2015

To Becky Helfer

"... love is strong as death ..."
—Song of Solomon

❧ prologue ❧

Summer before sophomore year

"I realize this is upsetting news," said Ms. Daniels, watching me and Olivia across her enormous wooden desk.

There was no way I was letting her see me cry. I bit my lip and stared at the wall behind her.

It was hung with photographs of ballerinas—on stage wearing elaborate tutus; in leg warmers and cutoff T-shirts, draped over the barre; at dressing tables, the lights around their mirrors casting a halo as they stared soulfully at their own reflections. Across the bottom of each was a scrawled message and an autograph, the first letters of the signatures dwarfing the rest of the name like principle dancers before the corps de ballet. It didn't matter that you couldn't decipher all the names. If you had been dancing as long as I had, if you had been in the ballet world your entire life, each of the women on

Ms. Daniels's wall was as recognizable as the president of the United States.

Olivia and I had dreamed that one day our photographs would be on Ms. Daniels's wall too.

But apparently, they were not going to be.

Ms. Daniels had called us into her office immediately after the final class of the summer intensive, and now she sat and fussed with a heavy-looking silver pen that lay on the center of her immaculate blotter. We had known it probably wasn't good news she was going to deliver when she asked to see us; girls who met with Ms. Daniels after class almost always walked out of her office crying. So we'd been ready to hear we hadn't performed as well as we should have this summer and that we were going to be repeating a class in the fall.

But not this.

We'd never imagined this.

Out of the corner of my eye, I could see Olivia's bare arm. The strap of her leotard had slipped off her shoulder, and as I watched, she slid it back up. I would have done the same thing—as NYBC dancers, we'd been warned for years about the ramifications of looking sloppy at school—but suddenly the gesture struck me as insane.

Who cared if we looked sloppy anymore?

Ms. Daniels abruptly put her pen in the drawer and glanced at her watch.

Olivia cleared her throat. "We both . . ." Her voice caught, and for a second I thought she was going to start crying, but she just swallowed and went on. "Zoe and I worked very hard this summer."

"I realize that," said Ms. Daniels. "Unfortunately, hard work is not always enough." She touched her tongue to her lip, then slipped it back into her mouth when she saw me notice.

Olivia and I had been dancing with the elite NYBC—the most competitive ballet school in the country—since we were nine years old. The year we'd auditioned, eight *hundred* other girls had tried out for twelve spots. We'd planned on auditioning for the studio company when we were juniors in high school. If we'd been accepted, senior year we would have left Wamasset High to take dance classes at NYBC full-time, earning our high school diplomas by correspondence class. We'd get our own apartment in Manhattan and have glamorous tours through the capitals of Europe, brilliant reviews in *Dance Magazine* and the *New York Times*, thrilling romances with visiting dancers from Moscow and Paris.

Little girls would put posters of us on their walls.

"I appreciate that this is difficult news to process, so I want to make sure what I am saying is completely clear," said Ms. Daniels, looking from me to Olivia. "There is no longer space for you at NYBC."

If I even tried to answer her, I was definitely going to start bawling. For five years, Monday through Friday, we'd come into Manhattan from New Jersey. Saturday mornings, while other girls were sleeping late or shopping at the mall or playing sports or doing homework or going to birthday parties, we went back to the city and danced some more.

And now, according to the school's director, we were finished.

Did she really think her message might somehow be *unclear*?

"We understand." My voice was shaking, and suddenly I felt Olivia's hand on mine. It wasn't until she touched me that I realized how tightly I had been squeezing the arm of the chair.

For a second, I took my eyes off Ms. Daniels and looked at Olivia in the chair next to mine. She was still staring straight ahead, and as I watched, her profile morphed into Olivia in the dressing room at the New Jersey ballet school where we'd met when we were four. *Can you help me?* she'd said, walking over to me with the barrette that had slid out of her long blond hair.

Well, there was no way I was going to be able to help her with this.

I looked back at Ms. Daniels. She adjusted the pin shaped like a toe shoe that held her elaborate silk scarf in place. Once again, her tongue flickered at the corner of her mouth.

The silence deepened. Finally, Ms. Daniels stood up. Then we did too.

"I hope you will both see this not just as an end but as a beginning." She gave a small, sad smile. "Dance is one thing to do with your life. But it is not the only thing."

The words were professional. Smooth. I imagined her polishing them semester after semester as she spoke to girls just like me and Olivia. Girls who had worked hard. Who had worked so hard they had done nothing *but* work. Girls who had given everything they had to dance. But who were still never going to be good enough.

I made this weird noise, half laugh, half cry. It must have sounded as if I was choking, and Livvie slipped her fingers into mine.

Ms. Daniels didn't acknowledge the sound, just held her hand out to me. Not knowing what else to do, I shook it with my free hand, then turned away and walked across her office to the door, my toe shoes silent on the thick beige carpet.

"Good luck," said Ms. Daniels. "Keep in touch."

"Thank you, Ms. Daniels," said Olivia as automatically as she'd adjusted the strap of her leotard. Then she followed me out of Ms. Daniels's office and pulled the door shut behind us.

We looked at each other. Neither of us spoke.

This is the worst thing that will ever happen, I thought, and as I stared into Olivia's enormous green eyes, I knew she was thinking the same thing. *This is the worst thing that will happen to us in our entire lives.*

❧ part 1 ❧

Fall,
junior year

1

Since it was the first day of school, Olivia's brother Jake gave us a ride, and as he slid into an empty space in the parking lot, Emma Cho, a wildly enthusiastic cheerleader who'd been trying more or less since birth to make Jake her boyfriend, hurled herself at us so violently that for a second I thought Jake had hit her with the car. But the blinding smile she flashed Jake as we got out and the "He-ey, Jake!" she sang to him made it seem unlikely she'd just been rammed by his Honda.

"Hey," he answered. Jake was a senior, *and* really good-looking *and* he was on the football team, so while Emma might have been the most determined, she was hardly the only girl who was madly in love with him. He and his best friend Calvin Taylor, who was the QB, should have listed *beating girls off with a stick* as an extracurricular activity on their college applications. Jake hugged Emma back, but he didn't linger, just said "See ya" to all of us and headed over to join a bunch of senior guys who were standing near the edge of the parking lot. When he did that, Emma looked briefly forlorn, then threw her arms around Olivia.

"Hi, Livs!" Her red-and-white cheerleading skirt flared out above her knees. High, *high* above her knees.

"Hey, Emma," said Olivia, hugging her back. Right after we got the ax from NYBC, Olivia started teaching a dance class for at-risk girls at this rec center in Newark where her mom's on the board. A lot of people from our high school satisfied their community service requirement there—including the cheerleaders—and somzetimes Olivia had lunch with the squad on Saturdays after they taught their classes. That my best friend regularly hung out with cheerleaders was one of the great mysteries of my life.

"Zoe!" Emma squealed, hurling herself at me when her hug with Olivia came to an end.

"Oh. Hey. I mean, hi. Hi, Emma." I patted her awkwardly on the back. The cheerleaders were always nice enough to me, but I couldn't help feeling like they saw me as this weird birth defect of Olivia's, something she would have been wise to have removed but for some reason chose to live with.

"I *still* can't believe you guys didn't try out for cheer squad last spring," Emma said, stepping out of my lackluster embrace and shaking her head in amazement.

"I couldn't. Soccer," I answered immediately, even though after one awful season as the world's worst soccer player, I'd dropped it.

"Dance class," said Livvie.

Emma made a pouty face. "But *we* do the tumbling class *and* we cheer. You could do *both*."

"I *know!*" said Olivia, ignoring Emma's implied criticism. "You guys are awesome."

I smiled vaguely.

Placated by Olivia's praise, Emma waved good-bye to us, made Olivia promise to have lunch with the squad on Saturday, then skittered off to join her fellow cheerleaders. As I watched her go, I spotted Bethany and Lashanna. They waved at me and I waved back. I'd been nervous that they'd be mad when I didn't go out for soccer again this year, but they'd seemed to understand.

Taking Livvie by the hand, I started walking toward them, but she pulled me back, reaching into her bag and pulling out her phone. "Wait a sec."

I groaned but stayed put while Livvie fussed with her phone, then swiped at a lock of heavy blond hair that had dropped over her eyes. Until last summer I'd also had long hair, though my hair is so black it's almost blue. But the day after we were thrown out of NYBC, Livvie came with me to Hair Today, Gone Tomorrow and watched me get approximately three feet of hair chopped off my head. When the woman

13

asked if I wanted to take a lock to remember it by, I just stared at her like, *Why would I want to remember my hair?*

No more dance. No more soccer. I shivered slightly. My parents and my guidance counselor were on my case to pick an extracurricular activity and to pick it fast. I'd played some tennis up at my grandparents' this summer, but was I seriously going to try out for the tennis team like I'd told my parents I might? Livvie slipped her arm around my waist, and we stood shoulder to shoulder as she held the camera up at face level. "Say, 'Olivia is so cheesy.'"

Glad to be pulled out of my thoughts, I repeated, "Olivia is so cheesy," and she snapped the picture. To say Livvie had dealt better than I had with our being dumped from NYBC would be an understatement. Sometimes I wondered if the secret to being well-adjusted wasn't blond hair.

"Nice," she said, angling the screen toward me. Livvie and I were almost exactly the same height—five seven—so our faces were right next to each other. Olivia was grinning widely, her dimple pronounced, her eyes sparkling.

"You look like a prom queen," I told her. "I'm all 'Take me to your leader.'" I have big eyes, which I'd always known but which I hadn't fully appreciated were quite so enormous until I got my pixie cut. I looked exactly like a cartoon drawing of an alien.

"You're beautiful. Your eyes are seriously *awesome*. No joke." She hip-checked me absently, still studying the screen.

"Am I crazy or do I have a picture of you wearing this exact same shirt?"

I glanced at the cap sleeve of my dark blue T-shirt. "That's impossible. I've never worn this shirt before."

"Hmmm . . ." Livvie bit her upper lip and stared at the image, then shrugged. "Well, whatever." She dropped her phone into her bag, took me by the hand, and led me toward the front steps of Wamasset High, so named because on this site a proud tribe of Wamasset Indians made their last stand against a group of British settlers who were ultimately successful in their attempt to brutally exterminate every last one of them.

"Do you think it's comforting to the dead Wamasset that the descendants of their murderers attend a high school named in their honor?" I asked.

Livvie'd been trying to get me to have a more positive outlook on life, and now she turned around and pointed her finger at me threateningly. "Stop that."

I held my hands up in a gesture of surrender, and we headed into the lobby. The noise was deafening. Bethany and Lashanna weren't anywhere to be seen, but half a dozen cheerleaders were, including Stacy Shaw—one of the captains of the cheerleading squad—and Jake's would-be girlfriend Emma.

STACY: (*Screaming.*) Aaaaah!

EMMA: (*Also screaming.*) Aaaaah!

(*They embrace.*)

STACY: (*Wails.*) I wish you'd gotten captain. (*She bursts into tears.*)

EMMA: (*Also bursting into tears.*) Staaaaaaay!

STACY: Emms!!!!

EMMA: I love you so much.

STACY: I love *you* so much. (*They continue to embrace, weeping.*)

Olivia and I made eye contact. "You regularly lunch with those people," I pointed out.

"They're not as bad once you get to know them," she insisted.

"Let me guess: That's what you tell them about me, right?"

Laughing, we turned out of the lobby and down the two hundreds corridor. When we got to my homeroom, Livvie hugged me good-bye.

"Fortress after school, right?" she asked, even though odds were we'd have at least a couple of classes together.

"Right," I agreed. As I hugged her back, I realized something. "Hey, Livs," I said, pulling away. "You're not just my best friend—you're my extracurricular activity."

Livvie pressed her hands to her chest and got a dreamy expression on her face. "I've always longed to be an extracurricular activity." Then she kissed me lightly on the cheek and headed down the corridor. "Love ya," she called over her shoulder.

"Love ya," I called back.

I stepped into the classroom, nervous for a second that no one I hung out with would be in homeroom with me, but then I saw Bethany. She saw me, too, grinned, and moved her bag off the desk next to hers. Grinning back at her, I made my way across the room. Just as the bell rang I slipped into my seat, and then Ms. Evans raised her head from the papers she'd been shuffling on her desk, walked over to the door, and shut it. She looked around the room at all of us as we slowly got quiet. "Welcome, everyone!" she announced, the tight curls of her perm bobbing as she nodded and smiled at us. "I hope you all had a wonderful summer."

It was official: junior year had begun.

2

In Olivia's backyard was an enormous beech tree that had to be about a hundred years old. In it was what we call the fortress.

The fortress was a . . . thing her dad and Jake built in the tree a few summers ago. It was supposed to be a place that would lure the twins, Tommy and Luke (they were eight now), outside for hours of fun so they wouldn't drive their mom batshit with their running around in the house.

Everyone called it the fortress, but really it was just a platform. The plan had been for it to be a *real* fort, with walls and a ceiling and everything (I remember looking at some pretty complicated architectural drawings her dad commissioned), but then Jake made the football team and wasn't so into building it and Tommy and Luke said a tree fort was babyish and now Livvie and I were pretty much the only ones who used it.

At five o'clock, we climbed up for what we felt was a much-deserved break. It didn't seem possible that we had so much homework already, but after an hour and a half of working in Livvie's kitchen, neither of us had put a dent in our assignments. It was only the first day of school. How were we ever going to survive junior year?

We lay on the wooden planks of the fortress, half trying to get our heads around the amount of work we had to do, half watching Jake and Calvin Taylor toss a football back and forth.

"I can't believe they come home from football practice and play football," I said. We were on our stomachs, our chins resting on our hands.

"Zoe, we danced for, like, six hours a day, remember?"

I ignored her question, which was rhetorical anyway, and we watched Jake and Calvin in silence. Calvin leaped up to catch the ball Jake had just thrown. For a second he seemed to hang in the air before gently dropping to earth, almost as graceful as a dancer.

"I cannot get over how hot Calvin Taylor is," said Livvie.

I eyed him lazily. He and Jake were both wearing shorts and no shirts, and their skin was shiny with sweat. Jake wasn't fat, but compared to Calvin, who was long and lean, he was definitely thickish. You couldn't see it from up in the tree, but Calvin had a beautiful face that was saved from being too pretty by his nose being a little crooked from where it got broken during some football game.

"I swear to you," Livvie continued, "we had a moment."

I groaned. "Are you *still* talking about that ice cream run you guys did? Livvie, that was, like, a *month* ago. Besides, you'd have to murder all those cheerleaders and then climb over their dead bodies to get to him."

Livvie smacked her lips exaggeratedly. "It might be worth it."

I must have been the only girl at Wamasset who didn't think Calvin Taylor was God's gift to our zip code. He'd moved here late—the summer before his sophomore year—and immediately made varsity football and every girl's top-ten list. He and Jake started hanging out a lot, and at first I didn't think he was so bad, but then I found out what an asshole he really was.

That year, my freshman year, I had this . . . well, I guess you couldn't say boyfriend since we went on exactly one date. His name was Jackson, and his sister was in my and Olivia's class and he was a sophomore like Jake and Calvin. Livs and I went to a Halloween party at his sister's house, and Jackson and I ended up hanging out a little, and the next night he called and asked me out on a date. Like a real date—a dinner-and-a-movie date. The whole thing would have been awkward enough (what with our barely knowing each other and his parents driving us to the mall), but then when we got to the theater (we were going to see the new

James Bond movie), pretty much the *entire* football team was there. Most of the guys tried to be cool about it, just all, "Hey, Zoe; hey, Jackson," and kind of pretending they didn't see us, but Calvin kept giving us these knowing looks while we were waiting on line to buy snacks. And then he came over to our seats during the previews with a bag of popcorn that he said was "special delivery from the guys for the lovely young couple." Jackson laughed, but I seriously wanted to punch Calvin. It was hard for me to even think about whether I was glad Jackson was holding my hand during the movie because I was so busy hating Calvin, and later, when Jackson and I were waiting for his dad in this darkish part of the parking lot and Jackson started kissing me, I could barely concentrate because I kept expecting Calvin to jump out from between two parked cars and be all "Surprise!" Jackson's family moved away the day after our date (okay, it was more like a month later, but between football and dance we never found a time to go out again), so I guess you could say Calvin Taylor not only ruined my first date *and* my first kiss but also my first (and only) relationship.

The idea that my best friend might be falling for my nemesis was more than I could take.

I rolled my eyes. "Calvin's the worst, Livs. Don't be another notch in his belt."

She was still watching him and Jake. "I'm telling you I'm, like, bizarrely drawn to him."

Thinking a different tactic might be more effective, I got to my hands and knees and crawled toward Olivia. "He's so handsome and magnetic. And he lives in that mansion up in the Estates. Beware! Maybe the reason you're so drawn to him is because he's really a *vampire*! *Raarh!*" When Livvie laughed, I growled, baring imaginary fangs, then rolled onto my back and stared into the leaves of the tree. I could barely feel a breeze, but their shimmering proved that there was one.

"Liv?"

"Mmm?"

"What do you think I should do?"

"About what?" She yawned. "Sorry. I'm so tired. Did I tell you I almost fell asleep in physics? I jerked awake at the last second, but I think Mr. Thomas is onto me."

"About my *life*. What should I do with my life?" I sat up and looked over Olivia's enormous Victorian house and across the hedges at the edge of her yard. Up and down the block were other houses, and in each of the houses were people. What did *they* do with their lives?

"Teach the dance class with me," said Olivia, and she rolled onto her side and leaned her head on her hand. "The girls would *love* you."

"No dance," I said, shaking my head. It was amazing to me how . . . accepting Livvie had been of our being cut from NYBC. She taught a ballet class once a week, organized the spring recital for her dancers, then led a dance camp for two weeks over the summer. She even kept the photo from our first dance recital on her desk—the two of us smiling at the camera, our pink tutus squashed because we're standing so close together. I, on the other hand, in an attempt to escape my failed dance career, had joined (and then quit) the soccer team, ripped the posters of ballerinas off my walls, thrown out all my dance paraphernalia, and forbidden anyone from uttering the word "ballet" in my presence. I couldn't help envying her a little, but Livvie had always been the one to take things in stride.

Why should this be any different?

I watched her face, seeing her make the decision not to push me on the dance thing. "And you're *sure* you don't want to do soccer?" she asked.

"Positive." The girls on the soccer team were awesome, but everything about the sport had felt so *wrong*. I'd gone out for the team because I wanted to get as far away from dance as possible, but instead of making me forget dancing, soccer had only made me miss it more. I remembered standing on the soccer field, all that sky and grass and the feeling that without ballet, there wasn't enough gravity to keep me connected to earth.

A leaf dropped onto my foot, and I picked it up and tore a thin strip from the edge. It was incredible how our bloody, blistered feet had healed so beautifully over the past year. My toes shimmered with the pale pink polish I'd chosen when

Livvie and I had gotten pedicures on Labor Day.

Livvie stretched her arms over her head, then reached for my ankle and patted it. "Just tell me *why* you won't do the dance class," she said sleepily.

I tried to put into words exactly how I felt. "I just . . ." I tilted my head and studied the canopy of leaves over our head, as if the answer might be written there. My explanation came slowly. "I thought . . . it was going to be my whole life, Livs. It *was* my whole life. And now it's . . . what? A hobby? That feels so *wrong*."

Livvie squeezed my foot to show she understood. "You could do something else at the rec center, you know? It wouldn't have to be dance. There's the tumbling class."

I raised my eyebrows at her. "You aren't seriously hooking me up with the cheer squad, are you?"

"The kids in the class are adorable," she said, not answering my question. Then she yawned again.

I turned away and snorted. "I'm not even dignifying that suggestion with a response." I thought about how freshman year she and I had satisfied our community service requirement with the performances of *The Nutcracker* that NYBC did for the city's public schools. Last year, I'd spent half a dozen afternoons cleaning up garbage at a nearby nature preserve with the soccer team. It was weird how far-reaching extracurricular activities were. Just because you did one thing, a whole bunch of other things—who you had lunch with, where you did your community service, what parties you went to—fell into place.

If you *didn't* do something, on the other hand, you had no place to fall into.

I was so busy thinking about how I needed a place that I almost didn't hear Olivia when she asked quietly, "What do you love, Zoe?"

I made my voice deep and mock-seductive, glad to be distracted from my depressing train of thought. "You, baby!"

But Livvie didn't laugh. After a minute, I looked over at her. Her eyes were closed, and she was breathing rhythmically.

It had been a long day, and though the sun was low, it was still warm out, warm enough that I could imagine how easy it would be to drift off into sleep. Still, no one fell asleep just like that. Was she faking it?

I nudged her calf gently with my foot, but she didn't stir. She really was asleep.

Wrapping my arms around my legs, I leaned my cheek on my knees, thinking about what Livvie had asked. It was too embarrassing to admit the truth, like confessing you loved a guy who didn't know you existed.

Still.

In my head I heard the music start, felt the grip of my toe shoes, the butterflies in my stomach. The tension in my legs intensified, as if I were a racehorse eager for the starting gate to be lifted. For years, every moment I wasn't dancing was a moment I was waiting to dance. Dancing had been how I knew I was alive. How I knew I was me.

Without it, I somehow . . . wasn't.

So there was only one answer to Olivia's question.

"Dance," I whispered, so quietly that even if Livvie had been awake, she wouldn't have heard me. "I love dance."

❧ 3 ❧

Mostly to get my parents off my back I went to the first meetings of the yearbook and the newspaper staff. My mom kept telling me I should try out for the play, but one look at the drama club was enough to let me know that it was the last place I wanted to spend my free time. The actors at Wamasset had all the bitchiness of the NYBC dancers, and the idea that I'd spend my free time with a bunch of backstabbers *not* dancing was laughable. I might have been lost, but I wasn't insane.

But at least the drama club's single-mindedness felt familiar. All the other activities—Model Congress, yearbook, Science Club—just seemed like things people were doing to pass the time or to make colleges accept them. I couldn't see building my life around the passage of a fake Senate vote or the taking of the perfect photo of the volleyball team. It all seemed so . . . pointless. If I was going to do something, I wanted to give my life over to it, to love it, to wake up in the morning for it like I had for dance.

Was I seriously going to get out of bed every day for Chess Club?

By the time Saturday morning rolled around, it was starting to feel like my extracurricular activity was convincing my parents how busy I was without any extracurricular activities. My mom got up early and went to the gym, but I told her I had too much homework to join her. When I made the mistake of wandering out to the back deck, my dad asked if I wanted to help in the garden. I told *him* I had homework, and he asked if I could at least walk Flavia before I started working. I did, then sat in the kitchen—just out of his line of vision—with a cup of coffee cooling on the table in front of me. The thought of spending my Saturday morning writing an essay on imagery in the opening chapters of *Madame Bovary* was more than I could bear.

I am doing nothing, I thought to myself. *If anyone asks me what I did this weekend, I can say, I literally did nothing, and it won't be that annoying thing where people say literally when they mean figuratively.*

Then I got Olivia's text.

coming 4 u 4 lunch. no thank u helping of cheer squad.

A "no thank you helping" was what you got at Olivia's house if her mom was serving something you didn't like. For example, if she were to say, "Can I offer you some calf brain?" you might say, "No, thank you." And then she would put a tiny bit of calf brain on your plate because Mrs. Greco believed a person should try everything at least once.

In the past when Olivia had invited me to go to lunch with her and the cheerleaders, I'd always taken a pass, but if I was still sitting at the kitchen table when my mom got home from the gym, my only options would be starting my essay or discussing with my parents (once again) my future.

The choice was clear. I got to my feet.

Mrs. Greco's right, I thought as I dumped out the remaining coffee from my cup and put the mug in the dishwasher. *You should try everything once.*

Except, I quickly discovered, having lunch with Stacy Shaw, Emma Cho, and the rest of the Wamasset cheer squad. Because even the tiniest calf had a bigger brain than they did.

We were seated in a horseshoe-shaped booth big enough for eight. Emma was between me and Olivia. Immediately after we ordered, Emma turned to Olivia, gave her a hug, stroked her hair several times, then rested her head on Olivia's shoulder with a sigh. "I wish you were my little sister," she said. "You are just so *awesome.*"

Despite her general tolerance for cheerleader behavior, Livvie was clearly taken aback by Emma's petting her as if she were a cat. She didn't say anything, though, just sat there looking uncomfortable.

I turned my head and asked Emma, "Is that your way of saying you wish you were married to Olivia's brother?"

"Oh, *snap!*" said Stacy. She reached across the table to high-five me as the other members of the cheer squad laughed. Emma looked embarrassed, and I felt bad. Maybe I'd needed to rescue Livvie, but did I have to do it by being a total bitch? It wasn't like Emma had ever done anything to me. Still, there was Stacy's hand, hovering halfway between us. I guess I could have *not* high-fived her, thereby alienating both Emma *and* Stacy in one fell swoop, but I chickened out and gave Stacy a limp high five back.

"You guys, aren't those kids *sooo* cute?" wailed a sophomore named Hailey, thankfully changing the subject. Since sliding in next to her in the backseat of the car, I'd observed that every word that came out of Hailey's mouth was a cry of some kind. It was as if she lived in a state of constant emotional suffering so great she could not contain it, not even to order her salad with dressing on the side.

"They are," Olivia agreed. She stretched her arms over her head and rolled her neck. The gesture was graceful, but tired. It made me wonder if what I'd thought was discomfort earlier was really exhaustion.

"You guys, I am literally crying for those little girls," said Emma, who, for the record, was not actually crying. "Their lives are, like, really hard. One of the new girls in the class told me that her brother's in *jail*."

Sitting in the two chairs at the end of the table were identical twins on the cheer squad, seniors named Margaret and Jamie Bailor, who as far as I could tell had received less than their fair share of the squad's IQ. One of them said, "That's why it's really good that we're teaching them tumbling and stuff."

"Seriously," agreed whichever twin had not made the initial point. "They need something in their lives. Tumbling is so much better than drugs."

That night we lay side by side, Livvie on her bed, me on the trundle bed. The sprinklers were twirling a soothing rhythm outside her window.

"Okay," she said, "I sense today's lunch did not help us make strides toward your teaching tumbling with the cheer squad."

A few glow-in-the-dark stars were still stuck to her ceiling from where we'd put them up in middle school. We'd planned to do an exact replica of the constellations in the northern hemisphere, but halfway through the Big Dipper we'd just started sticking them up any which way.

"An excellent deduction," I said, yawning.

It was quiet for a minute, and then Livvie yawned also. "It's so crazy that we're juniors. Remember when we were freshmen? The juniors were older than Jake! We're now older

31

than people who were older than Jake used to be." We both laughed at how nonsensical the last part of her sentence was.

I thought about freshman year, watching the juniors and seniors stand at the doors to the parking lot, swinging their car keys as they waited to go out to lunch with their friends. They'd seemed so . . . grown-up. So sure of themselves. I rubbed my forehead as if to remove the image of those confident upperclassmen from my brain and said, "I feel like people are going to expect us to know things we don't actually know."

"Yes!" There was the rustle of the sheet as Livvie rolled over. In the faint light coming under the door, I saw that she'd propped herself up on her arm and was facing me. "Driving! SATs! College. It always seemed so far away, but it's not. It's *here*." She lay back down. "I don't feel ready."

"It's still kind of far away," I pointed out.

"Emphasis on the *kind of*."

I could hear footsteps on the floor above us, and I knew it was one of Livvie's parents checking on the twins. Then I heard someone coming down the stairs, then her mom talking to her dad. The hall light went off, and the room, which had seemed dark already, became nearly pitch-black. I pulled the soft sheet up to my chin, smelling the familiar smell of the detergent Livvie's mom used.

"Calvin really *looks* at you when you talk to him." Livvie's voice was growing sleepy. "It's intense."

"That's what you said about Milo Bradley," I pointed out.

Milo Bradley was this boy who went to private school in Manhattan and took classes at Juilliard. He was a couple of years older than us, and Olivia and I met him freshman year right after Christmas break at a café we always went to when we had time between classes. He was cute in this nerdalicious way, and the three of us started getting together for coffee on a regular basis. He and Livvie would have these long, intense conversations, and it seemed pretty clear they were into each other, so I'd try to make myself scarce by doing stuff like staring intently at the screen of my phone and going to the bathroom every thirty seconds. Olivia went to watch him rehearse a few times (he played the piano) in these private practice spaces they have at Juilliard. It was kind of a big deal because we had to lie to her parents about how *we* were having extra rehearsals just so she could sneak away with him.

Each time they went off together, Livvie and I were sure they were *totally* going to fool around, but they never did. Once, when they were sitting next to each other on the piano bench, he kissed her hand, and another time he put his arm around her, but that was it, even though Olivia was practically *dying* to make out with him. She was too scared to ask him what was going on, so finally she just started telling him she was busy whenever he called to make plans. The third time it happened, he said, "I don't get it. Are you breaking up with me?" I was with her at the time, and when she said, "I guess I *am* breaking up with you," I just *lost it*. I mean, were they even going *out*? She had to practically beat me to death with a toe shoe to get me to stop laughing loud enough for him to hear me.

It had been a while since I'd teased her about dumping her clearly gay boyfriend, but Milo's being a really good listener had been something she'd referenced constantly, so her saying the same thing about Calvin Taylor seemed a good reason to bring him up.

"Don't remind me about Milo," she wailed. "I'm begging you."

I yawned. "Calvin's annoying." But I was too sleepy to really care if she liked him or not.

"Mmmm," she answered, and I heard the rustle of sheets as she rolled over. "Don't worry about finding something to do, Zoe," she mumbled after a pause. "Everything will work out. I can tell. This is going to be a great year."

I could feel myself dozing off, surrounded by the sounds and smells of Livvie's house, as familiar to me as my own. My last thought before I fell asleep was that Olivia was right. This was going to be a really great year.

∽ 4 ∾

Livvie woke up with a fever Sunday, and she missed school Monday. Monday night when I talked to her she said she'd be in school Tuesday morning, but then she texted me and said she'd woken up with a fever again and her mom was taking her to the doctor.

I called Livvie at the start of lunch Tuesday, but she didn't pick up the phone. I was standing by my locker, finishing leaving her a message, when Mia Roberts turned down the corridor.

Mia was the girl on the soccer team I knew the least. She'd been new freshman year (before coming east she'd lived in L.A.), and unlike the rest of the team (who hung out pretty much exclusively with one another), Mia hung with a lot of different people. And she didn't just not hang out exclusively with the team; she also looked nothing like the other girls we played with, all of whom—whether white or black, Asian or Hispanic, freshmen or seniors—were very . . . American-looking. Clean-cut. Like, you could use any one of them in photos for an antidrug campaign.

But Mia's hair was bleached white except for the tips, which were blue. When she wasn't wearing her soccer uniform, she wore black pretty much exclusively, down to black motorcycle boots or Doc Martens.

"Hey," she said. Today she was wearing a pair of black leggings with lace at the bottom and a black tank top. Her dark eyes were heavily made up with black liner.

"Hey," I said. I put my phone in my bag.

"You heading to lunch?" Mia asked. I nodded, and she gestured for me to accompany her. "Let's do it." She was chewing gum, and while I watched, she blew a small bubble, then cracked it loudly between her teeth.

I fell into step beside her. "I love cracking my gum. It drives my mom batshit when I do it, though."

"Well, your mom's not here now, is she?" Mia reached into her bag and pulled out a pack of Juicy Fruit.

I eyed the pack suspiciously. "I don't know. Sugar gum. Kind of a gateway drug, isn't it?"

"Try it," she said, wagging the pack at me. "The first slice is free."

I reached for a piece, unwrapped it, and popped it in my

mouth. "Oh my God," I said as the fruity taste exploded on my tongue. I had to close my eyes for a second to savor the experience. "This is the first nonsugarless gum I've had in years."

"I know, right?" said Mia, smiling triumphantly. "The dentist loves me. My mom says I'm sending his kids to college."

"It's worth it," I assured her.

We passed a circle of football players, including Calvin and Jake. Each guy was surrounded by a healthy harem of cheerleaders. Jake looked up, saw me, and waved. I waved back. Calvin glanced my way also, but even though we were both at the Grecos' practically every day, his glance slid over me as if I were some exchange student he'd never seen in his life.

Inwardly I rolled my eyes at what an ass he was.

"So," said Mia, "how come you don't do soccer anymore?"

"Um, because I so totally sucked at it?" I offered.

Mia laughed, but she didn't correct me, which I appreciated. "Does that mean you went back to dancing again?" she asked.

Here was concrete proof of how little anyone outside the dance world understood it. I imagined a universe in which Olivia and I had randomly decided to take a year off from dancing and then—equally spontaneously—decided to return to it. I let myself see the two of us as Mia must have seen us. In control. Masters of our destiny.

The fantasy was awesome, which may explain why I lied to her. "Nah. I was kind of over dance."

"Got it." We turned down the hallway toward the cafeteria. It was more crowded here, with some people shoving to get in and others shoving to get out.

"You know," said Mia, turning to me, "freshman year I was überintimidated by the two of you."

I practically choked on my gum. "You *were?*"

"I *was!*" Mia imitated my tone exactly, then laughed. "Is that so surprising? You're both tall and gorgeous. And you disappeared into Manhattan after school every day." We stepped into the river of kids headed to the cafeteria. "I saw you once at *The Nutcracker* when my mom and I took my niece. I mean, I didn't *see* you see you. Like, I couldn't pick you out. But your names were in the program."

I shook my head, as much at the idea of Mia's being at the ballet as at the thought of her searching for us in a sea of dancers. "That's so weird. I mean that we were on your radar like that."

Mia raised an incredulous eyebrow at me. "It's not weird, Zoe. You and Olivia were famous. I figured you were way too cool to hang out with regular people like me."

"*Really?* You thought we were *cool?*" I squeaked, so uncool that both Mia and I laughed. She held open the door to the cafeteria and I followed her in. As we joined a table, I composed a text in my head to Livvie, telling her about how cool and terrifying the population of Wamasset had once found us.

◆ ◆ ◆

I was irritated that Livvie didn't respond to my text, which was, frankly, hilarious. Wasn't she just sitting in the waiting room of Dr. Weiss, our pediatrician? Or sitting at Driscoll's Pharmacy waiting for her mom to fill a prescription? Or sitting and waiting for me to call her? I didn't stay home sick from school all that often, but when I did, that was my routine. The bell rang, ending math, our last period of the day, and Mr. Schumacher nodded in my direction. "You'll give Olivia the homework."

"Sure," I said, then muttered under my breath, "if she ever texts me back."

I went to my locker and slowly made my way outside. It was sunny but way cooler than it had been that morning, and I shivered, wishing I'd worn a jacket. The football team was heading out to the field all the way on the other side of the campus. I considered asking Jake if he knew where Olivia was, but the team was so far away I couldn't even figure out which of the uniformed guys he was.

Just as I decided it wasn't worth bothering, since Jake wasn't going to have any idea anyway, my phone rang. *Livvie!* Finally. I dug my phone out of my bag.

But it wasn't Livvie. It was some 212 number I didn't recognize. This was getting so *annoying*.

"Hello?"

"Zoe?"

It *was* Livvie. But why was she calling me from an unfamiliar number?

"Livs!" I was so glad to hear from her I wasn't even mad that she hadn't called me back earlier. "Where have you been all day? Whose phone are you calling from?"

"My phone's out of juice. Zoe, I have to tell you something." Olivia's voice sounded thin, as if she were calling from far away on a line with a bad connection. It didn't help that it was super noisy in front of the school, where all two thousand members of the student body seemed to have chosen to gather before heading off to their afternoon activities. I pressed my free hand to my ear, trying to hear better.

"Where are you?" I moved away from the crowded concrete circle by the front entrance and onto the lawn.

"Zoe, I'm . . . I'm at the hospital."

"The *hospital*?" For some reason, I thought of the twins. Could one of them have been in an accident? The possibility made my heart drop. Tommy and Luke could be super annoying, but they were also adorable. Last year, when they were in second grade and neither of them had their front teeth, Tommy would pronounce Zoe "Thoe."

"I'm sick, Zoe," said Livvie.

"Wait, *you're* sick?" I was still thinking about the twins. "Hang on a second . . . what?"

"I'm at UH," said Olivia.

University Hospital was only a few blocks from the Fischer Center, where NYBC was located. We'd driven by it every day on our way to and from dance classes and performances, its glass towers telling us we were just minutes from our destination or that we'd begun the journey home.

"But you were just at the doctor's office." I knew, even as I said it, that it was a stupid thing to say. It wasn't like there was no way to travel from the doctor's office to the hospital.

Olivia's voice was freakishly precise. "The doctor found a bruise on the back of my leg," she said.

"I saw that!" I shouted, remembering the bruise from when I'd slept over Saturday night. It was dark purple and spidery, and I'd almost asked her about it, but then we'd started talking about something else and I'd forgotten.

Livvie continued. "Well, she saw it and she asked how I'd gotten it, and I said I didn't know, and then she found this other one on my arm—on the back—"

"I didn't see that one," I admitted. Why was I interrupting her? I pressed my lips together to get my mouth to stop asking questions.

"It's there," Olivia told me, as if I'd doubted her. "I saw it in the mirror. Anyway, then the doctor started asking about the bruises, and how long I've had the fever, and then my mom said that I'd been really tired lately and she asked if maybe I could be anemic. And Dr. Weiss said she wanted us to go to the Med Center."

The Med Center was a cross between a doctor's office and an emergency room. They had X-ray machines and doctors and stuff, but I didn't think you would go there if you were having a heart attack. "Yeah," I said, "I know where that is. Remember when my dad stepped on a nail last summer? My mom and I took him."

Looking back at that conversation, I can't help wondering: Did I know? Did I know what was coming, and did I think that as long as I wouldn't let Livvie say the words, they wouldn't be true?

"They took blood," she went on. "And they found abnormal cells."

"Abnormal cells," I echoed.

"Abnormal cells," she repeated. "And they said they wanted us to go to UH so they could do a bone marrow aspiration. That's when they take some bone marrow out of your pelvic bone with a needle."

"A *needle?* Oh God, Liv." I clutched my arm in sympathy, even though I knew that wasn't where your pelvic bone was.

"My dad came," Livvie said. Her voice caught for a second, but she didn't cry. "He came to meet us, and the doctor said that they'd found blasts in my bone marrow."

"What does that mean?" I whispered.

"They admitted me," she went on, ignoring my question, "and they put in this thing called a central line. It's so the medication gets right into your body."

"The medication?" My voice was a whisper.

"I have leukemia, Zoe."

I gasped.

"But that's . . . that's impossible." It *was* impossible. I knew it was impossible. How could Olivia have leukemia? "There's a . . . I mean, there has to be some mistake. How could you be getting medicine already?" Somehow that was the most implausible part of what she'd told me. I'd slept at her house Saturday night. She'd been fine. I'd talked to her *this morning*. Eight hours later she was in the hospital and getting medicine? How could they even diagnose what she had that fast?

"It's true, Zoe." Olivia's voice quivered. I heard a voice in the background, and Livvie said, "My mom wants me to get off the phone. The doctor just came in. Can you come? I need to see you." It sounded like she was starting to cry.

"I'm on my way," I said, my voice fierce. Then I said it again, as if maybe she would doubt me. "I am *on* my *way*."

"Okay," said Livvie. "Love ya."

We *always* said *Love ya*. We ended every phone call, every chat, every conversation the same way.

See you tomorrow. Love ya.

Gotta go. Love ya.

My mom's calling. Love ya.

I have leukemia. Love ya.

"I love you, Livs," I said, my voice nearly breaking on her name.

"I love you too, Zoe," she answered. I could hear that she was crying. And then she was gone.

I stood on the edge of the lawn, the phone still pressed

43

to my ear. Cars pulled in and out of the parking lot, and kids tumbled from the building, taking the stairs two at a time as they raced into the liberty of the afternoon. The sky over my head was almost painfully blue, the grass a bright and vivid green. It was a crisp, beautiful, perfect fall day.

All that beauty was completely wrong. The sky should have been black, the grass withered, the students wailing with grief. *Olivia is sick!* I wanted to howl. *What are you people doing? My friend is sick!* It was impossible—the sky, the cars, the kids walking around as if it were a day like any other day. Nothing made any sense.

Before I could start screaming, I turned and raced for home.

∽ 5 ∾

My dad was in Washington on assignment, but I didn't even think to be relieved when I saw my mom's car in the driveway—what if she'd been at the gym or a meeting and I'd had to wait for her to return my call and come home, had to sit there on the front porch cooling my heels and losing my mind while Olivia stared at the door of her hospital room, expecting me to walk through it any minute? I flew up the wooden steps of our front porch and into the house. Flavia barked as I entered.

"Mom! Mom!" I could hear the hysteria in my voice.

My mom's an architect, and her office was in the back of the house, but she must have been in the kitchen because she appeared in front of me about a second after I threw open the door. "What is it? What's happened?" She was holding the coffeepot, like maybe she'd been pouring a cup when she heard me yelling.

Still panting from my sprint home, I managed to choke out, "Livvie's . . . she's sick. She's in the hospital. We have to go."

"Olivia's sick?" My mom's eyes popped wide with concern.

"We have to go, Mom. She's at UH. We have to go right now." I started pulling on her arm, like when I was a little kid.

"She's in the *hospital*?" My mom grabbed my elbow.

"That's what I *said*." Why was she not moving? "Now let's go."

"Zoe, sweetheart, you have to explain what's going on." Instead of racing for her keys and shoes, she put her hand on my shoulder. "Calm down. What's wrong? What's wrong with Olivia?"

"Mom, I *told* you! She's sick. She has leukemia. She's in the—"

"She has *leukemia*?" She dropped my arm and pressed her fingers to her lips. "My God! When did this happen?"

"When do you *think* it happened?" I slapped my forehead. "Oh, yeah, it happened last week, only I forgot to tell you about it."

"Zoe, there's no need to get—"

"Why aren't you *hurrying*?" I ran over to the stairs and grabbed a pair of shoes. "We have to *go*." My voice was shrill, and my eyes stung.

For a second, my mom stared at me from across the room as I stood there, holding her black ballet flats out to her. If she didn't put on her shoes and get in the car, I was seriously going to take the keys and drive myself. I had my learner's permit. I'd been driving (with one of my parents in the car) for months. I would make it.

As if she'd read my mind, my mother crossed to where I was standing. Her hand shook, and she had trouble slipping her feet into the shoes. By the time she was done, I'd grabbed her bag and gone to the front hall. Without saying another word, we headed out the door.

My mother's a talker. It's like the monologue most of us have running in our head at any given time is, in my mom's case, dialogue. *Should I have the chicken salad sandwich . . . oh, it's kind of crowded in here . . . I better not forget to write this down . . . it's really taking a long time for the light to change . . . I think I should buy this T-shirt in blue* and *black.* The whole drive into Manhattan she talked and she talked and she talked.

"You know, honey, I went to school with a girl who had leukemia, and she was *fine.* And that was *years* ago. They've got treatments now that are much, much better than the ones they had then."

"Mmmm-hmmm." What *was* leukemia? I didn't even know exactly. I knew it was terrible. I knew people could die from it. But what *was* it? Olivia said they'd found something in her blood. . . . I picked at a split nail on my thumb, biting and pulling at it.

"And University Hospital is the best. Just the *best*. If any one of us got sick, I'd want us there. And do you remember my friend Beth? Her brother-in-law is the head of . . . cardiology there, I think. Or it could be dermatology. Anyway, he's a big, big deal. Maybe I'll ask Beth to call him. It's always good to know a doctor who's on the staff when you're a patient."

"There's nothing wrong with Livvie's heart, Mom. Or her skin." The nail split low, and I peeled it off, glad to focus on the pain.

"Well, it's always good to know a doctor," she repeated. We were driving up West End Avenue. The Fischer Center and NYBC were just north of us; my mom and Olivia and I must have done this drive a thousand times. Ten thousand times. Our being in the car together driving to Manhattan after school would have been perfectly normal if Olivia had been sitting with us and my mom hadn't put her blinker on for another five blocks.

"Now . . ." She leaned forward and peered out the windshield, then braked for a yellow light. I wanted to scream at how slowly she was going. The back of the hospital loomed to our left. "I *think* the main entrance is right around the corner, so I'm going to . . . No. Wait. I can't turn here." She clicked off her blinker, even though there was no one behind us. "Maybe I'll just look for a spot." She leaned forward again and squinted. "Does that sign say 'no parking any time'?"

The light was still red. My finger where I'd peeled off the nail throbbed. Something inside me felt tight, as if I were a balloon that had been blown up too big. I reached for the door handle. "I'm going to meet you inside."

"Just give me a second to park."

I opened the door. The cool breeze made me realize how stuffy it had been in the car. Why had we driven all the way with the windows closed?

"Zoe, wait!" The light south of us must have changed. Cars came up behind ours and started honking. My mom's voice was shrill. "Zoe, the light's changing."

Actually, it had already changed, but I was out of the car. I slammed the door shut, ran three long steps, and, without even meaning to, did a grand jeté onto the curb as if I'd turned back the clock and Livvie and I were still ballerinas together.

↬ 6 ↫

My mom had been right—the main entrance to the hospital *was* just around the corner. I felt guilty for abandoning her and waited a minute, thinking maybe she'd be right behind me. But she wasn't, and I couldn't take standing there. I pushed through the revolving glass door and crossed the lobby, my sandals silent on the white marble floor. There was a sign next to an enormous desk directing visitors to show their ID. I'd left my wallet in the house not thinking I'd need it, but luckily the security guard didn't ask me for anything except Olivia's name. He looked her up in a computer and waved me to a bank of elevators off to the right. On the black-and-white visitor's sticker he'd written *ROOM 1238* in blue Sharpie.

When the elevator doors opened on the twelfth floor, I

found myself looking at a dark gray sign that read PEDIATRIC ONCOLOGY.

Oncology. The word was like a punch. *Oncology.* Leukemia was cancer.

Olivia had cancer.

As I stepped out of the elevator, a little boy, maybe three or four, walked toward me down the hallway. He had no hair, and he was holding a stuffed animal, chatting with a woman who looked like she was probably his grandmother. The woman asked him a question and he said, "Of course!" and she laughed.

He has cancer. That little boy has cancer.

They walked by. Had Olivia seen the boy? I wanted Olivia not to have seen him. I had some idea it would be upsetting to her to have seen a little boy with cancer. But of course Livvie had cancer, so maybe seeing a kid with cancer *wouldn't* upset her. *How can kids get cancer? That is so completely screwed up.* I could feel myself getting mad, not at God—who I don't believe in—but at people who believe in God. Because what kind of a fucked-up God would make a world where kids can get cancer? I headed down the hall in the opposite direction from the boy, but the numbers were going down, not up. The mad feeling was feeding on the tight feeling, and I was actually having trouble catching my breath. I turned around. The boy and his grandmother were gone. I half walked, half ran along the hall back the way I'd come, until I got to room 1238. Next to the room number, a piece of paper had the handwritten words *Olivia Greco*.

I pushed on the door. It was big and heavy-looking, and I shoved it hard, expecting a lot of resistance, but it shot open. "Sorry," I said by way of greeting, as everyone in the room jumped at the sound of the door slamming open.

The room was small, maybe half the size of Olivia's room at home. Livvie, wearing a blue hospital gown and a pair of blue sock-like booties, was sitting on the bed with her mom. Her dad was sitting in a pinkish pleather chair next to the bed, and Jake was sitting on the radiator under the window. There was a gorgeous view of the Hudson River, which looked in the afternoon sun as if someone had painted the surface of the water a vivid, almost neon, orange.

Guess what, kids! The bad news is: You have cancer. But hey, check out these views!

Olivia was pale, like maybe she still had a fever. But except for that and the IV disappearing into the sleeve of her hospital gown, she looked exactly the way she'd looked when I'd left her Sunday morning after our sleepover.

"Hi," I said.

"Hi," she said.

I felt relieved to be seeing her but also strangely shy. I wasn't sure if it was okay to go over and sit with her. Not that there was enough room on the bed for me, Olivia, and her mom. And not like I could ask her mom to get off. Unsure of what to do, I just hovered near the door.

"Hi, Zoe," said Mrs. Greco, giving me a sad smile. "You were so good to come right over."

Olivia's mom was always dressed beautifully. She didn't work, but she did a lot of volunteer stuff—raising money for a wildlife sanctuary near us, serving on the school board. I could picture her getting dressed this morning. She'd chosen a white blouse and pale yellow suit. She'd slipped a string of pearls around her neck and snapped the clasp. Before her committee meeting or her charity lunch, she'd be taking Olivia to the doctor. Brushing her bobbed blond hair, she'd expected to hear her daughter had strep throat or maybe a virus. Nothing out of the ordinary. As she'd slid her feet into her beige suede pumps, could she possibly have imagined that before the day was over, she'd be wearing them while sitting on her daughter's hospital bed?

"Hey," said Jake. He came over and gave me a hug.

"Hi," I said. He was wearing his football uniform, and he looked pale, paler even than Olivia. His pallor inspired an insane fantasy—that Jake was the one who was sick. Without even meaning to, I conjured up the phone call from Olivia that could have been. *I have terrible news. My brother has leukemia.* I pictured coming to the hospital to see Jake or one of the twins, and as I did, I felt my heart leap with joy. Then I felt awful. I was wishing sickness on a healthy person. But no, it wasn't like that. This was a *trade.* A sick person for another sick person.

A different sick person. An eye for an eye.

An eye for an eye? Was that even what that saying meant?

And since when did I quote the Bible?

Livvie patted a spot on the bed, but before I could move toward it, her mom stood up, clearly preparing to block my approach. "Zoe, can you clean your hands very carefully?" She nodded at the Purell dispenser on the wall.

I quickly crossed to it and doused my hands, rubbing the Purell in even when it stung my finger where I'd ripped off part of the nail. Then I went over and sat next to Livvie, who shifted to make room for me. I put my arm around her, letting my shoes hang off the edge of the bed, and she laid her head on my shoulder. I wanted to say something. Anything. But everything I thought of saying sounded completely stupid and awful. Of all the bizarre things that had happened today, my being tongue-tied around Olivia might have been the strangest.

"Well, this completely sucks," she said finally, and then we laughed. The laughter felt a little bit hollow and a little bit forced. Still, it felt good to be sitting next to Olivia and laughing. It felt normal. Olivia looked normal. She sounded normal. Everything about this moment was totally normal.

Except that it wasn't.

"You are going to be *fine*," said Livvie's mom, patting Olivia's hand.

"My mom keeps saying that," Olivia whispered, loud enough for her mother to hear.

Her mother smiled and kept patting. "Because it's true," she said.

"Okay," said Livvie. There was a little frustration in her voice but none of the venom that had been in mine when I was screaming at my mother earlier. Even with cancer, Olivia was a nicer person than I was.

"How are you feeling?" I asked. "Are you feeling okay?"

"I feel . . ." She considered the question carefully, then turned her head to face me. "I feel like I'm having an out-of-body experience. Like none of this can really be happening." Her voice shook a little bit on the word *happening*.

I squeezed her shoulders, worrying after I did it that I'd somehow mess up her IV.

The door opened less dramatically than it had when I'd entered. I expected it to be my mom, or maybe one of Olivia's grandparents, but instead Calvin Taylor walked in. He was also in his football uniform. His hair was messy and there was a long scrape on his forearm. In his hands was a cardboard tray with four cups of Starbucks coffee.

"Piping hot," he said to the room. Then he went over to Olivia's dad and handed him one of the cups. Without getting off his phone, Mr. Greco nodded his thanks.

"You were so sweet to run out and get these," said Mrs. Greco as she took a cup from him. "And after you drove Jake all the way here."

"I didn't mind," he said. "Really." Then he looked at Olivia.

"Sure you don't want one?" He touched her foot gently and smiled at her.

She shook her head. "No, thanks." I glanced at her, but there was no obvious response to Calvin's being in her hospital room or touching her.

He thrust his chin vaguely in my direction by way of greeting, then went over to where Jake was sitting and stood beside him. "Hey, man," he said, handing him one of the two remaining cups. Jake said something to him, and Calvin said, "Sorry," quietly, and went over to the Purell dispenser.

What was Calvin Taylor doing leaving football practice to drive Jake into the city and go on a coffee run for the Grecos? He wasn't part of the family. Not that I was part of the family, but I was pretty damned close. Calvin had only lived in Wamasset for a few years. I'd known Olivia for more than a *decade*.

I felt irritated that the Grecos were asking Calvin to help out and then irritated at myself for being irritated. The Grecos needed support now. If Calvin offered Jake—or any of them, really—that support, I should be happy to see him in Olivia's hospital room.

Still, I wasn't. And it wasn't just because he'd teased me about Jackson. There was something about Calvin—the way every girl at school drooled over him, the way the school newspaper ran his picture on the sports page every five seconds, the way he was too important to bother to acknowledge me.

Even his whole I'm-so-helpful-let-me-be-your-chauffeur-and-delivery-boy routine, which the Grecos were clearly falling for, rubbed me the wrong way.

Was I the only one who could see that he was a self-satisfied ass?

The door opened again. This time my mom walked in. "Hi, guys," she said quietly, and then she used the Purell dispenser. I was surprised that she knew she had to do that.

Olivia's mom stood up and went over to my mom. They hugged and then started talking quietly, too quietly for me to hear what they were saying. Over by the window, Calvin and Jake talked. Olivia's dad typed on his BlackBerry. Even though there were almost half a dozen people in the room with us, I felt like we were suddenly alone together.

Olivia must have felt the same way because when she started talking, it was clear that she was talking just to me. "I really think I'm going to be okay," she said. Her eyes had purplish circles under them. How long had they been there? How had I not noticed? "I was freaking out before, but . . . I don't know, I just *sense* that I'm going to be okay."

Immediately I said, "Of *course* you're going to be okay." Then I regretted saying it. I hoped I didn't sound too much like her mom.

The door to the room opened again, and this time a woman in a white lab coat came in. She was short, with gray streaks in her brown curly hair.

"Hello!" She gave a wave to the room, then pressed the Purell dispenser and rubbed her hands together. "I'm glad to see Olivia has so much company."

"We don't want to tire her out, Dr. Maxwell," said Mrs. Greco quickly.

"If you think it's better for everyone to go, we'll send them all home," said Mr. Greco, getting to his feet.

The way Mr. Greco—who was a big partner at his law firm and who talked to pretty much everybody as if they were his employees—spoke to Dr. Maxwell, I could tell she was important.

Dr. Maxwell smiled at Olivia. "Are you tired?"

Olivia gave a little shrug. "I'm okay."

"Good." Her round tortoiseshell glasses caught the light and made it seem as if her eyes were sparkling. Under her lab coat she had on a pretty silk blouse. She came over to the bed. "You must be Zoe," she said, and when I nodded, she went on. "Olivia told me about you. She's really going to need her friends right now." Her voice was matter-of-fact, like, *Just to be clear, having cancer is not something good.*

"Of course," I said.

Dr. Maxwell slipped up the sleeve of Olivia's hospital gown, checked something on Olivia's chest briefly, then nodded. "It all looks good." She glanced over her shoulder at the IV line hanging from the pole. "How are you feeling? Are you nauseated?" Her tone was the same as it had been when she'd told me Olivia would need her friends, and I started to get the sense she was just matter-of-fact about everything.

Olivia shook her head. "Not yet. I have a funny taste in my mouth." Livvie ran her tongue along her teeth and made a face. "It's weird."

"Unfortunately, I can't help you with that, but if it's making you nauseous, let me know. Like I said before, it's hard to get the horse back in the barn once he's out."

I had no idea what she was talking about, but Olivia must have because she nodded. Dr. Maxwell looked around the room. "Everything seems okay for now," she said. "Olivia's off to a good start."

I hadn't noticed how quiet the room had gotten while Dr. Maxwell was examining Olivia, but as soon as she gave her assessment, the buzz of conversation that started up again made me feel the silence her presence had generated. It reminded me of how it had been in a dance class when Martin Hicks, the NYBC director, would pay one of his occasional visits. You didn't realize how tightly you'd been holding everything in— how high you'd been lifting your leg, how far you'd extended your arms—until he left and you felt the collective tension seep out of the room as everyone literally gave a sigh of relief.

Now people went back to their conversations. Dr. Maxwell stood next to the bed. "So," she said, "Olivia and her family and I had a long talk earlier, but she asked me to come back and explain some things about her illness to you."

I looked at Olivia. "Really? You wanted her to explain everything to me, too?"

Livvie nodded. I loved her so much right at that instant I almost cried.

"Now, what do you know about leukemia?" asked Dr. Maxwell.

"It's got something to do with Olivia's blood," I answered, purposely not using the word *cancer*.

"Good," said Dr. Maxwell, and even though we were talking about a deadly disease that my best friend had, I felt glad to have gotten the answer right. "It does have to do with blood. Specifically, it's a cancer of the blood."

"Actually, I was trying to avoid the *c* word," I explained.

Olivia laughed, and even Dr. Maxwell cracked a smile. "We use the *c* word a lot around here," Dr. Maxwell assured me. "Now, there are different types of leukemia. Most children and teens get something called acute lymphoblastic leukemia, or ALL. Olivia has acute *myeloid* leukemia, or AML. It's a cancer more commonly associated with males in their sixties."

Livvie turned to me. "I have old-man cancer. Isn't that so humiliating?"

"It *is*, actually. But I won't tell anyone," I promised.

Dr. Maxwell was shaking her head. I couldn't tell if she was amused or irritated by the way we were talking. "In a healthy person," she went on, "blood is formed inside the soft, spongy part of the big bones in your body, such as your femur. You know what your femur is?" I nodded. Our first year at NYBC, a girl in our class had had a skiing accident and broken her femur. I still remembered when one of the worst dancers in our class had pulled us aside to tell us about the accident. *She may never dance again.* Her face had been bright pink with the drama of the moment.

"Your femur's here." I hit my thigh as I said it.

"Correct," Dr. Maxwell said. "So blood is born—formed—in the bone marrow. There, immature cells called blasts grow into mature blood cells: white blood cells, red blood cells, or platelets. Think of bone marrow as a school. Or a house. The kids grow up, learn a trade, then leave home and go to work at a job.

"But leukemia stops blood cells from doing that. In a person with AML, instead of making normal blasts, which grow into normal blood cells, the bone marrow starts making cancerous cells. They divide quickly and uncontrollably. They don't do their jobs. And they fill up the bone marrow so that there's no room for normal, healthy cells to be made or to grow. The immature cells are strong and hard to kill. They're like child soldiers."

Dr. Maxwell pointed behind her at the IV bag hanging on the pole beside Olivia's bed. "The drugs we're giving Olivia right now are drugs that target rapidly dividing cells, such as myeloblasts."

"And hair," Olivia said. Her voice was quieter than it had

been. I patted her arm, not sure what else to do.

"And hair," Dr. Maxwell said, and now I was grateful for how matter-of-fact she was about everything. "Because chemotherapy targets *all* rapidly dividing cells, it unfortunately doesn't *only* get cancer cells."

I'd always wondered why people with cancer lost their hair. "Why can't they invent drugs that target rapidly dividing *sick* cells only?" I asked.

"Well, we're working on it," Dr. Maxwell said. She pushed her glasses up on the bridge of her nose. "I promise you. We're all working on it."

I couldn't take Dr. Maxwell's being so nice. It made me want to cry. Instead I asked, "Will she get sick? I mean, will she throw up?" Livvie made a face. She hated throwing up. Not that anyone *likes* it, but Livvie really *really* hated it.

"She may experience nausea and vomiting," Dr. Maxwell said. "Chemotherapy triggers a chemical response in the brain that makes some people sick to their stomach. But the good news is we have a lot of drugs to make Olivia comfortable. Hopefully she'll only have very mild side effects."

"That's kind of lame good news, Dr. Maxwell," said Olivia.

"It is," Dr. Maxwell agreed, and she stroked Olivia's forehead gently. I'd never seen a doctor do something like that.

"When can she come home?" I asked. If she was home by Friday, I could spend the weekend at her house with her. We could watch distracting movies all day.

Dr. Maxwell's voice was businesslike. "Three to four weeks."

Three to four weeks? I tried to keep my voice neutral. "I thought . . . I thought maybe she'd be home this weekend."

Dr. Maxwell shook her head. "The chemotherapy itself only lasts for about a week, but it destroys so many blood cells that a person is very vulnerable to infection. We keep her here until her blood counts go up."

My head spun. How could Livvie be in the hospital for an entire *month?*

They were both staring at me. I had to say something, but my panic had parched my lips and my tongue felt glued to the roof of my mouth. "Well . . ." I cleared my throat, hoping to make my voice more normal. "And then . . . that's it, right? She's done?"

Livvie shook her head. "That's just the first round. Then I have to do it three more times."

"*Three more times?*" It came out like a wail, which I immediately regretted.

My response triggered something in Livvie, who suddenly looked distraught. "And I might not be able to go to school between treatments *at all.*"

"Wait, you're going to miss *months* of school? I—" I bit my tongue. Literally. Because here's what your best friend doesn't need to hear you say when she's just found out she has cancer: *I can't deal with that.*

"This is a lot to take all at once, I know," said Dr. Maxwell.

She furrowed her forehead in a way that somehow managed to be concerned and not pitying. "And it's not the last time you'll be able to ask me questions." Dr. Maxwell put her hand on Olivia's shoulder. "I'll see you tomorrow, but if something comes up during the night, they'll page me."

"Okay," said Olivia. "Thanks, Dr. Maxwell."

"Yes," I said, trying to capture an optimistic tone. "Thanks for explaining all of this to me."

She smiled at me. "Olivia is very lucky to have a friend like you."

Dr. Maxwell said good-bye to everyone, and when the door had closed behind her, Mrs. Greco clapped her hands together once. "Now I'm sending everyone home. Our girl needs to get her rest."

I was surprised that Olivia didn't object, but when I looked at her face, she seemed tired, and I thought maybe she was relieved that everyone was leaving.

My mom came over and gave Olivia a long hug, then touched me lightly on the shoulder. "I'll meet you outside."

Calvin and Jake said good-bye. When Calvin was hugging Livvie, she gave me a little wink and a thumbs-up behind his back, and I actually laughed.

I got off the bed and stood over Olivia. Maybe it was a trick of the light, but she looked somehow frailer than she had when I'd first walked in, as if she'd gotten smaller over the past thirty minutes.

Not wanting her to read my thoughts, I bent down and hugged her. She squeezed me back. There was nothing frail about her hug, and the strength in her arms made me feel better.

"This is going to be okay," I whispered into her shoulder. "You're going to be okay." She gave a tiny squeak, and I could tell from the way her body shook that she was crying. It was hard to believe that just a minute ago she'd given me the thumbs-up about Calvin Taylor's hugging her.

Remembering how my getting upset earlier had made *her* get upset, I forced myself not to cry as I pulled away. "I'll see you tomorrow, 'kay?"

"Thanks, Zoe," she said. She wiped the tears off her cheeks, and no new ones fell. "I love you."

"I love you too, Liv."

The whole way home, my mom talked. She talked about how Mrs. Greco was going to arrange for Olivia to Skype her classes. She talked about how the doctors felt there was every reason to be optimistic. She talked about how Olivia was getting the best medical treatment there was. She told me she'd called my dad, who was on his way home. Every once in a while, she turned to me and patted me on the knee or stroked my hair.

"You okay, honey?" she asked about twenty times.

"I'm . . . yeah. I'm okay," I said each time. I couldn't find the words to describe the tight feeling that had disappeared for a little while when I was with Olivia but had come back again now that we were in the car. *Months.* She was going to be out of school for months. She had to go through round after round of chemotherapy. My mind danced from one detail to another, skittishly skimming the surface of the situation. I would picture Dr. Maxwell's glasses, then the dark circles under Olivia's eyes. I felt Olivia's shoulders shaking as I hugged her. I lowered my window all the way, hoping the chilly night air would focus my thoughts, but it did nothing except make my face cold.

Since I'd gotten my permit, every time we got in the car I begged my mom to let me drive, but even if we hadn't been driving in Manhattan (where out-of-state residents can't drive until they're eighteen), I was way too distracted to even contemplate operating a motor vehicle. I kept thinking about how on the way to school I'd been pissed because on B days after lunch I have history, then physics, and then math. And I'd thought, *I hope Livvie's in school, because if she's not, this day is going to suck even worse than it will if she's not in school, which is a lot.*

If you'd asked me on my walk that morning to list ten things I was worried about, I would have started with a pop quiz in history, because I'd only kind of done the reading. If you'd asked me to come up with ten more things, chances are global warming might have made it onto the list. And if you'd asked me to list *another* ten, I might have added something

66

about bioterrorism, because sometimes when it was late at night and I couldn't sleep, I worried about how my parents and I would get out of New Jersey if there were a terrorist attack.

But no matter how many multiples of ten you'd added, I just don't think *I'm worried that Olivia has cancer* would have made it onto one of my lists. Because there are some things you worry about. And then there are some things you *don't* worry about.

You don't worry about them because they're too awful to contemplate worrying about.

We pulled up into the driveway. I followed my mom up the stairs to the front porch and waited while she fished for her keys. She opened the door and flipped on the light. From the kitchen came a whimper.

"Oh my God," my mom whispered. "We forgot all about Flavia."

She raced into the kitchen, and I followed her. Flavia was lying on the floor, his paw covering his face as if he were ashamed. A few feet away was a small puddle of pee.

It was my job to give Flavia his afternoon walk. I pictured him waiting for me to get home from school, imagined how confused he must have been when I raced into the house and then raced out again, taking my mom with me instead of him.

I went over and dropped to the floor. "I'm so sorry, Flavia," I said, putting my arms around him. "I'm so sorry." For a second he seemed to resist my hug, and then he gave a little sigh and rested his head on my lap as if to say, *I understand. I forgive you.*

"I just forgot. Livvie's sick, and I just forgot." Flavia blinked at me. The last time I'd walked him, I'd gone over to Olivia's house after. She hadn't been sick then. Except she had been. I pictured her bone marrow, full of terrifying child soldiers, the kind that were sometimes featured on the front page of the *New York Times*, with their dead eyes and their automatic weapons. They'd been hiding out inside her, their numbers growing for weeks. Months. Maybe years? We were driving in and out of Manhattan and dancing and planning our glamorous futures, and all that time, an enemy deep in Olivia's DNA was plotting and waiting and getting ready to strike.

"She's okay, Flavia," I said. "She's going to be okay. Really. She is. You don't need to worry, Flavia. She's going to be fine." And then I wrapped my arms around his body and the tight feeling inside me burst and I cried and cried into his soft, warm fur.

7

I would have said that after Livvie's diagnosis nothing could shock me, but the next morning, when I pushed open the door to Wamasset High School minutes before the first bell, still bleary-eyed from my night of tossing and turning, it turned out there was something for which I was *completely* unprepared.

No sooner had I entered the lobby than there was an ear-splitting scream, followed by the cry, "Oh my *God, Zoe!*"

It was as if I'd tripped some personalized burglar alarm. I stood, frozen, waiting to see where the voice had come from.

The lobby was wall-to-wall people, but the crowds parted as Stacy, Emma, and the Bailor twins flew toward me, hurled their bodies at mine, threw their arms around my shoulders, and—and here I am not exaggerating—began to sob.

"Zoe, it's so awful!" Stacy dug her chin into my shoulder.

Her ponytail slapped my face.

"It's just so awful!" Emma echoed. She was clutching my arm and patting the side of my head.

Within seconds, the rest of the cheer squad had gathered around us, all of them damp-eyed, a few with tears running down their faces.

Stacy released me from the hug, then grabbed my hand. "Zoe, we just love you so much."

The cheer squad loved me?

"It's true," Emma asserted, though I hadn't spoken my doubts out loud. She dropped her head onto my shoulder. "Have you seen Jake this morning?"

"Listen," Stacy continued, "last night we were talking about doing a fund-raiser for the Leukemia and Lymphoma Society. And I just know that I speak for everyone at Wamasset when I say that we will *all* participate as we work to find a cure for this deadly disease."

"Are you . . . planning a speech or something?" I asked.

She nodded. "To Principal Handleman. I'm going to propose we do a car wash and blood drive. Do you think Olivia would like that?"

They stared at me, waiting for an answer.

Do not be a total bitch. Do not be a total bitch.

"Um, yeah, that's really nice of you guys. I'm sure something like that would mean a lot to her," I said. My phone buzzed, and I checked the screen. *OLIVIA.*

"I have to go," I said. I would have been relieved to hear from her anyway, but given my situation, her phone call was doubly welcome.

"Oh my God," wailed Hailey. "Is that Olivia?"

"Yeah," I admitted, "it is, actually." I am not exaggerating when I say a reverent hush fell over the girls surrounding me, as if I had just told a group of nuns that Jesus Christ himself was on the line.

"Hi," I said into the phone, ducking my head slightly so I wasn't looking into all those eager faces. "Um, I'm standing here with the cheerleaders."

There was a pause. Then Livvie said, "Seriously? But you hate those guys."

I glanced up. Everyone was still staring at me. "Olivia says hi."

"Hi, Olivia!" they shouted. "Tell her we love her!" a couple of voices added.

"They say they love you," I repeated.

"Oh," said Olivia. "Thanks."

"She says thanks," I said. Then I made a gesture to indicate I was having trouble hearing what was being said at the other end of the phone and began sliding toward my locker.

"Bye, Livvie!" cried Stacy. She began to wave, and the other cheerleaders followed suit, as if I were a cruise ship pulling slowly away from the dock.

"Zoe, you have to help us plan the car wash!" added

Emma. I nodded and nodded and made the same I-need-to-go-somewhere-I-can-hear gesture and then I was blissfully out of the lobby and on my way down the two hundreds corridor.

"Jesus Christ," I said. "This is really weird. They want to do a car wash."

"I know," said Olivia. "Stacy sent me a text last night. And this morning I got an email. She signed me up to receive daily inspirational messages. Today's was all about the goodness within me."

"Holy shit! Did you puke immediately?"

Olivia gave a tired laugh. "Already did that."

"Oh, honey." I leaned against my locker. "Are you okay?"

"I don't know. Yeah. I mean, I'm okay." She had this brave but tired voice that I'd never heard her use before. It made me want to crawl through the phone and curl up next to her on the hospital bed. The warning bell rang.

"I heard that," said Olivia. "You've gotta go."

"I don't care," I said. "Whatever. I'll be late."

"Actually, I'm kinda cooked," she admitted. "I just wanted to say hi."

"Right," I said fast. "Of course. I'm sorry. You get some rest. I'll call you later."

After we hung up, I opened my locker, but I didn't take anything out or put anything in. My hands were shaking, and I leaned the side of my head against the cool of the metal shelf. On my locker door was the picture she had taken the first day of school. We were tan. Our smiles were wide, and I realized Livvie's dress was blue and white and so was my shirt, almost as if we were wearing some kind of uniform. *You two look like salt and pepper shakers.* That's what my mom used to say when we both had long hair. *You're a couple of salt and pepper shakers.* And now here I was, just a stupid, lonely pepper shaker. What was the point of a pepper shaker without a salt shaker? I didn't even *like* pepper.

"Hey, Zoe." It was a boy's voice. I figured it was Jake, but when I turned around what I saw was Calvin Taylor, who, apparently, had decided to acknowledge my existence.

"Oh," I said. "Hey." I was still thinking about Olivia's voice. It had been so frail.

"How are you?" he asked. He was taller than I was, and he leaned down a little when he asked. Maybe because he was such a professional stud I'd imagined him smelling of cologne or aftershave or something equally . . . studly, but he just smelled like the outdoors.

I shrugged. "I'm great. Just, you know, peachy."

He raised an eyebrow at me. "Okay, why do I doubt that?"

"Well," I snapped, "I mean, how do you think I am, Calvin? I suck, okay? I can't even . . ." Why the hell was I confessing my feelings to Calvin Taylor of all people? I sighed and turned to the contents of my locker, but I couldn't register them. Survive a month of school without Olivia? I might as well try to cross the Atlantic Ocean on an empty refrigerator box.

73

"You can't even what?" Calvin asked. He'd moved around to stand next to me, but I didn't turn my head to look at him, just kept staring at the spines of my textbooks and binders.

"I can't even get my mind around it. I can't even *see* it." I lifted my hands and looked down at them. "First I think of Livvie, and that's horrible. And then I think of her family and I feel so awful for them. And then I feel bad for myself." I shook my head. "I do. I feel really sorry for myself, okay? Because I'm just that selfish." I seriously could not figure out what books I needed for first period, and even if I could have, I didn't give a crap about having them, so I just shut my locker and snapped the lock on it. Then I turned to face Calvin.

He was leaning against the locker next to mine. His snug T-shirt showed off his upper body, and he was wearing fitted but slightly low-slung jeans that made you know he had six-pack abs to match his broad, muscled (but not *too* muscled) shoulders. His hair was damp and sexy-shaggy. He pushed it off his forehead, revealing eyes that were an intense greenish-brown. Our eyes met. And as they did, I suddenly remembered the joke I'd made to Olivia about his being a vampire.

That's when I started laughing. I couldn't help it. I kept picturing him lowering his head and sinking his fangs into my neck. *Now you are among the undead, foolish girl! You will worship me as do all the girls at Wamasset. Ha ha ha!*

Tears of laughter ran down my face. Uneasily, Calvin asked, "Did I miss something funny?" but I couldn't catch my breath long enough to answer him.

"You're just so . . ." But I was laughing too hard to finish my sentence, and I didn't even know for sure what I would have said if I could have spoken. "Nothing," I gasped finally. "I'm sorry. Did you come over here to tell me something?"

He must have decided to write my laughter off as some kind of best-friend-has-cancer-induced hysteria because he continued talking without addressing it. "I just wanted to say . . ." He put his hand on my shoulder. His voice, when he spoke, was calm and soothing. "It's going to be okay."

Wait, had he seriously just said, *It's going to be okay?*

Was that, like, supposed to comfort me?

Wiping tears of laughter out of the corners of my eyes, I reached up and squeezed his shoulder, then attempted to imitate his condescending tone. "Thanks, Calvin. I can't . . . I can't tell you how reassuring it is to hear you say that." I started laughing all over again, and I was still laughing when I turned away from him and headed for physics class. *Livvie,* I wanted to scream, *it's bad enough that you have cancer. But why did you have to fall for such a cheese ball?*

8

I'd been expecting to find Olivia asleep or maybe vomiting into a basin, but when I got to the hospital after school, she was sitting up in bed dressed in a pair of jeans and a plaid button-down shirt we'd gotten together at this old-school army-navy store last year. It was good to see her in regular clothes rather than a hospital gown. Her hair was in a thick braid down her back, a style she hadn't worn in a long time. Her mom was sitting in the pleather chair next to the bed.

"You look really pretty," I said to Olivia. She did, too. Young, but pretty.

She gave me a thin smile. "They started this new antinausea medication, so I'm supposedly feeling better already."

"Well, that's supposedly good news," I said. "Hi, Mrs. Greco."

"Hello, Zoe." Mrs. Greco looked way more tired than she had the day before, and I wondered if she'd had as bad a night's sleep as I had. "Would you Purell your hands, please?" She smiled at me, but it was a smile I'd never seen on Olivia's mom's face before. There was a brittle edge there, like any second it could crack and something sad and scared and ugly would poke through.

I went over to the Purell dispenser, hearing Livvie and her mom talking in whispers behind me. When I turned around, Mrs. Greco was still smiling that creepy smile. "Okay, girls," she said. "I'll give you some time. But half an hour. That's it." She fussed briefly with Olivia's bed, and I noticed that someone had brought Olivia's comforter from home. "Well, that's better," said Mrs. Greco, having fixed whatever was bothering her. "Okay. I'll see you both in a bit."

As soon as her mom left, Olivia sighed and dropped her head back against the pillow. "She is driving me crazy."

"She's freaked out," I said, making my way over to stand by the bed.

"I wish she'd stop smiling for a minute," said Olivia. "It's freaking *me* out."

"Yeah, that smile is fucking *bizarre*," I agreed.

Livvie leaned toward me and took my hands in hers, then split her face into a terrifying grimace. "How are you feeling, honey? Are you tired? Would you like to eat something? Is it too cold in here? Is it too warm in here? Do you want to walk down the hall? Do you want your book? Can I get you anything? Anything at all?" With each question, she made her smile wider and more frightening. Then she flopped back and let go of my hand. "That's why I finally let her braid my hair. I figured at least I wouldn't have to look at her smiling while she did it."

"It does look nice," I said.

"I look like a third grader," Olivia corrected me.

"A *very pretty* third grader," I assured her.

She rolled her eyes at me.

"How are you?" I asked.

"I don't know." She shrugged. "I had to call Mrs. Jones at the rec center and tell her I was sick. They're going to find someone else to teach the ballet class."

"Oh." I sat down in the chair her mom had vacated. "Well, I mean, that's good, right? That they won't have to cancel it or anything."

"Yeah, I guess." But her voice was sad.

I leaned toward her. "Livs?"

She toyed with the edge of her shirt, not meeting my eyes. "I *like* teaching the class, okay? And I'm just . . . I'm just feeling sorry for myself. Forget about it, okay? I mean"—she waved her hand around the room—"it's not like I can teach the class from here. So let's . . . let's talk about something else. Tell me about your day."

"Livvie . . . ," I started, and I reached for her hand.

But she shook her head and shut her eyes tightly, not facing me. "Tell me about your day," she repeated. "Please."

"Sure," I said, not sure what else I could do. "Of course."

Thirty-one minutes later, Mrs. Greco followed me out the door of Olivia's room and down the hall. "Thanks for coming today, Zoe," she said. "It means a lot to Olivia."

I hoped it had, but I wasn't so sure. Nothing, not even my Calvin-Taylor-really-is-a-vampire story, had seemed to cheer her up.

"I've spoken to Mr. Handleman," she went on, "and it looks like—when she's well enough—Olivia is going to be able to Skype her classes. But if there's work that can't be delivered via computer, I told him you or Jake could be the point person. I hope you don't mind." We were standing in front of the elevator, and Mrs. Greco pushed the down button.

"Of course not. I'm glad to help." My parents always said Olivia was a part of our family, but I didn't know if the Grecos felt the same way about me. Like, even though Livvie had been calling my parents Ed and Cathy since the day she met them, I still called her parents Mr. and Mrs. Greco. Sometimes I worried that they thought I was a bad influence on Livvie because our family wasn't religious, my parents let me go to R-rated movies, my dad was a freelance journalist, and my mom earned more money than he did. Meanwhile, the Grecos went to church every Sunday, Mr. Greco was a lawyer who wore suits and went into the city every day, and Mrs. Greco was a stay-at-home mom. Livvie said I was totally paranoid, but I wasn't so sure.

I didn't want to explain to Mrs. Greco my whole theory about her thinking my parents were agnostic lefties with no family values, but I wanted her to know how much I loved Olivia. "I really hope you'll rely on me in any way you can."

I had this fantasy that Mrs. Greco would hug me, ask me to call her Adriana, and tell me that to her and Mr. Greco I was like family, but she just patted me gently on the cheek. "Of course," she said. "We know we can count on you."

"Thanks, Mrs. Greco," I said. The elevator doors opened and I got on. "That means a lot to me." And even though I was the one who said it, I couldn't decide if I was being sarcastic or not.

I missed the train to Wamasset by less than ten minutes, so I had to kill almost an hour waiting for the next one. Penn Station's got lousy stores, but whenever Livvie and I were stuck waiting for a train, we always managed to find something fun to do, even if it was checking out a shop full of lame touristy stuff or trying on tacky clothes we would never buy. Today, though, the time dragged while I wandered from Hot & Crusty to Duane Reade to New York Inc., finally settling in the waiting area, where I just sat and stared at the board listing the train departures. I couldn't stop thinking about how sad Livvie had been all afternoon. Not that she shouldn't have been. I mean, if getting a diagnosis of leukemia doesn't give you the right to be sad, what does? But the crazy thing was, she almost hadn't seemed sad about having cancer. It was like not teaching the dance class had been the straw that broke her back.

How was she going to last through weeks of treatment—*months* of treatment!—with nothing to look forward to besides Skyping her classes and receiving a daily inspirational message from the cheer squad? Thinking about her squeezing her eyes shut to stop herself from crying made me furious, and when I stood up after they announced the train to Wamasset, I was actually shaking my head, as if I were having an argument with the universe about the unfairness of it all.

And the worst part was, there was nothing I could do. I chucked my empty coffee cup in the trash and headed down to the platform. Dr. Maxwell's telling me Livvie needed her friends suddenly felt like a bad joke. What did she need her friends for—so we could bear witness to her misery?

It wasn't until the train was almost at my stop that I had my brainstorm. If Olivia could Skype her *school* classes, why couldn't she Skype *other* classes? My hands were practically shaking with excitement as I dialed her number.

"Hey," she said. She sounded really tired.

My idea burst out of me. "Let's teach the class together."

"What?"

I realized from how fuzzy her voice was that I must have woken her up, so I repeated myself, enunciating each word carefully. "Let's. Teach. The. Class. Together! The dance class. We can use our phones. Or I'll bring my dad's laptop or something."

There was a long pause.

"You don't have to do this," Livvie said finally. "I know you don't want to do this."

Was she serious?

"Livvie, come on. It's so nothing." Given what Olivia was going through, the idea that teaching her dance class with her was some big sacrifice had to be a joke.

I heard a voice in the background, and Livvie said, "I'm okay, Mom. Really."

"Do you have to go?" I asked her. "We can talk about this tomorrow."

"It could be a big job, Zoe," said Olivia, ignoring my offer. "I might . . . I might be pretty sick sometimes, and . . . I mean, you might have to do it by yourself." It sounded like she might be crying a little.

I made my voice mock angry. "Oh, so you think I can't run a ballet class for beginners? Thanks a lot, *bi-yatch*!"

Olivia laughed. Like, *really* laughed. "The recital's a lot of work—" she began.

"I'm not taking no for an answer," I interrupted her. "So just, you know, stick that in your pipe and smoke it."

There was another long pause. I stayed quiet, watching dusk turn the sky over New Jersey a deep purple.

"Zoe, are you sure?"

"Oh my *God!*" I cried, slapping my hand against the seat next to me. "Will you *stop* already? I'm doing it and that's final."

And suddenly Olivia didn't sound tired or sick at all. "The girls are so great," she said, speaking quickly. "I mean, they've just had the worst lives, but they're still really into dancing. This one girl, Imani, she's lived with *four* different foster families in the past *year*. Can you imagine that? *Four families!*"

I laughed. "Zoe, you don't have to convince me. It was my idea, remember?"

"Oh. Yeah," she said. Then she added, "Hey, wouldn't it be funny if I'd staged this whole cancer thing just to get you to teach the dance class with me?"

"Hilarious," I said. The computerized voice announced, "The next stop is Wamasset. Wamasset is the next stop."

I heard her mom in the background, and this time Olivia said, "I gotta go."

"Of course," I said right away. "I'll call you tomorrow."

"Thank you, Zoe." Olivia sounded slightly out of breath.

"Love ya," I said, and then she said, "Love ya," and we hung up. I walked to the door of the car. Even though I hadn't wanted to make a big deal out of it, I felt good. Really good.

Waiting was the worst. Waiting to visit Olivia. Waiting for her to get out of the hospital. To get better. To come back to school.

Doing something—even teaching a dance class—beat the hell out of waiting.

9

Jake had offered to give me a ride to the rec center, but it wasn't his car that pulled into my driveway at eight thirty on Saturday morning.

It was Calvin Taylor's.

Even before I saw Calvin's car, I was already in a bad mood. There was some problem with the hot water heater so my shower was freezing. Then I couldn't find a pair of ballet slippers. That might not be weird for most people, but all my life I'd had a minimum of a dozen pairs of ballet slippers and half as many pairs of toe shoes lying around my room at any given time. But like I said, when NYBC gave me and Livvie the ax, I chucked everything I owned that was ballet-related, so even rooting around in the attic and basement didn't turn up an old pair of shoes. On the one hand, it was kind of cool how thorough I'd been. On the other, I was fucked. I stood in my room fuming, surrounded by piles of everything I'd yanked off the floor of my closet and from under my bed. Finally, I just called Livvie at the hospital, and she said she'd tell her mom to give Jake a pair of her shoes to give to me. Livvie and I had the same size foot, and while you can't share toe shoes with another dancer since they mold to your feet, ballet slippers—especially ones you're not wearing for some major performance—aren't a problem.

I was running late and racing downstairs to grab something to eat before Jake picked me up and drove me to the rec center in downtown Newark, where—while I taught ballet and the cheerleaders taught tumbling—he and a bunch of the other guys on the football team would be teaching kids how to bench-press or tackle or rape or whatever it was that football players knew how to do well. I'd no sooner stepped foot in the kitchen than Calvin Taylor's car pulled up in front of my house, and I thought, *I now have objective proof that the universe is determined to screw with me.*

I yelled good-bye to my parents and ran out the front door, blaming Calvin for my missing the most important meal of the day.

"Hi," I said, sliding into the backseat of Calvin's vintage BMW.

"Hi," said Jake. Calvin didn't say anything.

"Oh," Jake said, "I'm supposed to give you these." He reached between the front seats and handed me a bag with the shoes inside.

Calvin backed the car out of the driveway. His car had soft leather seats. It was maybe ten or even fifteen years old, but it was in beautiful shape. It was one of the things that semiannoyed me about Calvin, how in addition to everything else he had this cool vintage car. Still, he *was* giving me a ride.

"Thanks for driving me," I said.

"Sure," said Calvin. His tone was clipped. I couldn't tell if it was I'm-mad-at-you-because-you-laughed-in-my-face clipped or It's-eight-thirty-and-I'm-not-a-morning-person clipped. Jake said something to him that I couldn't quite make out, and Calvin responded, "Not if he's still injured." Then Calvin turned up the music so I couldn't hear them at all, and I leaned back against the seat and stared out the window.

When Calvin turned into the parking lot of the rec center, which was surrounded by a barbed-wire fence, I figured the facility would be as awful as the rest of the block, but it was actually a pretty nice three-story brick building. There was a huge mural on the wall by the parking lot that had a black teenager guy being frisked by a cop. All around them were people holding cameras directed at the boy and the cop, and above the picture were the words LOVE YOUR CITY.

KNOW YOUR RIGHTS. It sounds depressing, but the colors were bright and the whole thing felt somehow energized and optimistic.

Calvin parked the car and the three of us got out. Jake put his arm around me as we walked toward the building.

"You doing okay?" he asked, squeezing my shoulders.

I loved Jake. Whether or not Mr. and Mrs. Greco saw me as family, Jake had always treated me like a little sister.

"Yeah, I'm okay," I said, squeezing him back. "You okay?"

"I don't know," he said, shaking his head. "This is seriously fucked up, you know?"

There really wasn't any other way to put it. "I know," I agreed.

"Jake! Calvin! Zoe!" Jake and I turned around. Stacy, Emma, the Bailor twins, and Hailey were piling out of Stacy's Lexus SUV.

"Come here, guys!" Emma called. She was gesturing us over frantically, as if the parking lot were on fire and she had discovered the only escape route.

Despite how annoyed he always seemed by Emma, Jake took his arm off my waist and headed toward the girls. "We'll give you a ride home," he said over his shoulder to me.

"Whipped much?" I teased him.

Laughing, he spun around in a full circle, pausing in my direction just long enough to give me the finger. "Just meet us back here after, okay?"

I shook my head, laughing also. "My dad's getting me. I think he thinks we need some father-daughter bonding time."

"Got it. See ya later."

"Later."

The girls literally swarmed Jake, and I watched him be engulfed by them. Emma managed to nuzzle in closer than all the rest, and when I saw him put his arm around her, I wondered if she felt triumph or just relief.

Stacy waved enthusiastically in my direction, but I just shook my head. It wasn't until she called, "Calvin," that I realized he was standing almost next to me.

"See you inside," he called back. Then he started walking toward the entrance.

Watching him go, I thought about how he'd barely talked to me in the car. It started to make me feel a little uneasy. Maybe what he'd said about how everything was going to be okay was idiotic, but it *had* been a little bitchy of me to laugh at him like that. I flashed forward: If when Livvie got better she still liked Calvin and they started going out, the last thing I needed was my best friend's boyfriend thinking I was a total asshole.

"Hey!" I shouted.

Calling after him made me feel a little like one of the cheerleaders.

He stopped and turned around. But he didn't say anything or walk over to me. I covered the distance between us.

"So," I began. "I . . . uh." I chuckled nervously. "I feel kinda bad about how I acted when you came over to me. You know. The other day. At my locker."

"Okay," he said. His arms were crossed over the word *Wamasset* on his gray T-shirt.

"That's it?" I crossed my arms also. "Okay?"

"Gee, Zoe, I'm sorry. I mean, I *want* to be good for a laugh. I just don't know if we have the same sense of humor."

Out of the corner of my eye, I saw the cheerleaders head into the rec center, Jake holding the door for them. Stacy and one of the Bailor twins had their arms around each other's waists.

I thought of Olivia and how before she got sick, I'd told her I wouldn't teach the dance class with her.

All at once I felt incredibly tired. "Just . . . just forget it, Calvin. Whatever." I took a step toward the building, but he put out his hand to stop me.

"'*Whatever*'? You're kidding me, right?" He gave an incredulous laugh. "Let me get this straight—Tuesday night, I'm at Jake's house. His phone is ringing off the hook. Aunts, uncles, grandparents. Fucking Emma *alone* calls, like, fifty times. And I'm just hanging out, watching him talk to the ten million people who are checking up on him, and suddenly I'm like, 'Wow!'" He made his voice thoughtful, reenacting the realization itself. "'I've never been in this house without Olivia and Zoe being here.' And then I'm like, 'I wonder if anyone is calling Zoe,' because it seems to me that you two don't hang out much with other people, and I don't know if you have a lot of other friends or anything. So Wednesday morning I decide to find you and see if you're okay, and the next thing I know, you're making me feel like a total dick."

"Look, I *said* I was sorry, all right?"

"Actually"—Calvin held up his index finger—"you *didn't* say you were sorry."

"Well, I'm *sorry*, okay? I'm sorry. I'm very, very sorry." I threw my arms wide. "Please, Calvin, will you forgive me?"

He cocked his head to the side and looked at me for a count of three. Then he smiled. "Yes. Zoe, I accept your apology." With that, he turned and walked into the building.

And even though there was objectively nothing left to say, I felt somehow that our conversation wasn't over.

Small letters on a plaque by the front door read THE REGINALD B. HARRIS COMMUNITY RECREATION CENTER. Inside, the walls were painted a creamy yellow, and there were black-and-white artsy-looking photos of Newark hanging everywhere. Next to the entry foyer was a sitting area with comfortable-looking overstuffed couches and armchairs. I could have been standing in the lobby of one of the swanky apartment buildings the girls at NYBC lived in.

I followed the signs to the main office, and when I explained who I was to the secretary there, she directed me to a door with a small black-and-white plaque that said RUTH

JONES, DIRECTOR. I knocked, and a woman's voice told me to come in.

Ruth Jones—if this was she—was an older African-American woman a little bit shorter than I was, and she was standing at a filing cabinet, holding a manila folder. Her office was small and neat, with two straight-backed chairs facing a desk covered in relatively organized-looking stacks of papers and folders. The walls were covered in color photos of smiling kids of a variety of ages.

"Can I help you?" Mrs. Jones's question had an edge to it, as if she thought I might be there to ask for a favor or something.

"Hi," I said, eager to disabuse her of the notion that *she* was somehow expected to help *me*. "Are you Mrs. Jones? I'm Zoe Klein. I'm Olivia Greco's friend. I'm going to be taking over the dance class while Olivia's having her treatment."

She didn't exactly jump up and down for joy. In fact, she just said, "Mmmmm-hmmm," and slid the filing cabinet drawer shut. Her lips were pressed tightly together. Once the drawer was closed all the way, she walked around to the front of the desk. I now saw that she was wearing extremely high heels. In her bare feet, she probably wasn't taller than about five feet. "Like I told Olivia," she said, "I'm not so happy with this entire . . . situation."

And what situation *might that be? My friend having cancer? Because I am just* soooo *happy about* that *situation.*

"This situation?" I repeated. "Do we have a situation?"

92

Even though I'd tried to keep the sarcasm out of my voice, her eyes narrowed slightly. "Yes, we do have a situation, Miss Zoe Klein." I heard the slightest hint of a southern accent. "And the situation is this: You did not apply for this position. No one interviewed you. I have no letters of recommendation from your teachers. I can't just have people walking in off the street to work with my girls. I *told* Olivia that I needed to take someone who'd gone through the application process, but she got upset. She said you were the only person she could work with. And I know she's sick. And our girls just love her, and she said if you did the class, she would be working with you. So what exactly am I supposed to say?"

And what exactly was *I* supposed to say? Olivia had *made* Mrs. Jones hire me? And what was all this talk about *hiring*, anyway? It wasn't like I was going to be getting a paycheck at the end of the month. This was just a stupid community service thing.

I stared at Mrs. Jones. Mrs. Jones stared back at me. Neither of us said anything, and I felt myself growing furious. My face burned and my fingers twitched.

It wasn't the first time I'd felt this way since Olivia's diagnosis. Just about anything could set me off these days—a seat belt that wouldn't snap shut, a bathroom stall with a broken lock, the stupid water heater and my freezing shower. Lately it felt like if I wasn't mad about something, I was *about* to get mad about something.

Olivia had gotten cancer and I'd gotten an anger-management problem.

I was seriously about to lose it at Mrs. Jones, but just as I opened my mouth, I saw Olivia, sitting in her hospital room, crying because she couldn't teach the girls ballet. Then I imagined calling Olivia up to inform her that I'd just told Mrs. Jones where she could shove her dance class.

I took a deep breath, squeezed my hands into fists, and managed to give Ruth Jones a wide and relatively sincere smile.

"Mrs. Jones," I said calmly, "I truly hope I'll be able to gain your confidence." My phone vibrated with an incoming text. I ignored it, keeping my eyes glued to Mrs. Jones's. Over and over as we stared at each other I repeated silently, *I am someone you can trust. I am someone you can trust,* willing her to get my telepathic message.

Finally, reluctantly, Mrs. Jones moved her eyes from mine. "I won't have my girls disappointed. They have to know they can depend on this place. The rest of the world lets them down. We lift them up."

When she said that, I knew I'd won. She was going to let me teach the class for Olivia.

"I won't disappoint them," I promised, almost adding *ma'am* at the last second and then deciding it would be overkill.

Out in the hallway, I checked my phone. The text was from Olivia.

don't be scared of mrs. j. she is ok.

I dialed Livvie's number. "That's information I could have used a little earlier," I hissed. "*And* she's not 'okay,' *and* nice of you to tell me she doesn't even *want* me teaching the class. I thought I was doing her some big favor."

"You *are* doing her a big favor," Olivia assured me. "As soon as she sees what you can do with these girls, she's going to realize that."

"Now I feel like she's just waiting for me to fail so she can fire me." Irritated by what I'd just said, I slapped the wall. "Listen to me. How can she fire me? *I don't even work here.*"

"Is this fun?" asked Olivia. "Are we having fun yet?" As Mrs. Jones had directed me to, I headed down the hallway and up a well-lit flight of dark wooden stairs.

"Your having cancer is a complete pain in my ass, Olivia Greco," I said.

"Tell me about it," she agreed.

～ 10 ～

Walking into the dance studio at the Reginald B. Harris Community Center was perhaps the strangest experience of my life.

Not because it was weird, but because it wasn't.

When I got to the second floor, I'd called Olivia back, this time with FaceTime, which we'd never used before. Her face filled the screen, which was so weird that I immediately cracked up. "Okay," I said, finally getting myself under control and making my voice deep and serious. "We are now walking down the hallway." I held the phone out in front of me and moved it around so she could see the hallway, then turned it back so we were looking at each other.

"Copy that," she answered, trying to keep a straight face and failing.

"Houston," I said. "We do not have a problem. I repeat: We do not have a problem."

"Roger, Captain," she squeaked, before totally losing it.

I was laughing so hard I could barely push the studio door open, but when I finally got myself more or less collected and crossed the threshold, the room looked identical to all the other dance studios Olivia and I had ever been in—a wall of full-length mirrors, a barre underneath the windows on the opposite wall, the floor a pale wood. The only difference between the studios Olivia and I had danced in at NYBC and this one was that this one didn't have a piano.

I had never been in this room before, but I knew it perfectly. The sensation made me shiver slightly, as if I'd somehow stepped into my own past.

The dozen or so girls clustered at the far end of the room and staring at me as I walked in were a welcome distraction.

"So, um . . . hi. I'm Zoe." I gave a little wave. Most of the girls were probably around eight or nine. One or two might have been a little older, and one girl was so tall I was sure she was at least twelve or thirteen. A couple of the smallest girls waved back at me. I put my phone down, reached into my purse for the bag with Olivia's ballet shoes, sat down, and slipped them on. The whole time, the girls watched me, not saying anything.

"Where's Olivia?" asked the tall girl finally.

"Ta-da!" I picked up the phone and held it out to them.

From their squeals of amazement, you would have thought Olivia had just materialized in the middle of the room. All traces of hostility gone from their faces, they gathered around my phone, calling out and waving hello to Olivia. A couple of them actually reached up and touched the screen shyly. Finally the same tall girl who'd asked me where Olivia was now asked *Olivia* where she was.

"Everybody sit down and I'll tell you." Olivia's voice was tinny and a little distorted, but word passed from one girl to another and soon they were huddled in a tight group on the floor. I held my phone directly in front of me. To the girls it probably looked as if Olivia's face was on my body.

After all these years, I was finally getting to be a blonde.

"I'm really sorry I'm not there," Olivia began once they were quiet. "But last week I went to the doctor, and it turns out I have an illness that has to be treated with an IV. See my IV?" The girls nodded, their faces serious. "I'll be better soon, but I have to take this medicine for about a week, and then I have to recover from taking this medicine, which is kind of crazy when you think about it."

"What do you have, Olivia?" asked an adorable girl with short, tightly braided hair and a high-pitched voice.

"That's a good question, Imani," said Olivia, and I realized I was going to have to learn all their names. I'm terrible at names. A person can tell me her name and I forget it five seconds later. While Olivia described what was wrong with her without once uttering the word *cancer* or *leukemia*, I watched Imani, trying to think of a mnemonic that would help me remember Imani. *Sounds like salami.* Nothing about her hair said salami to me. A few freckles. Freckles had nothing to do with salami either. I kept staring at her, noticing only when she reached up to scratch her chin that she was wearing a necklace that said *Imani.*

"But when are you coming back?" asked the tall girl suspiciously. She was so not falling for this whole Olivia-has-to-be-in-the-hospital-for-an-unspecified-period-of-time-but-everything's-fabulous routine.

I had to respect her unwillingness to buy the bullshit we were selling.

"Charlotte, what do you mean, when am I coming back?" asked Livvie, her voice upbeat. "I'm here now. And you're really lucky, because you not only get me, you get my very best best friend in the entire world. We're like the . . . super dynamic duo."

Even though Livvie said the thing about our being best friends and a super dynamic duo in this really light, funny way, to my surprise I felt my eyes getting damp. Fabulous. Just when Livvie had reassured these girls that everything was going to be fine, I was going to start blubbering.

Way to inspire confidence, Zoe!

"Now," Livvie continued, "I told Zoe all about what incredibly hard workers you are, so don't make me a liar, okay?"

A few of the girls nodded. A few others said, "Okay!" I made a mental note of how Olivia was talking to them—nice but firm.

I went across the hallway to an empty classroom, got a chair, and put my phone on it while the girls lined up at the barre. I turned on the CD player, and soft piano music filled the room as Olivia told the girls to stand in first position and then plié. For a minute I watched her face on my screen. She was smiling widely, totally in her element.

Meanwhile, I felt like I was being tortured. How could I be in a dance studio and not dance? My body ached to move, to bend and stretch with the music.

This isn't about you, I told myself firmly. *This is about them.* I took my eyes off Olivia and turned to look at the girls.

I'd always wondered how NYBC and other elite dance schools made their decisions about who to accept and who to reject, who to promote and who to cut. After dancing with the same girls for years, I definitely thought I knew which ones were the best, but it seemed to me that in just a few minutes of an audition, it would have been impossible to judge a dancer's true ability unless someone majorly fucked up.

Watching the girls follow Olivia's instructions, I immediately understood how it worked. All the girls stood in first position, facing the barre, bending and straightening their legs as Olivia told them to. But you definitely would not have used the word *graceful* to describe most of them. They kind of threw their knees out when they bent down, and they were almost all jerky in their movements, grasping the barre in a death grip as they stuck their butts out each time Olivia asked them to do a plié. A couple of the girls were okay, gently bending at the knee and holding their backs straight like they were supposed to. Still, if I'd been a scout sent to choose potential NYBC dancers from this group, I would have known at a glance to reject all of them.

Only one—the tall girl who'd kept asking questions earlier—had any real talent. Her arms were draped gracefully, and her fingertips rested lightly on the barre. When Olivia told the class to move to second position, she did a battement *tendu* so perfect I wondered if she'd studied ballet before Olivia had taught her. Because it wasn't just her skills. The whole way she carried her body was more expert and professional than any of the other girls. Once upon a time that had been me and Olivia—standing out from the crowd of girls who wanted to be ballerinas but didn't have the goods.

Until we didn't have the goods either.

After the girls were warmed up, Olivia had them move to the center of the room, and later she asked them to line up in pairs and had them *chassé* across the floor. Some of the girls definitely got better and more relaxed as class went on, but the tall girl was still the only one worth watching.

"Okay, guys," Olivia said when class was nearly over. "We only have a few minutes left, but let's try doing some chaînés. You may remember them from last week, but let's review. Zoe, can I ask you to demonstrate?"

"Sure," I said, glad to finally get out of my head and be useful.

I headed to the center of the room. I hadn't been actively avoiding looking at my reflection, but when I met my own eyes in the mirror, I realized I'd managed not to see myself for the whole time we'd been in class.

The funny thing was that my reflection, when I finally saw it, was the only strange thing in this otherwise familiar setting. At NYBC, girls wore pink tights and black leotards. Always. No exceptions. Since I was no longer in possession of either of these items of clothing—what with my having chucked my entire dance wardrobe—I'd put on black leggings and a cropped blue T-shirt to lead the class. Even though I was wearing ballet slippers, the image reflected back at me wasn't the one I'd watched for years. I could have been doing yoga or joining my mom for one of her exercise classes.

Olivia began talking me through a chaîné, which is the most basic turn in ballet. You start in first position, with your arms together; then you move your legs into second position while you open your arms; then you close your arms and your feet. All the while you're on pointe or in relevé, keeping your eyes on a single spot on the opposite wall as you turn.

I let Olivia's voice rather than my own brain control my movements. As she spoke, I moved across the floor doing one slow-motion turn after another. It was strange to break down a move I knew so intuitively, and I actually stumbled once, the same way that if you try to think about tying your shoes your laces suddenly get tangled up in your fingers.

When I arrived at the far wall, Livvie said, "Let's see that again, honey."

When we'd been at NYBC, the only day of the week we didn't have class was Sunday, and on Sundays, Livvie and I would sometimes go down to my basement and practice. We'd dance until our legs were shaking and we were watering the floor with sweat as we spun. Sometimes one of us would bark out commands, standing in the corner with her arms folded in imitation of Martin Hicks, NYBC's director. When the one who was dancing would finish, the other one would say, *Let's see that again, honey,* which was apparently (according to the girls we knew who had danced for him) his way of saying, *That fucking sucked, you lazy bitch.*

I looked across the room at Olivia's face on the tiny screen. The girls watching us faded into the background. It was just me and Livvie and our private joke. "I'm sorry, did you say, 'Let's see that again, honey'?"

"I might have." In Olivia's voice, I could hear the effort it was taking her not to laugh.

I put my hands on my hips and stared at her. "So, what are you saying, exactly?"

Still keeping a straight face, Olivia answered, "I think you *know* what I'm saying."

Out of the corner of my eye, I saw the girls looking from me to Olivia, trying to crack our code.

"I'll get you for that," I said. Shaking my head and laughing to myself, I held my arms out in front of me. Then I began to chaîné across the floor.

All of the awkwardness I'd felt while I was trying to demonstrate the components of the turn disappeared, and I felt my body turn to liquid as one position slid effortlessly into the other, my arms and legs moving together without my ordering them to.

I'd been doing chaînés since I was six years old, and they felt as natural a way to cross a room as walking. When I got to the far wall, I wanted to keep spinning, to push through the paint and plaster and brick and chaîné all the way to Manhattan. But then a bell rang quietly in the distance, startling me out of my reverie. I stopped abruptly, and to my surprise, the girls burst into applause.

"Zoe, that was amazing!" Imani cried.

"Oh," I said, suddenly self-conscious. "I mean, thank you."

"Yeah," agreed another girl, who also had tightly braided hair and who looked so much like Imani that I wondered if they might be sisters.

"Thank you, Zoe," said Olivia from the phone. "And thank you, class." I realized the bell meant class had ended.

"Thank you, Olivia," said the class in perfect unison, and they all curtsied toward the phone before gathering up their things. A few of them glanced my way as they were walking out. "Thanks, Zoe!" one called.

"Sure," I answered, and then quickly corrected myself. "I mean, thank *you*."

When the girls had left, I went over to my phone.

"That was fun, right?" said Livvie.

"I don't know." I shook my head, not sure how to describe how confusing it had been. "It's weird. Being here."

"You get used to it," said Livvie quietly.

It was the first time she'd even hinted at feeling weird about teaching the class, and I snapped my head to look at her. She was lying back on the bed, and now I could see that she was wearing a long-sleeved green T-shirt that we'd ordered together in August from J.Crew. The only time I'd seen her wear it was the day it arrived, which was when she tried it on and realized simultaneously that she hated it and that it couldn't be returned.

I'd planned to ask her what she meant about getting used to it, but seeing what she was wearing distracted me. "Nice shirt," I said. "Let me guess: Your mom packed clothes for you."

She gave me a tired smile. "Bingo."

"You look beat," I observed.

She nodded.

And suddenly, I felt overwhelmed with sadness. We weren't in the dance studio together. Thanks to technology, it might feel like we were. But we weren't. One of us was in a dance studio in Newark.

One of us was in the hospital.

"I'm sorry. Next time I'll do more," I told her. "I promise. I won't let you get so tired."

"Don't apologize," she said, shaking her head slowly. "I wanted to do what I did. Aren't the girls great?"

"They are," I agreed.

Her eyes were closed, and I thought she might have dozed off, but then she said quietly, "Wasn't it nice to dance again?"

"I don't know," I said. How could I explain that I felt as if I'd spent the past hour in a room filled with ghosts? "Sure. Yeah." Then I rolled my eyes. "Get some sleep." She gave a tired laugh at my nonanswer. "Hey," I added, "if you want, after my dad and I run errands, I'll go to your house and pick some clothes for you. I can bring them to the hospital later." I knew Livvie's wardrobe as well as I know my own—probably better, because since her mom was kind of conservative, we had to spend a lot of time debating what her mother's opinion would be regarding the appropriateness of certain items of clothing, including shirts with low necklines or any skirts that might possibly be modified using the adjective *short*.

She nodded. "You sure you don't mind?" She was so tired she was slurring her words.

"I'm ignoring you," I said. "Go to sleep. I'll see you soon."

I turned off my phone, and when the screen went to black,

Olivia's face was replaced with a reflection of my own. Soft classical music still played. The studio was empty. Should I stay and try to choreograph something for the recital? Livvie had said it was a lot of work. If I started now, there would be plenty of time. But it wasn't like I was supposed to be working on a routine for the recital by myself. Livvie and I would do it together.

I got to my feet and looked around. Part of me wanted to stretch out at the barre, really warm up, do something more complicated than a string of chaînés so I could—

So I could what? Get better?

Why bother? Who would notice? Olivia? The girls in the class?

If a dancer dances but NYBC isn't watching her, is she even dancing?

I hadn't signed on for these questions when I'd volunteered to teach the class. All I'd been focused on was helping Olivia. But here I was, feeling sorry for myself and thinking about things I'd promised myself I'd never think about again.

As fast as I could, I grabbed my bag and walked out the door of the studio.

I'd made my decision the day I got cut.

Dance held nothing for me anymore.

∾ 11 ∾

I went home, showered, changed, and walked over to Olivia's to get some clothes to bring to her at the hospital later. Tommy and Jake were playing basketball in the driveway, and they let me into the house.

There was something creepy about walking down the hallway to her room all by myself, but I couldn't figure out what. After all, it wasn't as if I'd never been in Olivia's room without Olivia. How many times had I run up here to grab something while Livvie waited for me in the den, the TV paused in the middle of a movie? Or raced back inside while my mom sat in the car and I retrieved my notebook or my backpack?

Standing in her bedroom, I dialed Livvie's number, but she didn't answer, and I plopped down on the bed, waiting for her to call me back. The comforter I was sitting on was her old one—her new one was on her bed at the hospital. This one was fire-engine red, and it clashed with the walls, which were a pale green. Before she'd redecorated (over the summer after seventh grade) her room had been all primary colors—red comforter, blue chair, yellow carpet. The day before the guys came to paint, Olivia had taken pictures of the room for her memory box, which was this gigantic box she had, filled with keepsakes. The whole time Livvie was taking the pictures of her old room, I'd kept telling her she was crazy. How could we ever forget her room? She'd lived in it since she was little, and I'd practically lived in it since then too. But now, studying the comforter that had covered her bed for the first eight years of our friendship, I found I couldn't re-create her old room in my head, not even when I closed my eyes. I thought about going into her closet and digging through the memory box for the pictures, but I didn't think I should without asking Livvie if that was okay.

The minutes passed. I lay back on her bed, my silent phone next to me. Outside, I could hear Jake and Tommy playing basketball. It seemed to me I'd been hearing that noise my entire life.

As I lay there, trying to remember what art had hung on the walls of her old room, out of nowhere I suddenly thought, *Olivia has cancer.*

My heart started racing.

Cancer. How could my friend have cancer?

Cancer killed people.

But Olivia wasn't going to die. We were sixteen. People who are sixteen, people you've known your whole life, don't die of cancer.

Why not? asked an ugly, scary voice in my brain. *Why don't they die of cancer?*

"Because," I said out loud, the sound of my voice startling in the quiet room. "They don't."

I got to my feet. Moving silenced the voice in my head. I slid open the middle drawer of her wooden wardrobe, where she kept her shirts. But staring at the top one, I found myself stymied all over again. Did she still like the red T-shirt with the three-quarter sleeves? I hadn't seen her wear it in a while, but she'd never specifically mentioned *not* liking it. Maybe it was just out of the rotation? I bit my lip, looking at her drawer of carefully folded T-shirts: long-sleeved ones on one side of the drawer, short-sleeved ones on the other. How had I never noticed how carefully Olivia folded her clothes? We'd always joked that she was neat and I was messy, but I'd never appreciated just how neat she was. Each shirt was stacked on top of the one below it as precisely as if they were on display at Banana Republic or the Gap, two stores that Olivia and I both hated.

Standing in her room, surrounded by her stuff but unable to know what she would want to wear, the voice in my brain informed me, *This is what it would be like if Olivia were dead.*

"Well, she's *not* dead!" I said out loud.

I reached for my phone. I needed to talk to her, even if she just told me to chill out or said she didn't care what she wore.

I dialed her number, but it wasn't Olivia who answered. "Hi, Zoe."

"Hi, Mrs. Greco."

Her voice was whisper quiet. "Olivia's just having a little nap."

"Oh," I said. My heart dropped. I couldn't ask Mrs. Greco to wake her daughter just because I was freaking out. "I was just going to ask her about some clothes. I'm putting a suitcase together for her."

"Yes, she told me about that," said Mrs. Greco. "She hates all the clothes I brought her. I guess I haven't been paying attention to what she wears."

Apparently neither have I, I thought, glancing down at the red T-shirt.

"Do you want her to call you when she wakes up? Assuming she's feeling up to it?"

"No, no," I said quickly, "I can figure it out on my own. I just wasn't sure about this one particular shirt."

"Okay," said her mom. "I know she's looking forward to your visit later. And not just because of the clothes."

That was nice. Mrs. Greco's saying that made me feel better.

"Thanks," I said. "I am too."

◆　◆　◆

I ended up just picking things I'd seen Olivia wear in the last few weeks of summer—a blue-and-white-striped T-shirt, a pair of white capri pants, a skirt with a pattern of faces that we'd bought because we couldn't decide if it was awesome or awful but that turned out to be clearly awesome—adding a couple of hoodies and some leggings and yoga pants because of the air-conditioning in the hospital. Then I zipped the suitcase, rolled it along the hallway, and bounced it down the stairs. When I opened the front door of the house, I expected to see Jake and Tommy still playing hoops, but instead I saw Calvin Taylor dribbling while Tommy watched from the sidelines. Calvin might have been the QB of the football team, but he was a damn good basketball player. His arm moved in a smooth arc as he seemingly effortlessly took the shot from far down the driveway. Just as I pulled the door closed behind me, the ball swooshed into the net. Tommy applauded. Neither of them saw me come out.

"Now you," said Calvin, bouncing Tommy the ball.

"I'm not going to be as good as you," Tommy told him.

Calvin didn't deny it. "Well, considering I've got about three feet and ten years on you, that seems fair, don't you think?"

"But I'm a prodigy," Tommy explained, grinning. The twins' smiles always slayed me. It was like the rest of their bodies hadn't caught up to their enormous new front teeth. "My goal is to be the only third grader who can dunk."

"Is that so?" Calvin asked, laughing. He dashed over, picked Tommy up, and raced him back to the hoop. "Quick! Quick!" he cried. "Do it. Dunk!" Sitting on Calvin's shoulders, Tommy was higher than the hoop, and he easily dropped the ball into it. "And the crowd goes wild," yelled Calvin. "Aaaah!" He ran around the driveway, Tommy on his shoulders, both of them cheering.

As they finished their victory lap, Tommy called, "Hi, Zoe!"

"Hey!" I waved to them. "Where are your brothers?"

"Jake's getting Luke at Aunt Margaret's house and then he and Calvin are taking us to the movies." He lowered his voice and informed me confidentially, "We're going to see a PG-13."

"In your *dreams*, little man," Calvin said. He lifted Tommy off his shoulders and put him on the blacktop next to him. Tommy gave me a knowing wink and went over to the grass on the other side of the driveway to retrieve the ball.

Calvin was breathing heavily from his lap with Tommy on his shoulders. He put his hands on his hips and cocked his head at me. "You running away from home?" he asked, nodding at the suitcase.

"Yeah." I shrugged and looked off to the end of the block. "You know how it is. Big dreams. Little town."

"Sure," he said. "I get it."

"Actually, these are just some clothes for Olivia," I explained.

"You packed her a suitcase?" he asked, genuinely surprised.

"Yeah," I said, surprised that he was surprised. "Does that seem weird to you?"

"I don't know." He wiped his sweaty forehead with his upper arm. "I can't imagine any of my friends going through my clothes."

I shrugged. "Maybe it's a girl thing." As soon as I said it, I was annoyed with myself. I hate gender stereotypes, like girls love princesses and boys like guns. All the guys I was with at NYBC had had to deal with being called fag and homo just because they liked dance. I mean, a lot of them *were* gay (or at least well on their way to being gay), and words like *fag* and *homo* are totally unacceptable whether or not people are gay, but my point is that tying particular behaviors and interests to a particular gender seems to be the major reason guys who like dance get called names.

"Or maybe it's a Zoe-Olivia thing," he said.

"Maybe," I agreed.

After our bickering earlier in the week and then my angry apology Saturday morning, this felt almost like a truce. Together we watched Tommy set up, shoot, and miss the basket by a mile.

"Good try," said Calvin. "Don't lean back so much."

Tommy headed to retrieve the ball, and I glanced over at Calvin. To my surprise, he was looking at me. There was something intense about how he was doing it—not anything gross, like he was checking me out, but more like he was watching for something or wondering about something, and he could only learn the answer if he studied me long enough.

I felt self-conscious about how I was staring at him or he was staring at me or we were staring at each other. "You're really good." As soon as the words were out of my mouth, I was mortified.

"What?" He smiled, but there was a confused look on his face.

"I meant I . . . I mean, I meant to say you're really good with *kids*." I looked away, watching Tommy because it was something to watch besides Calvin. "I'm not very . . . natural with them. It's a little awkward."

"I'm sure you're fine."

"Trust me. I'm not one of those people who say they're bad at things they're good at." Tommy sank his shot and Calvin gave a long, low whistle. "Nice job, T-dog!" Tommy did a brief victory dance.

"Are there a lot of those people?" asked Calvin.

"What people?" I was confused.

"People who say they're bad at things they're good at." He considered the possibility. "I thought people usually say they're good at things when they're not."

"Wait, what?" I pushed my hair off my forehead. My bangs were growing out, and lately they were always getting in my

115

eyes. "I'm sorry, I totally lost what we're talking about."

Calvin threw back his head and laughed just as Jake pulled into the driveway, honking, with Luke hanging out of the back window and waving.

"Come on!" Luke yelled. "We're going to be late."

"You need a ride?" asked Calvin as Tommy tossed the basketball onto the lawn.

"No," I said. "I feel like walking. Thanks, though."

"Anytime."

Calvin and Tommy headed for the car, and Jake waved to me. "You don't want a ride?" Jake asked.

I shook my head. It was less than a mile from my house to Livvie's, and I walked it all the time. "I'm fine," I told him. "Have fun at the movies."

The car drove down the block. I waved to them as they passed, thinking what nice guys Calvin and Jake were for entertaining the twins all afternoon. Calvin especially, since you could argue that Jake's being their big brother obligated him to look after them.

Pretty quickly I couldn't hear the car anymore. It was a warm afternoon; the only sound was birds calling to one another or singing or whatever it is that birds do and the occasional slam of a door or maybe a lawn mower going in the distance. The walk from Olivia's to my house was so familiar I could do it on autopilot, and as I made the turn onto my street, I realized I'd gone the whole way without once thinking of Olivia's being sick. I stopped, startled by the realization. I wondered what I *had* been thinking about, but when I tried to retrieve my thoughts of the last fifteen minutes, the file came up blank.

～ 12 ～

It's insane how fast the unthinkable becomes the normal.

By the middle of October, my new routine was as predictable as my old one had been. I went to class. I ate lunch. Sometimes I'd see Jake in the hallway or as I was walking into school, and we'd hug and he'd ask me how I was doing. If he was with Emma, she'd hug me and ask how I was doing also. Sometimes I'd just pass a group of cheerleaders without Jake, and *all* of them would have to hug me and ask how I was doing. Once, when Mia and I were coming back from Starbucks and we ran into Jake and Emma and Stacy Shaw and the Bailor twins in the parking lot, she witnessed this phenomenon and said there weren't enough minutes in a free period for her to do coffee runs with me anymore.

I went over to Mia's a couple of times, and the soccer team

had a party and they invited me, but all those things were just a way to pass the time. My life—my *real* life—was, just as it had been until sophomore year, with Olivia. Every day after school and every Saturday afternoon and every Sunday morning I'd get on the train or into my mom's or my dad's car and head into the city to Olivia's hospital room. We'd do homework together or not do homework together or talk trash or—when mouth sores from the chemo made it hard for her to talk—communicate via a sign language we invented that made us crack up but that drove everyone else in the room totally batshit. On Saturday mornings, we taught dance class together—or she taught the class while I said vague, encouraging things from the sidelines.

Instead of dancing together, we were waiting for Olivia to get better together. Everything had changed, but nothing had changed. It was still me and Olivia in our own world.

One afternoon, just as I was walking out of history—my last class of the day—and doing a mental check of what I had to get from my locker before I left the building to go home and meet my dad so he could drive me into Manhattan, Mrs. Greco called. Because it was her hospital room's landline, which Livvie called me from if her hands were shaky (which sometimes happened from the chemo), I'd assumed it was Livvie, so when I picked up, I said, "Yo!" in this way we have.

"Zoe?" said Mrs. Greco.

"Oh, Mrs. Greco. I'm sorry. That's just this dumb thing Livvie and I do. Yes, it's Zoe."

"No, that's fine," said Mrs. Greco. "I understand you two have your . . . things." Mrs. Greco was one of the people who was not especially fond of our private sign language. "I'm calling because Olivia is too tired to have visitors today. Her counts are so low—she's just wiped."

Even though the chemo was over, Olivia's red and white blood cells still had to come back, like flowers growing in a postapocalyptic landscape. While that was happening, she didn't have much energy. The day before, she'd dozed off twice while I was there. "I don't mind being there even if she's asleep," I said.

Mrs. Greco didn't come right out and say no.

"We're hoping a transfusion's going to give her some pep," she told me. "It's scheduled for later this afternoon."

"She's like a vampire," I joked.

I don't know if the idea was objectively funny or not, but I really think Livvie would have laughed.

Her mom did not. "I suppose so," she said.

"Anyway," I said, "I'm sure she'll feel better after she gets the transfusion."

"Of course she will," said Mrs. Greco firmly. "And then she'll be up for visitors again."

"Yeah. Maybe tomorrow."

"She'll call you," Mrs. Greco said.

At the far end of the hallway, I saw Jake and Calvin standing by their lockers. They were talking to each other. I almost went over to say hi to Jake, but Calvin had his arm draped around this senior girl, and for some reason that made me feel weird about going over to them.

When I got home, my dad was in the kitchen working on his laptop. I told him we wouldn't be driving into Manhattan to see Livvie. Then I jerked the door of the refrigerator open, looked inside, grabbed a bottle of seltzer, then slammed the fridge shut loudly enough that my dad jumped a little.

"Are you okay?" he asked. "You seem a little mad."

"I seem a little mad? Yeah, I'm a little mad." I put my hands on my hips and glared at him, and it was like all those times I'd managed to contain my anger—all those annoying seat belts and bathroom locks and too-hot macchiatos that I'd been tolerating for the past several weeks—just exploded. "The stupid doctors give Olivia all of this medication that's supposed to make her healthy, and meanwhile it makes her feel like total shit. I mean, what the hell are they doing?"

He lowered the lid of his laptop and frowned. "It's lousy. It's really lousy." He shook his head.

"It's not lousy; it's criminal," I corrected him. "They're, like, carpet bombing her body and just hoping it will make her better. Livvie said some people who get chemo get *brain damage*."

"Well, I think that's pretty rare," my dad said, folding his hands under his chin.

"Oh, so that makes it okay?" I waved the bottle of seltzer to emphasize my point. "What if *your* kid got brain damage from all the toxic chemicals the doctors were dumping into her body to quote unquote cure her?"

He pushed his chair back, stood up, and came over to where I was standing. Then he put his hands on my shoulders and looked down at me. "Everyone is doing everything they can to make sure Olivia gets better. They're using the tools they have. It's no one's fault that those tools are primitive."

"Why are you defending a bunch of random doctors you don't even know?" I demanded, jerking free of his hands and crossing the room to get a glass. "Since when are you a cheerleader for the medical community? Aren't you the one who's always saying we need a single-payer system?"

My dad gave me a confused look. "I'm not exactly sure what this has to do with a single-payer system."

"Can't you see how our whole medical system is completely fucked up?" I slammed the glass and the seltzer bottle on the counter and threw my hands wide in the air. "I mean, wasn't cancer supposed to have been cured, like, fifty years ago?"

My dad's expression softened. "Honey, we're all worried about Olivia. But it's no one's fault she's sick."

"Oh, *really?*" I snapped. "That's your professional opinion."

"Not everything is somebody's fault."

"Don't give me that, okay? I'm really tired of hearing that."
I looked at the bottle in front of me. "You know what? I don't
even *want* a fucking glass of seltzer." I left the bottle there and
stormed up to my bedroom.

"Maybe we could watch the language a little bit, okay?" my
dad called up after me.

"Whatever," I yelled back, and I slammed my door.

The stupid thing was—the *embarrassing* thing was—I wasn't
even mad about Olivia's blood counts. I'd been all psyched for
the day her chemo ended, but then Olivia had told *me* that
Dr. Maxwell had told *her* that a lot of patients felt worse *after*
the chemo because they had such low blood counts. Given
how tired Livvie had been when I'd visited yesterday, I wasn't
exactly shocked that she was too zonked for me to visit today.

It was that word. *Visitors.* If Mrs. Greco had said, *Olivia
isn't up for seeing you* or *Livvie wants to see you but she feels like shit*
(not that Mrs. Greco would ever use the word *shit*, but still), I
wouldn't have minded so much. *Visitors.* Like I was Emma, who
was always offering to go with Jake to the hospital, ostensibly
because she was worried about Livvie but really because she
wanted to be Jake's official girlfriend as opposed to what she
was, which was the sad girl who threw herself at him.

God, that was so me. The sad girl throwing herself at the
Greco family.

My phone rang. It was the hospital landline again. Mrs.

Greco? I picked up. Before I could say anything, Olivia spoke. "Check your email." I could tell her mouth was still bothering her, because she articulated her words carefully.

I logged on. There was a forward from Olivia.

"It's from fucking Stacy Shaw?" I screamed. "Oh my God, is this one of those inspirational messages?"

"Just read it," Olivia said patiently. "I want to hear you read it."

I read it out loud.

Dear Olivia,
We are all *freaking out* that you are sick. We just love you so much. You are the sweetest person and we are going to do *everything* we can for you! Starting with raising money for the Leukemia and Lymphoma Society and the National Bone Marrow Registry with a . . . drum roll, please . . . car wash! Also a blood drive! I talked to your mom, and she said that you might be able to come if the weather's warm and it's outside (car wash, outside, so totally!), so we're scheduling it for the last Saturday in October. We're all going to sign up with the registry, so if you need a bone marrow transplant (hopefully not, right?!) you can have one from one of us!!! We love you! We're cheering for you!
Love, Stacy (aka Captain, lol!)

"Oh. My. God," I whispered as I reread the message, silently this time.

"Mmm-hmmm."

I didn't even want to think about Olivia's needing a bone marrow transplant. The only reason she would need that would be if the chemo failed and she relapsed, which was so not going to happen. After getting some early postchemo blood work, Dr. Maxwell had said it was "unnecessary" to think about Livvie's having a bone marrow transplant, which clearly meant she was responding well enough to the chemo that she was definitely not going to need one.

"I don't care if it costs you your life," I said. "You *cannot* get Stacy Shaw's bone marrow. I'm serious." God, talk about brain damage.

"I promise," Livvie whispered.

"How are you feeling?" I asked. Over the weeks she'd spent in the hospital, I'd begun to crack the code of Livvie's answers to this question. *Good* meant *not bad*. *Fine* meant *pretty bad*. *So-so* meant *awful*.

"So-so," she said.

"Oh, honey."

"But the good news is"—I heard a slurp, and I knew she was eating one of the frozen pops that made her mouth feel better—"they're sending me home Sunday."

"They *are*? Livvie, that's amazing." I jumped to my feet. If they were sending her home, that meant she was getting better. All this time I'd been so focused on how lousy the chemo was making her feel that I hadn't paid attention to the fact that it was actually curing her.

"I know," she said.

"I'm so happy," I said, and then I started to cry. I thought I was managing to keep my snuffling on the DL, but then Livvie asked, "Are you *crying?*"

"A little," I admitted.

"Geez," she said, her voice sounding stronger than it had during our entire conversation thus far, "you are such a wimp." The fact that she had used the word *geez* (very close to *Jesus*) made me know her mom wasn't in the room.

"You're not supposed to be on the phone, are you?" I realized.

"I'm supposed to be resting," she admitted. "But I had to call and tell you the good news." Her saying that just made me cry harder.

"Can you do me a favor?" Livvie asked, speaking carefully. I thought she was going to ask me to stop bawling in her ear, but instead she said, "Could you teach dance class alone Saturday morning? I just feel too—"

"Oh my God, of course!" I said, wiping my face. "Of course I can."

"I know we were going to try to start choreographing something for the recital—"

"Livs, please! Don't even worry about it. I'll figure something out. I'll work on it."

"Thanks," she whispered. "Don't worry about anything. Just have fun with them."

"Sure," I said. "Of course."

"I love you."

"I love you too."

I hung up. When Livvie had good news, she called me. When something funny happened to her, she called me. When she needed something, she called me. When she wasn't allowed to be on the phone, she called me anyway.

Maybe Mrs. Greco thought of me as a visitor.

But Livvie didn't.

Later, my mom and I went to get takeout from Mr. Chow's. We were sitting in the little waiting area by the cash register when out of nowhere my mom reached over, pulled me to her, and gave me a hug so tight it actually hurt.

"Ouch, Mom!" I complained. "You're hurting me."

To my surprise, my mom's whole body suddenly convulsed in a single enormous sob. A second later, she pulled away. There were tears on her face.

"I'm sorry," she said. Her voice was husky.

I felt bad for pushing her away, and I reached out and patted her hand. "It's okay."

"I just keep thinking of how awful this is for Adriana. For all of them," she added quickly. "But for Adriana especially. I think it must be the worst for her. To have your daughter . . ." Her eyes filled up and more tears spilled onto her cheeks. She didn't bother wiping them away.

127

"It's the worst for Olivia," I corrected. "She's the one who's sick."

"I know," said my mom, digging around in her bag. She pulled out a tissue and blew her nose. "I know it's awful for her. But I just think about what if it were you and how your dad and I couldn't—" Her voice broke, and she buried her face in her tissue.

"Mom, please." It wasn't just that I didn't want the woman who worked the register at Mr. Chow's to see her. There was something about her saying how awful it would be if it were me who was sick that made me feel guilty, almost like she was saying she was glad it was Olivia and *not* me.

She took a deep, shuddering breath and wiped her eyes. "I'm sorry."

I slipped my arm around her waist and hugged her. "Anyway, it's *not* me, Mom."

"I know," she repeated. "I know that, honey." She blew her nose again and put her arm around my shoulders.

"And she's coming home," I pointed out. "That's really good news. It means she's getting better." I smiled and poked her gently in the side. "Then we can finally take that mother-daughter trip to see Fallingwater you've always talked about."

My mom was kind of obsessed with the idea of a mother-daughter trip somewhere. She and Mrs. Greco would bring it up now and then, but somehow it never seemed to happen. Olivia's and my theory was that that was because nobody but my mom thought it would be fun to see Frank Lloyd Wright's most famous house, which, unfortunately, is in Nowheresville, Pennsylvania.

I'd said the thing about the mother-daughter trip as a way of throwing a bone to my mom, totally expecting her to start chattering on about how wonderful it would be for all of "us girls" to go somewhere together.

But she just said, "Mmmm," and squeezed my shoulders again. I waited for her to start talking (which is like waiting for the Home Shopping Network to start selling you something), but she stayed quiet. When our food came out from the kitchen and the woman called our name, my mom paid for the food and took the bags. She handed me one, then held the door for me as we exited the restaurant. But she didn't say a word about our trip, and she didn't say what a wonderful thing it was that Olivia was on her way to being cured.

13

Saturday morning when I ran down the driveway to meet Jake, who was driving me to the rec center, I assumed one of the two people sitting in the backseat must be Calvin, but two other guys from the football team—Sean Miller and Delford White—were there instead. They said hi to me, and I said hi back.

"So, are you psyched about Olivia coming home tomorrow?" Sean asked me. "Jake was just telling us about it."

"Totally," I said. "I can't wait."

"My mom's home right now sterilizing everything," said Jake. "Prepare to be boiled."

"Happily."

Jake turned up the volume on the radio, and no one said anything for the rest of the song. When it ended, I asked where Calvin was.

"He's got some family thing this weekend. In Pennsylvania," Jake answered, slowing down for a red light and jumping to another song.

"Oh," I said. "Well, that sounds like fun."

Jake shrugged. "I guess." The light changed, and he drove on. It was weird, because for a minute it almost felt like I was disappointed by the news that Calvin was away for the weekend.

But of course I wasn't.

I mean, why would I be?

The second I walked through the door of the dance studio, the girls swarmed me. Charlotte reached for my phone, crying, "Hey, Olivia! Hey, hey, Olivia!" I pulled it to my chest protectively as another girl who'd been smiling at the screen as if she could already see Olivia on it pushed her face toward me. "Careful," I said as she bumped into me. Stepping back, I landed on someone's foot, and she yelled, "*Ouch!* Watch *out!*" and I was like, "I'm *trying* to watch out," and then I shouted in this really loud voice, "Everyone just take a step *back!*"

It was as if I'd flipped the silent switch. Everyone not only took a step back; they all froze, staring at me as if I'd raised my arm to slap them.

"Sorry," I said quickly. "I'm really sorry."

But they were suspicious now. Their eyes wary, they watched me. My hands were on my hips as if I were angry, and

I dropped them to my sides.

"Where's Olivia?" asked a voice, either the girl who'd asked before or someone else.

"Yeah, how come she's not on your phone?" said Imani.

"Olivia's not feeling well. The medicine she's been taking made her feel sick, and so she's sleeping." I didn't know if she was sleeping, but it sounded better than saying she was recovering from getting a transfusion.

"Did she die?" Charlotte demanded, glaring at me.

"Did she *die*?" I echoed, my voice incredulous. "You think I would be here if she *died*?" As soon as the words were out of my mouth, I realized they were the absolutely wrong response. I tried to make my voice like Olivia's—firm yet kind. "What I meant to say is no, she is not dead." I looked around the room and smiled, then added, "Come on, guys, how could she be dead? She was just here last week."

They must have been satisfied by my insisting that Olivia was alive, because no one pointed out that it was possible to be alive one week and dead the next. I took advantage of their silence to ask them to go over to the barre so we could start class.

They warmed up, then moved into the center of the room to do some floor work. Everyone was being pretty giggly, and I kept having to repeat my instructions to them. Were they like this when Olivia led the class? I couldn't remember, and I decided to ignore their not paying perfect attention. It wasn't like I could be mad at them, today of all days. Olivia was coming home tomorrow! Thinking about that, I wanted to giggle along with the girls. Dr. Maxwell had said that it was even possible Olivia might come to school for a while, assuming her counts continued to go up. *We try to keep teens' lives as normal as possible,* she'd told Livvie. *We believe that mental health is tied to physical health.* Livvie would be going to the hospital for blood tests every few days, and maybe, just maybe, one of them would say she could have a normal life for a little while before she had to go back for her next round of chemo.

"Zoe? Do you want to see it again?"

Startled, I looked over at a girl I was pretty sure was named Aaliyah, who had been the first person to chaîné across the floor.

"What?"

"Do you want us to do it one more time?"

"Sorry," I said quickly. "No. You don't have to do it again. That was great!" I clapped wildly. The CD ended. The room was perfectly still.

"Let's work on sauté," I suggested.

"Again?" asked Charlotte. "We did that all last class."

In my head I saw the hours and hours, the days and weeks and *years* Olivia and I had spent perfecting our sautés. And Charlotte was tired of doing them after a single class.

But it wasn't like these girls were going to be professional

133

dancers. So what was the point of their perfecting anything, really?

"We don't have to work on sauté," I practically shouted. "Not if you don't want to. I mean, what *would* you like to do?"

Charlotte stared at me. "Aren't *you* supposed to know?" she pointed out. "You're the teacher."

"Right." I laughed fakely. "Of course."

But suddenly my mind was a total blank. The only word that would come into my brain was *sauté*; a decade of taking ballet and there wasn't one stupid step I could think of besides the one they were tired of doing.

How could I not have choreographed something for them to learn? I'd promised Olivia that I'd start working on a routine for the recital, and I'd just let it slip my mind. What kind of a dance teacher was I?

But I wasn't a dance teacher. I was a replacement dance teacher. A *temporary* replacement dance teacher. It wasn't like I'd signed on to have all this responsibility.

Only I had. Livvie had warned me. *It could be a lot of work.* Those had been her exact words: it could be a lot of work. And I'd been like, *Work schmerk, no problem.* Except that it *was* a problem because I *hadn't* done the work that I'd said I'd do, and now I had nothing.

We stared at each other, me at one side of the room, them at the other. I smiled nervously, but none of the girls smiled back.

Just have fun with them. That was what Livvie had said. *Just have fun with them.* But dance wasn't fun. Dance was work. Only they didn't really want to work, and I couldn't really see the point of *making* them work. So we weren't working *and* we weren't having fun.

The silence grew.

Okay, this is a disaster. This is a total fucking disaster.

And right at that second, Mrs. Jones opened the door and stepped into the room.

"How you all doing?" she asked, her voice gentle. She was wearing a dark gray skirt and jacket and a white silk blouse. Around her neck was a choker of large pearls, and she touched her thumb to them gently as she spoke.

"We're okay," I said immediately. I smiled at her. How pissed was Olivia going to be if I blew this dance class thing right when she was probably getting healthy enough to come in and teach it live? "It's going great, actually. The girls just finished doing some chaînés." The French word sounded official.

"That's good." She was smiling, but she wasn't looking at me. "You doing okay, Aaliyah?"

Aaliyah said she was doing okay.

"Good. Good." Mrs. Jones looked around the rom. The girls shuffled uneasily. "How about you, Charlotte? Everything all right?" When Charlotte didn't answer right away, Mrs. Jones turned to me and added, "Because I was just down in the

135

gym, and they have more high school girls down there than they need. I could send a few of the cheerleaders up here to work with you."

She wanted to send one of the *cheerleaders* to help me teach an introductory ballet class? Why didn't she just put a bullet through my brain?

"I think we're okay," I said evenly. But Mrs. Jones didn't respond. It was clear I wasn't the one she was waiting to hear from.

Finally, from the far side of the room, Charlotte said, "We're okay, Mrs. Jones."

Mrs. Jones waited another minute as if she was sure somebody would contradict what Charlotte had just told her. When no one did, she said, "That's good. I'm glad you're working hard. We're all looking forward to the spring recital. It was so beautiful last year. And I know it's going to be just as wonderful this year." Then she said good-bye to us, and the girls and I said good-bye back.

When the door shut behind her, I could feel that collective sigh of relief. Apparently the effect of the boss— whether it was Martin Hicks, Dr. Maxwell, or Ruth Jones— was universal.

"Thanks, guys," I said, genuinely touched that they hadn't ratted me out for sucking so totally. "Next week Livvie will definitely be back, so, you know"—I laughed—"you won't have to deal with me so much, okay?"

I expected the girls to laugh also, but they just looked at the floor and shuffled uneasily. Once again, I'd said the wrong thing, but for the life of me I couldn't figure out what was wrong with it.

14

Saturday afternoon, Olivia was running a fever.

"They won't discharge me with a fever," Olivia told me. She sounded better than she had the last few times we'd talked, but apparently she wasn't.

I couldn't believe what I was hearing. "But I thought they want you out of the hospital. Isn't that what Dr. Maxwell said? That it's more likely you'll get an infection in the hospital than at home?"

"I know. I just want to get *out* of here."

Livvie's frustration fed my own. "So they're keeping you in the place where you got the infection until the infection goes away and they can send you someplace where you'll actually be safe from infection. That is seriously fucked up." I was sitting in my living room, and I hit the couch for emphasis. Outside, it was pouring; sheets of rain slapped against the plate-glass window as if expressing my mood.

She didn't say anything.

"Sorry," I said, annoyed with myself. "I'm supposed to be cheering you up." I took off my socks and rolled them into a ball, then threw them toward the basement stairs. I made my voice bright and cheery, like her mom's. "It's going to be *okay*, Livvie. Everything is going to be *great*."

That finally got a laugh out of her. "Yeah, well, at least you're not on my mom's *list*. She's *obsessed* with finding out who exposed me to this, and since you haven't been here in a couple of days, you're in the clear."

"Well, that's good news, I guess." Was this what we were supposed to be happy about now? *The bad news is: Olivia's been exposed to a dangerous infection. The good news is: totally not your fault.* I walked over to the window.

"Hey, how did dance go?" Livvie asked.

"Oh, yeah." Our property was on a hill, and since the house sat at the top, our living room felt almost like a tree house. Right now, though, it was rainy and misty enough that you couldn't see the trees; you just had to believe they were there. "Um, it was okay. You know. The girls really miss you."

"Did you guys do any work for the recital?" She yawned. "We really need to get started on that."

"Definitely," I said. "But you should get some sleep. I'll call you later."

"Mmmm. And remember, my fever might go down. I still might be able to come home tomorrow."

But Livvie's fever didn't go down. It went up. It went up and up and up until it hit 105. On the phone, her mom tried to explain what was happening, but you could tell she was totally frantic.

"She has no immune system," said Mrs. Greco. "Her body has no way of fighting this."

A wave of terror washed over me. Ever since Olivia had been diagnosed, I'd been hearing the same thing. *Infection is the big danger now. We need to make sure she doesn't get an infection. The biggest threat to her health right now isn't the leukemia; it's an infection.* All these days and weeks I'd been Purelling my hands when Mrs. Greco asked me to, but part of me had rolled my eyes at her obsession.

And now Olivia was sick. Someone hadn't washed her hands carefully or had carried a germ in on a purse or backpack or overcoat. A cart rolling along the hospital floors had picked up a virus and deposited it in Olivia's room. Just last week we'd been doing our math homework (or sort of doing our math homework), and Livvie's pencil had dropped on the floor. Without thinking anything of it, I'd picked it up and handed it to her.

Was she going to die because of something on that pencil?

"Is there anything I can do?" I asked. My voice was desperate.

"There's nothing—" Mrs. Greco's voice broke. "There's nothing any of us can do."

And then she hung up.

My parents stayed with me. They'd had dinner plans with friends, but they canceled them. My dad cooked, but I couldn't eat anything. I couldn't even stay at the table with them while they ate. Was I supposed to just sit there quietly, my brain spinning out horrible fantasies of what was happening to Olivia while my parents enjoyed a tasty dinner at our kitchen table, cozy and safe and warm as the rain lashed the outside world? As soon as I sat down in my chair, I knew there was no way I'd make it through the meal.

It was an unbroken rule in my house that you could not, under any circumstances, watch television while you ate. Even when I was *sick*—really sick, like with the flu or strep, not faking sick to get out of school for the day—I had to do something other than watch TV while I ate (talk to someone, read, stare at the walls of my room). Tonight, for the first time ever, my parents brought their plates into the den and sat with me on the couch while I channel surfed, anxiously looking for something—anything—that might distract me. They didn't even complain when I settled on *Law and Order*, a franchise my dad had called both *absurd* and *the nadir of Western civilization* on more than one occasion.

My parents went to bed just after midnight, and they

made me wash my face and get in my bed when they went to sleep, but I lay awake all night, my brain buzzing with terror. When my dad came downstairs at about seven thirty, he was startled to find me sitting at the kitchen table, where I'd been since sunrise.

"Did you get any sleep at all?" he asked, rubbing his unruly hair.

I shook my head. By now I was in such a panic I couldn't form words.

Our landline rang.

"Oh my God," I whispered. "It's awful news. I know it."

My dad turned completely white. He crossed the kitchen and grabbed the phone from the wall. "Hello?" His voice was harsh. "No, no, that's fine, Carlo. You didn't wake us." My stomach clenched. Carlo. Why was Mr. Greco calling my house? In all the years Olivia and I had been friends, Mr. Greco had never called my house.

My dad stared nodding. "That's wonderful," he said. "Yes, we were all very worried here. I appreciate your calling right away. We're very grateful to you." He smiled. "I know Zoe will be so happy to hear that. Yes, of course. Good-bye, Carlo." He hung up and turned to me. "Olivia's fever broke at about three thirty in the morning. She's sleeping comfortably now. They're talking about sending her home tomorrow."

I opened my mouth to say something, but all that happened was a huge sob escaped. I curled over the table, holding my stomach and crying. My dad came to sit next to me, and he put his arm around me and held me. "Oh, honey," he murmured. "Oh, honey."

"What happened?" asked my mom. I hadn't even heard her come down. "What is it?" I didn't look up as my dad told her what Olivia's dad had said. "Oh, thank God," she said, coming around the table and embracing me from the other side.

"Why are we always talking about God in this family?" I cried. "We don't even believe in God."

My mom laughed and wiped some tears off her own cheeks, then reached over and wiped my tears away. "I don't know, honey. That's a really good question."

We sat without talking for a while, my parents softly rubbing my back. I tried to get my head around the idea that Olivia was okay, that she was coming home.

"Listen," said my dad, his voice serious. "I think we all need to keep in mind that Olivia's illness is a marathon, not a sprint."

"What do you mean?" I pushed my bangs out of my eyes so I could look at him.

"It means," my dad continued as my mom patted my back, "that there are going to be a lot of ups and downs as long as Olivia is sick."

"*And* it means," added my mom, "that it doesn't help Olivia *and* it isn't good for you if every time Olivia has a setback, you spend an entire night preparing for her to die."

I knew they were right. I knew I had to be strong, that I couldn't collapse every time something went wrong. It wasn't like Dr. Maxwell had said Olivia would need her friends during treatment because it was going to be so easy.

Still, somehow knowing that and living it were turning out to be different.

"Yeah," I said. "I know." I wanted to say more than that, but my brain couldn't form the words. My parents must have read on my face how tired I was.

"Why don't you go up to bed?" my dad suggested.

"Yeah," I said again. "Okay."

Without consciously making the decision to move, I got to my feet and headed out of the kitchen and up to my room, where I escaped everything with a day of dreamless sleep.

15

When I got Livvie's text Monday that she was home, I didn't even consider going to my last two classes of the day. Despite the driving rain, I was halfway to her house by the time the late bell rang for English.

Luke answered the door. Behind him, over the stairs, was a banner that read *Welcome Home, Olivia!* and, beneath that, *We love you!* I recognized the twins' handiwork—*Welcome* was spelled with a *k* and without an *e*.

"Hey," I said, "aren't you supposed to be at school?" Though really, as a fellow truant, I probably shouldn't have brought the subject up.

"We got to skip! It's a holiday! Livvie's home!" He took my hands and danced me around in a circle, then led me toward the back of the house, both of us laughing. Everything around me felt different, and it wasn't just the banner or the mouthwatering smells coming from the kitchen. The antique wallpaper in the foyer, the brightly lit chandelier in the dining room—it was as if the house itself were celebrating Olivia's homecoming.

I followed Luke into the kitchen, expecting to find Livvie there. Instead, I saw Mr. Greco sitting at the table. His father was sitting across from him, and his mother was at the stove, cooking. I'd met Mr. Greco's parents tons of times—they lived in Florida, but they came to New Jersey a lot.

Mr. Greco senior looked like an older version of Mr. Greco, and his mother looked a little like I could imagine Olivia looking when she got old. They had the same green eyes, and Mrs. Greco dyed her hair a color close to the blond that Olivia's hair was naturally. To me it was always a little startling to see such bright blond hair on a seventy-five-year-old woman, but I guess she thought it looked nice.

Mrs. Greco senior came away from the stove and hugged me. "Zoe, honey, you're soaked." It was true. I'd walked over without an umbrella or a coat. She wagged her wooden spoon at me. "And you're too thin. Both of you girls are too thin."

"Mary," her husband chastised her, "of course she's thin. She's had chemotherapy. Would you leave her alone? The poor girl can't eat." I went over to where he was sitting and shook his hand. The skin felt smooth, almost like paper. I was pretty sure he was older than his wife, but it might just have been that he didn't dye his hair.

Mrs. Greco turned on her husband. "What chemotherapy? Zoe hasn't had chemotherapy."

He slapped the table with impatience. "I know *Zoe* hasn't had chemotherapy. *Olivia* had chemotherapy."

"You think I don't know my baby had chemotherapy?" She sighed. For all the confusion, this was actually a relatively linear, lucid conversation to be having with the Grecos. Livvie said it was because they were Italian, but whenever Mr. Greco's family was over, there were about ten conversations going on at once, and most people were participating in several of them simultaneously. Now Mrs. Greco pointed the spoon in her hand at her son, Livvie's father. "I still remember the day you brought her home from the hospital." Suddenly her eyes welled up with tears. "And now this." She started crying. "Why is this happening? And why does she have to go back for more chemotherapy? Why are they torturing her?" Mr. Greco stood up, walked over to his mother, and put his arms around her. "Come on now, Ma. Come on."

As soon as his wife started crying, Mr. Greco senior started crying. I didn't know where to look or what to say, so I just stared silently at the kitchen floor.

Olivia's mom came through the swinging door from the dining room. "Zoe! Olivia thought it might be you, but I said you were still at school."

"Oh, yeah. I got out early."

"Well, that's convenient," Mrs. Greco said. I couldn't tell if there was suspicion in her voice. "Livvie's so excited to see you, but we need to keep it short. I don't want her getting tired out. And you're feeling okay? You don't have a cold or anything?"

"No," I said quickly. "I mean, yes, I'm feeling okay. No, I don't have a cold."

"Good." She took a deep breath and actually smiled. "It's good to have her home, isn't it?"

"Yeah," I said. "It's really good."

"Wash up in the front bathroom, okay? Dr. Maxwell suggested visitors use their own bathroom."

"Sure," I said. After Livvie's fever, I had a new understanding of the word *visitor*, and I could see how as long as my house had different germs from Livvie's house, I was one.

I headed to the bathroom in the front hall. This was totally the visitors' bathroom; in all the years of coming to Livvie's house, I couldn't think of one time when I'd used it. The faucets were gold-colored, the towels were thin linen with the letter G embroidered on them in pale blue, and there was a tiny soap dish with little seashell-shaped soaps. The last time I'd been in there it was spring, and Livvie and I had been sent to check that it was ready for a dinner party Livvie's parents were having.

The seashell soaps were gone, replaced with two plastic dispensers, one of antibacterial soap and one of Purell. The embroidered towels were gone too. On the shelf next to the

148

sink was a pile of paper towels. I washed my hands, dried them carefully, then doused them in Purell.

The light was on in Livvie's room, and I slid the door open gently. She was sitting on her desk chair in a T-shirt and jeans, surveying her surroundings.

It was the most beautiful sight I'd ever seen. "Hi," I said.

She looked up at me. "Hi," she said.

I'd been looking forward to this moment for so long, but now I wasn't sure what to say or do. I went over to her bed and sat down at the edge of it. "I saw your grandparents," I said.

"My grandmother keeps hugging me and crying," said Livvie. "It's starting to get on my nerves."

"Yeah, I can see how that might be trying."

Livvie gave a little smile. She was still looking around her room. My hair was damp, and I rubbed it between my palms, waiting for her to speak.

"I was just thinking . . ." She hesitated, then continued. "I was just thinking that the last time I was here, I wasn't sick. I mean, I was *sick*," she corrected herself quickly, "but I didn't know I was sick. I just thought I had a virus or something." She glanced at me. "Isn't that crazy?"

"It is," I agreed.

"Zoe?" Her head was down, and she seemed to be watching her toe, which she was using to trace the dark green pattern that ran through the rug's pale green background.

"Yeah?"

She waited to close the swirl she'd been following. "Look." Then, without raising her eyes, she put her hand on her head and ran her fingers through her hair.

When I had long hair, I was always shedding. I'd brush my hair and the brush would be full of strands, or I'd take off a sweater and find half a dozen long black hairs stuck to it.

But what I was looking at now was something completely different. In Olivia's hand was a fistful of hair, more than I'd ever seen not on someone's head. I thought of my haircut after we got kicked out of NYBC, how it had seemed that with all the hair on the floor, there couldn't possibly be any left on my head.

This was like that.

I felt panicky, as if Livvie had just shown me a gaping wound that I needed to close. We looked at each other. Her eyes were glassy with tears.

Because I couldn't think of anything else to say, I just said, "It's going to be okay."

As soon as the words were out of my mouth, I wanted to snatch them back.

"What is? Being bald? Oh yeah, that's really okay." Olivia's voice was as close to nasty as I'd ever heard it.

"Oh, Livs." I got off her bed and walked over to the chair on my knees, then put my arms around her waist and hugged her tightly.

"They told me it would start falling out after a few weeks,

but I didn't believe them." Her voice was thick with tears. "I really thought . . . I think I really thought . . ." Now she was crying too hard to speak, and for a few minutes that was the only sound in the room. I started to cry also, the tears sliding silently down my face and onto Olivia's shirt. "I'm so embarrassed," she sobbed.

"What? What are you embarrassed about?"

"I thought . . ." She took a deep breath. "'Not *my* hair. My hair's too pretty to fall out.'" On the word *out* Olivia made a sound I'd never heard a person make before. It was like a howl.

"Don't be embarrassed," I whispered, hugging her still more tightly. "Please don't be embarrassed. Your hair *is* beautiful. It's so beautiful. It's going to grow back and it's going to be just as beautiful as it is now." I didn't know what to say, but I just kept talking.

"Why is this happening to me, Zoe?" Olivia whispered, her voice hoarse. "It's so unfair."

I could feel a huge sob growing in my chest, and all I wanted to do was let it out, wail as loudly as Olivia just had. I swallowed hard, pushing it down, down, down, scared that if I let it out, I'd never be able to stop.

"It is unfair, Livs," I whispered back. "I hate everything because of it."

"You hated everything before I got sick; you know you did," she whispered.

And then, out of nowhere, Olivia started laughing. It

wasn't a slow buildup, like a giggle into a belly laugh. She just burst into laughter. It was slightly hysterical laughter, but it was definitely laughter. "I have no idea why I'm laughing," said Olivia, catching her breath. "Maybe the chemo went to my brain." The possibility must have struck her as funny because she cracked up again.

"This is seriously fucked up," I said, and then I started laughing too.

"What, my having cancer or our laughing about it?" She swiped at her cheeks with the backs of her hands. "Zoe, what am I going to do?" she asked, and now she was crying again.

My hoodie was damp with the rain, but I used it to wipe her cheeks. "What if we braid it? I could do a long French braid, like your mom did the other day."

"Okay." She sniffed. "Yeah. Let's try that." Her eyes were shiny, but she sounded relieved.

"I'll get a brush," I said, jumping to my feet. Livvie directed me to her cosmetics bag, and a second later I was standing behind her chair, holding her brush in my hand, a hair band snapped around my wrist.

But it was like herding cats. Every time I ran the brush through her hair, it would fill up, and I'd have to go over to the garbage can and dump a fistful of hair into it before trying again, at which point the whole process would start over. After about three strokes, Olivia snatched the brush from my hand.

"Forget it," she snapped. "This was a stupid idea."

"It wasn't stupid," I assured her. "It was worth a try."

From where she was sitting, she couldn't see into the mirror on the back of her closet, so she got to her feet and walked over to it. "I shouldn't even care, right? I mean, it's just hair."

In the pale light of her bedside lamp, Livvie's beautiful blond hair glowed, as if it were its own light source. She looked away from her reflection and turned to me. "Come on," she said. She walked over to the door of her bedroom.

"Where are we going?" I asked.

Her voice only shook a little bit. "We're going to shave it off."

∽ 16 ∽

When Mrs. Greco, who we passed in the hallway, found out what we were about to do, she wanted us to go to the hairdresser's, but Livvie said absolutely not, and she reminded her mom how many people would be in the crowded public space that was Hair Today Gone Tomorrow. In the end, Mrs. Greco agreed that as long as we used Livvie's dad's electric razor and not a disposable one that might give Livvie a cut that could get infected, we could do it ourselves. She said she was going to leave us alone, but you could tell she was hovering outside the bathroom door. It wasn't until Livvie shouted, "Mom, you have to go!" that she finally said, "Okay," and went downstairs.

While that would have been a pretty mild exchange between me and my mom, it was unprecedented for Livvie to snap at her mother that way. I didn't comment on it, just ran a cotton swab doused with rubbing alcohol over Mr. Greco's electric razor like Mrs. Greco had told me to.

Livvie had a beautiful bathroom. Technically it wasn't hers; it was down the hall from her room, and there was a bedroom next to it, but that was a guest room, so she was the only one who really used this particular bathroom. It was very small, barely big enough for a sink, a bathtub, and the toilet, but there was a stained-glass window and these old fixtures and a huge antique mirror over the sink. When we were in fourth grade, without asking permission, Livvie and I hid out in her bathroom and shaved our legs, and before Livvie was allowed to wear makeup, she and I would come up here and experiment, slathering our faces with contraband lipstick, mascara, rouge, and eye shadow that we'd borrowed from girls at NYBC, and then frantically washing it off when her mom would call us to dinner.

The weird thing was, this almost felt like one of those crazy afternoons from elementary school. First of all, we couldn't figure out what to do at all. We tried just shaving the hair, but that was impossible—it was too long, and the razor kept getting stuffed with hair and then jamming or pulling on the strands so hard it hurt. The third or fourth time I tried and failed to shave off more than a strand or two at a time, Livvie started giggling.

"You seriously suck at this, you know?"

"Oh, I'm sorry, I didn't realize you had a PhD in head shaving." Laughing, I handed her the heavy black razor. "Here. You do it."

"I can't see the top of my *head*," she said, pushing the razor away. "Just . . . try again." But it was impossible. Finally I asked Mrs. Greco for scissors, and together Livvie and I started cutting. Once we got into it, there was something satisfying about the work, the sharp snap of metal on the long, delicate strands.

"When you think about it, they're just dead cells," I pointed out. The more hair we cut away, the bigger Livvie's eyes looked, exactly what had happened to me. Her ears were small and delicate, which I'd never noticed before.

"Yeah," said Olivia. She had a towel draped over her shirt. There was hair everywhere—on the counter, in the sink, all over the floor. My hoodie was covered with long blond strands.

The only place there weren't long hairs was on Olivia's head.

"We could leave it like this," I offered. A spiky, somewhat uneven layer of hair covered her skull. "I mean, I'd even it out and everything."

Olivia stared at her reflection. At first I thought she was considering what I was suggesting, but then I saw that she was looking into her own eyes and wasn't seeing her head. "No," she said, dropping her eyes to the counter and feeling around for her dad's electric razor underneath all the hair. "It all needs to come off."

Twenty minutes later, we were done. Olivia's scalp was

shiny and smooth, her forehead running up to the top of her head without any way to tell where her face ended and her scalp began. A small blue vein showed just above where her hairline must have been. Her eyes were even bigger than they'd been when her hair was short, but overall she looked small and fragile. We made eye contact in the mirror.

"So," she said. "This is me bald." Her voice shook a little, but it didn't break.

I pulled on a lock of my hair and held the scissors to it. "I think I should join you. Sisters in baldness."

But Livvie's hand shot up. "No!" she said.

"I don't care," I assured her, not letting myself think about whether or not I cared. How could I care? "We'll grow our hair back together."

She took the scissors from my hand. "It's only hair, anyway." She looked at herself in the mirror, staring hard at her reflection. "Dr. Maxwell said I can go to school next week if I wear a surgical mask." She paused briefly. "Bald with a surgical mask. Look! There goes that girl with cancer." Her eyes welled up again, but then she shook her head forcefully and took a deep, audible breath. "I'm going to get a hot pink wig."

"Fantastic!" I said quickly. "I love it already."

Livvie surveyed the hairy bathroom. "What a mess."

"You go lie down," I told her. "I'll clean it up."

Olivia hesitated for a second, but then she said, "Okay. I am kind of tired."

"Do you want me to leave?" I asked quickly. "I could clean it up and just go so you can sleep."

She shook her head. "I want you to stay. If I fall asleep, just wake me, okay?"

"Okay," I promised.

Hair apparently has a life of its own. No matter how many times I went over the bathroom with a broom and a wet paper towel, there was still hair everywhere, almost as if each individual strand split into a dozen more every time I turned my back. Finally Mrs. Greco came by the bathroom. When she saw Olivia's hair all over the place, she pressed her lips together into a tight, thin line, but she didn't say anything and she didn't cry. Then she disappeared, and a minute later she came back with the vacuum.

"How is she?" she asked.

"I don't know," I said.

Mrs. Greco put her hand on my shoulder. "I'm so glad she has you."

I was scared I was going to start bawling. But I swallowed hard. "Thanks," I said. "I'm lucky to have her, too."

"We all are," her mom said. "I thank God for her every day."

I didn't know what to say to that. How could you thank God for Olivia when God was the one who'd made her sick? That was my problem with religion. It didn't make any sense.

When I went into Olivia's room, she was curled up on her bed, fast asleep. Even though she'd told me to wake her, I couldn't bring myself to do it. Instead, I went over to her desk. On it I placed a thick lock of Olivia's hair that I'd salvaged from the bathroom.

The room was dimly lit, but the hair in my hand seemed to gather whatever light there was, glowing—just as it had on Olivia's head—with an intensity that almost made it seem alive. I glanced from the hair to Olivia, her shiny head all that was visible of her body, which was buried under her comforter.

I wished I could think of what to say to her. Maybe if I could have, I would have woken her up. But all I could think was, *It doesn't matter*. And even though I knew that was true, I also knew that it wasn't.

I grabbed a pen from the Lucite holder on the desk and slid a piece of paper out of the top drawer of her desk.

For the memory box. Call me when you wake up. Love ya.
xoxo, Me

I put the note next to the hair. Then I slipped out of the room and downstairs, leaving the house without saying good-bye to anyone.

17

"Don't forget to get your car washed on Saturday! All proceeds go to fight leukemia! Bake sale and car wash!"

There was a phalanx of cheerleaders around the front entrance to the building, all of them wearing their uniforms and handing out bright pink flyers. Stacy was standing on the bottom step, and when she saw me coming up the walk, she gave a yelp of joy, ran down, and threw her arms around me. Then she stepped back and handed me a flyer.

"'Save a life: Get your car washed,'" I read out loud. I looked up at her. "Who knew that was all it takes?"

"What?" she asked. Then she laughed. "Oh, I get it. Well, you know . . . it's just meant to get people psyched and stuff." When she blinked, her sparkly blue eye shadow shimmered in the early morning sun.

"No, I know." I shook my head. "Sorry, I'm just a bitch sometimes."

Stacy looked genuinely surprised. "No you're not." She gave me another hug. "Don't forget to bake something for the bake sale! And just wait until you see our cheer at Friday's assembly." She stepped back and kicked one leg high in the air, then placed her hands firmly on her hips. "*Goooo, Olivia!*"

There was something beautiful—almost balletic—about Stacy's sharp, precise movements. "Hey, that was really good," I said. "You're a really good cheerleader." I meant it too. For what might have been the first time in my entire life, I was talking to Stacy Shaw without being even a tiny bit sarcastic.

Stacy shrugged almost shyly. "I know. Well, gotta go." She waved the flyers in my direction. "Can't go home holding any of these." Then she turned back to the crowd. "Save a life! Get your car washed!" she cried.

If I believed in that kind of thing, I might have seen some link between what the cheer squad did for Olivia at Friday's assembly and the text I got from her twenty minutes later. Was it possible that their shouting her name and kicking their legs and waving their pom-poms had led to the four miraculous words that appeared on my screen halfway through math?

MY COUNTS ARE NORMAL!

Immediately I asked Mr. Schumacher if I could go to the bathroom.

"Livvie, that's amazing!" I said as soon as I was safely ensconced in the girls' room. I knew she'd been getting stronger, that her counts were going up. But normal was huge. Normal meant . . .

"If it's warm tomorrow, Dr. Maxwell said I can go to the car wash," she crowed.

I screamed and pounded on the tile wall. "You're free!"

"Is that dumb?" Suddenly Livvie sounded embarrassed. "Maybe it's dumb for me to want to go. I mean, it's kind of a stupid event, right?"

"God, Livs, it's not dumb. It's an event in your honor. Of course you should go."

"Did I tell you that Stacy's mom sent over dinner for my family a couple of nights while I was in the hospital?" Olivia asked.

"She did? Wow, that . . . that was really nice of her." To my embarrassment, my first thought was, *Did my mom think to send dinner over to the Grecos?*

Livvie was already on to a different subject. "My mom made an appointment for me to get my wig on Saturday morning. So at least any little kids at the car wash won't run screaming when they see me."

"No one's going to run screaming from you, Livs. You're beautiful even when you're bald."

"Yeah, well, just imagine how beautiful I'll be when I'm rocking that pink wig!"

It was obvious just from her voice how much happier she was now that she was out of the hospital. Why did she have to go *back* for more chemo? It was so awful I could have cried. But then I remembered what my dad had said about how anticipating bad things wasn't helpful to Olivia. Here she was all excited to come to the car wash on Saturday afternoon, and here I was upset about her having to go back to the hospital soon.

I was the antifriend.

"Livs, you are *so* going to be rocking that pink wig," I agreed, and when she laughed—really laughed, even though it hadn't been much of a joke—I felt grateful to my dad for pointing out the obvious.

Team Livvie needed to look on the bright side.

While Livvie and her mom went into Manhattan to get her wig, I headed to Newark to teach dance class. I'd come up with some steps for the recital, which had been surprisingly fun to do. It was harder than I'd thought, not so much trying to fit together pieces of a jigsaw puzzle as trying to create a jigsaw puzzle out of thin air. So I was excited to show the girls what I'd done and to see if any of them had ideas for building on what I'd choreographed.

But even though I'd been looking forward to teaching the class, when I got there, nothing went the way I'd planned. It was hard to get them to focus, and I ended up getting impatient with them. I didn't want to lose my temper, so instead I made a few snarky jokes to get them to stop fooling around. At one point Aaliyah kept doing cartwheels while she was waiting for her turn to glissade across the room, and finally I snapped, "I guess *some* people don't know the difference between tumbling and ballet." I laughed right after I said it, but she could tell I was irritated.

At least she stopped doing cartwheels.

But even if the cartwheels stopped, the class didn't improve. No one seemed excited about coming up with their own steps, and everyone was fidgety. It felt like they could tell how much time I'd put into preparing and they were trying to let me know what a waste it had all been. I thought of how obedient the students at NYBC were—we'd have just as soon stripped naked and run through the streets of Manhattan as messed around during a class.

The more I resented how they weren't taking class seriously, the more frustrated I got, and the more frustrated I got, the worse they behaved. It was looking like they'd be performing twenty minutes of standing still when that recital date rolled around.

Luckily, before I actually started screaming at the girls that they didn't deserve to study steps that dancers had been working their asses off to perfect for centuries, the bell rang. Everyone started packing up, and I crossed the room to shut off the music, rolling my eyes to myself as soon as my back was turned on the class.

Right when I hit stop, I felt someone throw her arms around my waist. It was so startling I gave a little yelp, and then I looked down and saw the top of Imani's head. Her whole body was wrapped around mine; she'd even wound her feet around my calves.

"Thanks, Zoe," she said. "That was really fun."

Surprised, I hugged her back, a little bit of my frustration dissolving. "Really?"

She arched her neck so she could look up at me, her expression puzzled. Then her face suddenly split into an enormous smile. "I get it," she said. "That was a joke." She laughed. "You're the funny one," she explained.

Now it was my turn to be confused, and not just because my *Really?* had been genuine. "What do you mean?" I asked, unraveling her from my body and kneeling so our faces were level.

"You know, with Olivia." She smiled and shrugged. "You're the funny one."

"Then what's Olivia?" I asked. I poked Imani lightly in the side and made my voice deep and my face mock stern. "The serious one?"

"Not exactly," said Imani. I had the feeling she was debating whether or not to add anything, but she just gave me one more quick hug and a wave, then ran out of the room to join her friends.

Washing my hands in the bathroom after class, I was still thinking about what Imani had said. Or hadn't said. If I was the funny one, what was Olivia?

It took me about a thousandth of a second to answer my own question: the nice one. She was the nice one, and I was the funny one. Which was kind of just another way of saying Olivia was the nice one and I was the bitch.

God, what was wrong with me? Even little kids knew I wasn't nice. I had to be nicer to people. I looked at myself in the mirror. "I vow to be nicer to people."

A second later, the bathroom door opened and Stacy Shaw walked in.

"Really?" I said to the universe. "You're *seriously* testing me on this right now?"

"He-ey," Stacy said, giving me an enormous grin. "Are you on the phone or something?"

"No, I'm just talking to myself."

"Oh," said Stacy. "That's cool. I do it all the time." She looked at herself in the mirror, fluffing her hair. "We'll see you at the car wash later, right?"

"Of course. I mean, I don't have a car or anything. But my mom and dad do."

"Oh, good," said Stacy. She opened her purse and fished out a large cosmetics bag, from which she removed a lip liner. "You can donate blood, too. If you're seventeen."

I shook my head. "Not yet."

"That's okay." Carefully tracing her lips, Stacy continued. "I just want, like, everyone to come out to show support for Olivia,"

As irritating as she was, I had to be grateful to her for all the work she was doing. I mean, it wasn't like I'd been busy recruiting people to come to the car wash.

"Are you going over to school now?" I asked, unable to take my eyes off Stacy as she slathered her lips with gloss. "I mean, to set up?"

"Oh, not yet." She blotted her lips with a tissue. "We've got an away game."

"You're *cheering* today? And *then* you're doing the car wash?"

"Mmm, yeah," said Stacy. She smiled at me. "So, I'll see you later?"

"Yeah," I said. "Later."

"I mean, I actually kind of have respect for Stacy," I said to Livvie. We were sitting in the backseat of her dad's car en route to the car wash. I had a container of brownies on my lap that my mom had helped me bake for the bake sale. Olivia's dad was driving; her mom was in the passenger seat. On the radio, jazz played quietly. "It's weird."

Livvie shook her head. "I hear you. But don't try and tell me about weird. I spent the morning wig shopping."

"It looks amazing, Livvie!" I assured her once again.

167

"Seriously. You did *such* a good job."

She put her hand to her head. "Do you think so? It feels . . . I don't know, artificial."

Despite her plans to get an outrageous wig, Livvie had actually gone with one that was almost exactly like her real hair, only shorter and with bangs that the wig seller had said would make the hair look more natural. It did look natural. Kind of. If you didn't look too closely, you couldn't tell, except that Livvie's real hair had been such a distinct color that the wig was blah in comparison. But it wasn't like there was anything she could do about having the most beautiful blond hair in the world.

"It doesn't look artificial," I assured her. "Actually, your *real* hair probably looked more artificial than the wig does. Everyone probably thought you dyed it to get it that color."

"Okay, that's, like, the weirdest compliment ever," she said, but she was smiling.

Her dad pulled onto Westerly Road. Even though the car wash had only started about twenty minutes earlier, there was already a line of cars waiting to get into the school parking lot. A banner nearly fifty feet long hung across the fence next to the road.

BAKE SALE, BLOOD DRIVE, AND CAR WASH TODAY! WASH YOUR CAR. SAVE A LIFE. SUPPORT OLIVIA GRECO!

She slid down a little in her seat. "This is weird."

She was right. It *was* weird. As we pulled forward, you could see all the cheerleaders, in their uniforms, washing cars. The football team was also washing cars, but they were in regular clothes. In the far corner of the parking lot a bloodmobile was parked, and a few people were lined up, waiting to donate blood.

"See, honey!" her mom said from the passenger seat. "Everyone loves you. Jake said the team couldn't *wait* to participate."

"The football team loves you," I whispered.

"I feel like such a tramp," she whispered back.

We pulled into the parking lot. "Do you want to get out and walk around?" I asked. "I mean, you're kind of the guest of honor."

"I don't know," she said. "It's weird. It's weird if I get out. It's weird if I don't get out." She rubbed her hands together nervously.

I turned to face her. "Liv, people really want to see you. They do. I make fun of Stacy and Emma and you know I really do think they're mentally disabled, but they seriously *care*." She laughed. "Stop! I'm being serious. Look, I know we joke about how it's just the two of us in our own little universe, but everyone's always asking about you. Really. Bethany and Lashanna and Mia and . . . just all the other girls on the soccer team. And in class. You know how I used to come to the hospital and say that everyone asked about you?"

"Yeah." She looked doubtful.

"Well, it's true. *Everyone*. I must tell a hundred people a day how you're doing. So, I mean, if you're tired, don't worry about it. But if you feel okay, you should get out of the car. People really *do* love you."

A tear rolled down Livvie's cheek, and she put her forehead on my shoulder. "I am such a cheese ball."

"No you're not," I assured her, laughing.

"Okay." She wiped her face. "Mom, Dad. I'm going in. I mean out." Olivia put her hand on the door and cracked it open. But before she could step out of the car, her mom stopped her.

"Wait." Mrs. Greco reached into her bag. "I'd feel better if you'd wear this." When she turned around, she was holding what looked like a piece of white fabric.

"What is it?" asked Olivia, puzzled.

"It's a surgical mask," said her mom. She smiled nervously.

"You want me to wear a *mask*?" Olivia sounded horrified. "Today?"

"Adriana," said Mr. Greco, his voice low, "I thought we agreed. Dr. Maxwell said she only had to wear it if she was going to be *indoors* in a crowd."

Her mother gestured to the lawn, which held a significant portion of the student population. "Are you trying to tell me this isn't a crowd?"

"But it's *outside*, Mom."

"That's enough," said her dad, glancing at Olivia in the rearview mirror. He didn't raise his voice, but Olivia got quiet. I would have also. If my dad said, *That's enough*, you might say, *Says who?* But there's no way you'd say that to Olivia's dad.

I was positive he was going to make her wear the mask, but all he did was put his hand on Mrs. Greco's hand. "Adriana, let her go."

There was a long pause. I could hear the hum of the car's engine and the muffled sounds of people outside talking and laughing. The car in front of us pulled up, but Mr. Greco didn't move.

Olivia's mom gave an almost imperceptible nod. "Okay," she whispered. Then she turned around. "You can stay. *For one hour.*"

"For *one hour?*" Livvie's mouth opened into a shocked O.

"Olivia." Her dad's tone required no elaboration.

"Fine," Olivia said. She started to get out of the car, but then she stopped and leaned forward. "Thanks," she said. Her dad stroked her cheek briefly, then gestured at the empty space in front of us. "Come on already! I gotta get my car washed here."

I hadn't realized that the air-conditioning was on in the car, but stepping out into the sticky warmth of the afternoon made me feel its absence. Still, I couldn't exactly be sorry that it was unseasonably warm for the last weekend in October. Thanks to climate change, Olivia could be outside.

The car wash was set up at the corner of the parking lot nearest the school. All around on the lawn people were hanging out, manning tables that sold T-shirts, mugs, and glasses. Tacked up to the building was a sign that said NATIONAL BONE MARROW REGISTRY. SIGN UP. YOU COULD SAVE A LIFE. Underneath it, an older woman sat at a table.

Mr. Greco pulled the car forward as Olivia and I walked over to the lawn. We passed a cluster of freshman and sophomore girls, and as we walked by, one of them whispered something to the others. "Hey, Olivia!" one of them called. Olivia and I turned. The girl was waving shyly.

Livvie hesitated. "What am I supposed to do?" she whispered.

I waved at the girl. "Hey!" I called to her. Through my smile I told Olivia to wave also, and Livvie raised her hand and waved.

"Okay, this is bizarre," she said.

"I think we can stop waving now."

"Hey, Olivia!" Lashanna and Mia were standing a few feet away, and we walked over to them. They were both wearing their soccer uniforms, with T-shirts over them bearing the logo for the Leukemia and Lymphoma Society.

"How's it going?" asked Lashanna.

"Okay," said Livvie. "Nice T-shirt."

"Thanks," said Lashanna. She spun around so we could

read the back, which said FUND THE CURE TO FIND THE CURE.

"Is it weird to be a cause?" asked Mia.

Livvie laughed. "Yeah, kinda."

Jake came over to where we were standing. "Hey, little sister," he said. "You gonna make yourself useful and wash some cars?" He wasn't wearing a shirt, and he was pretty wet.

"Sure," she said, laughing. He put his arm around her. "Come on. I'll take you over to say hi to some of the guys."

Livvie walked a few steps with Jake, then turned back to me. "You coming?"

"In a sec," I said. "I've got to drop these off." I indicated the container of brownies.

I watched Livvie and Jake make their way through the crowd. Everyone they passed, when they realized who Olivia was, wanted to hug her, but I saw Jake gently keep them away, more like a bodyguard than a brother. People's being so excited to see Livvie, their wanting to touch and talk to her, made me feel better about Wamasset High and a little stupid for how down on it I tended to get. These were good people.

These were Olivia's people.

I gave my brownies to the girls running the bake sale and bought a chocolate chip cookie for a dollar. While I ate it, I wandered over to the bone marrow registry table.

Sean Miller was talking to the woman sitting there. There was a pile of brochures lying next to them, and I grabbed one.

Every year, thousands of people wait for a bone marrow transplant. Could you be the one to save a life? There was a rainbow coalition of people in the photo on the front page. Inside were frequently asked questions. I skimmed through them, stopping on *Does it hurt to donate bone marrow?* According to the pamphlet, *Bone marrow is extracted from the back of the pelvic bone using a hollow needle designed for this purpose.*

Ouch. I stopped reading.

The woman handed Sean a Q-tip. "Wipe the inside of your cheek," she told him. When he'd finished, she slipped the Q-tip into a little container. "Okay," she said. "Thanks for registering."

"Sure," he said. "No problem."

He said hi to me and headed back to the car wash area. I stepped over to the spot he'd vacated. "I'd like to register," I said.

"Okay." She had bright red hair that looked dyed. Or maybe it was a wig. I wondered if she had cancer. "Are you eighteen or older?"

"Me?" For a second I considered lying. But it seemed unlikely a hospital wouldn't figure out my age at some point. "No. I'm almost seventeen."

"Are you a sibling?" she asked.

I shook my head. Once again family trumped friendship.

"I'm sorry," she said. "I know it's disappointing. But you should feel free to make a donation to the program." She handed me the brochure I'd put down.

"Thanks," I said. Having my parents write a check wasn't exactly the same as giving Olivia a life-saving bone marrow transplant.

The woman gave me an understanding smile. "If it's any consolation, the odds of nonrelatives being a match are low. Does your friend need a bone marrow transplant?"

I shook my head. "She's having chemotherapy. It's working really well, so the doctors don't think she'll need one."

"Well, that's good news at least. Still, consider supporting the registry." She took another pamphlet off the stack and went to give it to me, but I showed her the one already in my hand. Then I thanked her and headed over to the car wash area.

Olivia was talking to her brother, Stacy, and Emma. Except for Olivia, everyone was soaked, though the girls had managed not to get their hair wet. From a distance, with her wig, Livvie really did look normal. Her grandmother was right about her being too thin, but she'd always been thin, and in her long-sleeved T-shirt and skirt and leggings, you couldn't exactly tell how thin she was. While I watched, she said something to Jake, and he laughed. As soon as Jake laughed, Emma started laughing.

A few feet away, Calvin and Delford were washing a car. They were both wearing shorts and no shirts, and I found myself staring at Calvin. He really had a sick body. His arms and legs were muscular, and his abs were perfect. His shaggy hair was longer than most of the other football players'. I watched while he pushed it out of his face, then bent over to wash his sponge out in the bucket at his feet.

God, he was hot. He was *seriously* hot. Now that I didn't find his hotness irritating, I could appreciate its power. As I stood there watching Calvin spray water at the car, Livvie called my name.

I snapped around to look at her. She was smiling. "What's up?" she yelled. "You look like you're in a trance or something."

I walked over to where she was standing, laughing at her question and making a mental note to admit that, after having given her so much crap for liking him, I could now fully appreciate what she saw in Calvin Taylor (body and soul). When I joined them, Emma gave me a kiss on my left cheek while Stacy gave me one on my right cheek. "Hi-ii!" said Stacy.

"Bet you wish you were immunosuppressed right about now," said Olivia, smiling at me.

"You know it," I said. Stacy was annoying; there was no denying that. Still, she and the other cheerleaders had put this whole day together, which was kind of amazing. The fact that simply being cheerleaders gave them so much power was insanely stupid, but at least they were using that power for good, not for evil. I looked around me. Probably half the school had turned out for this event. More, maybe.

And suddenly, I had a brainstorm.

"Hey, Stacy, can I talk to you for a sec?" I asked.

"Totally!" Stacy said. As she and I stepped away from the group, Olivia gave me a puzzled look, but I pretended not to see. "So, what's up?" Stacy asked as soon as we were standing by ourselves.

"I kind of need your help," I said. And I sketched out my plan for Monday morning.

I'd been as disappointed as Olivia when her mom had said she could only stay at the car wash for an hour, but when the hour was up, even I had to admit that Livvie was clearly zonked. She wasn't exactly leaning on me and Jake as we walked out of the parking lot, but she was definitely moving slowly, and she practically fell into the car when her dad opened the door for her.

"You overdid it," her mom said, her hand pressed to Olivia's forehead. "Oh, I was so afraid of this."

"I'm okay, Mom. Really." She leaned against the seat and closed her eyes. "I'm okay."

But by the time we got back to her house, she didn't seem okay. She was shivering, and her teeth were chattering. Her dad and her mom helped her into the house and up the stairs. Then Mrs. Greco went out into the hall closet to get more blankets. Together, without saying a word, she and I covered Olivia with them.

I was scared. Olivia's hand felt hot to the touch, and she

was dozing in an unnatural way, like she wasn't falling asleep so much as she was being pulled under.

"I knew this was a terrible idea," Mrs. Greco said under her breath. "I just knew it." Her eyes scanned the room, and when they landed on me, I tried to make myself as small as possible.

I could hear Mr. Greco on the phone. "Yes, I'm calling for Dr. Maxwell," he said. Mrs. Greco went into the hallway as Mr. Greco gave whoever he was talking to his phone number.

"I think we should take her right to the ER," I heard Mrs. Greco say. Her voice was sharp.

Mr. Greco sounded calm. "I want to wait and hear what the doctor says."

"Who knows when she'll call back? You *know* how long it can take them to call back." Mrs. Greco sounded nearly frantic at the prospect of waiting.

"If it's an emergency, she'll call back."

"She's *unconscious*."

"She's *sleeping*. Dr. Maxwell said she might run fevers and that if she did, we should call. She did *not* tell us to bring Olivia to the emergency room. Her counts were up yesterday. She's nowhere near as vulnerable as she was last time this happened."

"You don't know that. I want to take her to the hospital now."

"If Dr. Maxwell doesn't call back in thirty minutes, we'll take her." For the first time since we'd gotten back to their house, Mr. Greco raised his voice. "Your getting hysterical isn't helping, Adriana! Now get ahold of yourself and go in there and help your daughter! I'll get the ibuprofen."

My parents bicker constantly, but I'd never heard the Grecos fight in public. Not that the hallway of their house was public, exactly, but still. I'd never heard them fight. Period.

Olivia moaned quietly. Or maybe it was a sigh. If I had to pick a side, I was on Mrs. Greco's. I wanted Olivia to be with doctors. I wanted her to be where people knew exactly what was wrong with her. What *could* be wrong with her.

Mrs. Greco pushed into the room. I tried to make my eyes convey that I was totally in agreement with her, but she didn't even look directly at me. "Zoe, I'm sorry, but I think it's too chaotic with everyone here." Since I was the only person there, it was clear that she meant for me to go home.

I didn't want to go. I was scared to leave Olivia, scared of what would happen while I was gone. But what was I going to do? It wasn't like I could say no to Olivia's mother.

Mr. Greco came in with a bottle of Advil and a glass of water. He didn't even seem to register that I was standing there, just walked around the bed to stand by his wife.

"How are we going to get her to take those? She's asleep," snapped Mrs. Greco.

"We're going to wake her up." He looked down at the bed. "Olivia," he said quietly.

"Mmm? I'm okay." She didn't open her eyes, just rolled her

head back and forth on the pillow.

"Olivia," he repeated, sharply this time. Then he slipped his arm under her back and sat her up. "Olivia, I need you to wake up now." Under the command, his voice sounded scared to me. His being scared made me scared.

"Zoe, I think you should go," said Mrs. Greco.

I thought I should stay, but I couldn't say that. I couldn't say anything.

Except good-bye.

∾ 18 ∾

The last place I would have expected to be six hours later was sitting with Mia and Bethany in the backseat of Lashanna's sister's car, driving to the blowout party Mack Wilson was throwing to celebrate our victory over Lancaster, a rivalry that in all my years as a Wamasset student I'd never understood or cared about.

Yet there I was.

What I really wanted was to be with Olivia, but when I called at eight, after waiting as long as I could stand it, her mom just said they were watching and waiting and that Dr. Maxwell "knew the situation." I asked if she could call me if anything happened, and she said she would. Almost the second I hung up my phone, it rang, and I was sure it was Mrs. Greco telling me Olivia had to go to the hospital. But it wasn't. It was Mia. She said there was a huge party at Mack Wilson's house and Lashanna's sister was giving them a ride and did I want to go. I said I didn't, that Olivia was sick and I was going to stay

181

home and wait to hear from her mom how she was doing. Mia said she understood, but five minutes later she called me back.

"I just heard Jake Greco's going to the party."

That didn't surprise me. Jake and his friends went to a *lot* of parties. You did not have to write the *Wamasset Herald*'s gossip column to know that Jake and his friends pretty much *were* Wamasset parties.

"And you're telling me this because . . ." I was lying on my floor staring up at my ceiling. Part of me wished I could just crawl under the bed and stay there until Mrs. Greco called me back with an update on Olivia.

"Because if her brother's going, that means Olivia must be okay."

It was kind of irritating how Mia was being all pushy about this. "She's hardly okay, Mia. She has cancer."

"Oh, *really?* I had no idea," said Mia. "And will your sitting at home and worrying about her be curing her cancer?"

"Ha-ha."

"Look, not to sound like a cheerleader, but at the car wash today, Lashanna and I were talking about how everybody was all worried about Olivia, but nobody was taking care of you. We were worried about you, okay? So sue us."

It was weird to imagine Mia and Lashanna talking about me. Worrying about me. It made me feel a little bit defensive and a little bit good. "I don't know what to say," I admitted.

"Just repeat after me," said Mia. "'I will come to the party.'"

Jake was going to the party. Would Jake go to a party if his sister were dying?

Once again, I heard my dad's voice. *It's a marathon, not a sprint.*

"Yeah," I said hesitantly. "Okay."

"Awesome," said Mia. "We'll pick you up in about an hour."

For a while after I hung up the phone, I stayed on my floor. Eventually I got to my feet and looked at myself in my full-length mirror. I was still wearing the yoga pants and the cropped T-shirt I'd put on to teach dance class that morning. It seemed impossible that so much had happened—the car wash, Livvie's fever—and I was still in the same stupid outfit. I stripped it off almost angrily and went to shower.

Normally my parents went out on Saturday nights, but my dad had a big deadline Monday, so they'd been planning on staying home even before Olivia started running a fever. When I went downstairs, they were sitting at the dining room table with my dad's laptop open in front of them. My mom was holding a glass of wine and reading something over my dad's shoulder.

"Yeah," my mom said, eyes on the computer screen. "That's much clearer. I mean, to a layperson. To me. As a stand-in for a generic layperson." They both laughed, and my dad said, "Great," then shuffled through a pile of papers on the chair next to him.

"Hey," I said. They both turned to look at me, and I felt

suddenly self-conscious. I gave a little wave.

My mom did a double take. "Honey, you look beautiful."

"Really?" I looked down at what I was wearing. "You think?"

"Let's see," said my dad, pushing his reading glasses up onto his head. "Oh, yes. Beautiful."

Earlier, as I'd stood in front of my closet debating what to wear, I'd gotten sad. Olivia and I always got dressed together— either in person or on the phone—to go out. Trying to get ready for a party without her was worse than sitting home and waiting to hear if she was okay. Wrapped in a towel, I'd gone over to the phone and called her house.

Her dad answered. "How's Olivia?" I asked, and then I blurted out, "Do you think it would help if I came over?"

Mr. Greco has a really deep voice, and the phone practically rumbled in my hand. "The doctor's going to call us back in half an hour. There's nothing for you to do right now."

"Oh. You have my cell, right?"

"Yes, Zoe," he said. "I'm sure we do." Then he hung up.

I don't think he'd meant to be mean, but *I'm sure we do* felt a helluva lot like *I don't care if we don't.* After that, I'd pretty much grabbed the first articles of clothing I'd found in my closet, thrown them on, and headed downstairs.

"It's really nice," said my mom, nodding her approval of my black skirt and pale pink tank top with the sheer, white, long-sleeved shirt over it.

The only thing I was wearing that Olivia hadn't helped me buy was my underwear.

"Are you going out or something?" my dad asked.

"Oh. Yeah. Sorry. I got invited to this party." I gave a little laugh.

"'This party'?" my mom echoed.

"Just this party. With a few girls. You know, from the soccer team."

My parents eyed me. To their credit, neither of them pointed out that it had been their idea for me to play soccer in the first place.

"I see," said my dad. "And will there be parents at 'this party'? The one with a few girls? From the soccer team?"

"God, Dad, of course."

"Well"—my mom stood up, came over, and gave me a hug—"have a good time."

As it turned out, there were not parents at this party. In fact, there were very *much* not parents at this party.

It was a cold night, and there were only a few people standing out on the lawn, but every person hanging outside was holding a cup of beer (if not two) in their hands. Inside, the enormous modern white house was packed with kids, and everywhere people were drinking.

This party had *my parents are out of town* written all over it.

The second I crossed the threshold, bumping into a drunk

girl who cried, "Oh, shit!" as she spilled her beer down her shirt, I knew that coming had been an enormous mistake. I couldn't relax. I couldn't have a good time. I so did not belong here. As Lashanna, Mia, and Bethany headed toward the sunken living room, I lingered by the front door, thinking I would just call my mom to pick me up.

"You okay?" asked Mia, turning and looking at me over her shoulder.

I shrugged. "I don't know, I'm—"

"*Zoe!* How's my girl?" Jake appeared out of nowhere, Emma trailing behind. He threw his arm around me in a drunken embrace, nearly clocking me in the face with a bottle he was holding, then sloppily kissed the top of my head. "Come here," he ordered. "Come hang with us."

"Yeah," Emma echoed, plucking nervously at the bodice of her tight red minidress. "Come hang with us."

It was easier to agree than to object, and before I could say anything to Mia, Jake had led me through the crowd and into a small room off the main hallway, where a bunch of guys were playing a video game on the biggest TV I'd ever seen. He sat down on an empty sofa and pulled me down next to him. Since there wasn't any room for her on the couch, Emma balanced on the arm beside Jake, who immediately turned his back to her.

"How are you? Are you doing okay?" Jake asked.

I shrugged. "Yeah. I'm okay. I guess I'm okay."

He handed me the bottle he'd been holding. "Try this. It's really good."

I took it from him and sipped tentatively. I'd drunk my share of wine and beer and even champagne, and my conclusion had been that I really didn't like the taste of alcohol. But clearly I'd never tasted anything like this before—it was sweet and sour and cold and delicious. It made me think of the word *ambrosia*. "What is it?" I asked. Without waiting for an answer, I took a deep swig.

"Cherry-infused vodka," Jake said, grinning. "It's good, right?"

"Yeah." I took another healthy swallow.

Jake put his arm around me. "This thing with Olivia is just so fucked up." I glanced over at Emma. We made eye contact, and from her glare, it was clear that she wasn't happy about how Jake and I were sitting.

"It's fine," I assured her. "Seriously. He's like my big brother."

Jake glanced up at Emma. "Oh, baby, are you freaking out? Don't freak out. Me and Zoe are just talking." While he explained the situation to Emma, I took a long, deep gulp of the cherry-flavored drink. It was so sweet. But it was also sour. Sweet and sour. That was like me and Olivia: sweet and sour.

"Hey, Jake," I said. "Do you think I'm *sour*?"

Behind Jake, Emma got up and walked out of the room.

"It's good, right?" Jake clearly hadn't heard me, but I didn't care. I took another swig from the bottle.

"Did you know I'm Olivia's donor?" he asked. "If she needs a transplant."

I pulled the bottle away from my lips, wiping a tiny dribble of liquid off my chin. "You *are*?" Jake wasn't even eighteen yet. Then I remembered the woman at the bone marrow donor registration table asking me if I was a sibling.

He nodded and took the bottle from me, then drank deeply before handing it back. "There's a twenty-five-percent chance a sibling will be a match. We all got tested." He shook his head. "I'm so glad it's me and not Luke or Tommy."

"Jesus." I shook my head, trying to imagine one of Zoe's little brothers having the procedure I'd read about earlier in the pamphlet. "But it's not like she's even going to need one anyway," I pointed out after taking another drink. "Dr. Maxwell said she's not going to need one." I'd been at the hospital a few times when Dr. Maxwell had come to see Olivia, and I was close to positive that one of the times when we'd talked about bone marrow transplants, she'd said Olivia was responding too well to the chemo to need one.

Jake took the bottle from me. After he drank, I took it back and drank some more. My body was getting warmer with each sip. I wondered if this was what it felt like to have a blood transfusion, and I giggled. "I'm having a vodka transfusion."

He reached for the bottle. "Gimme," he said. "I need a transfusion." We passed the bottle back and forth between us for a few minutes, watching the cars on the screen speed along urban streets before exploding into balls of flame. Then Emma appeared, placing herself between Jake and the screen, her hands on her hips.

"Can I talk to you for a minute?" She was quivering with rage.

"Uh-oh," Jake sang, "I think I'm in trouble." He stood up.

"Oh no you don't." I grabbed the bottle from him. He made a pass at retrieving it, but then Emma took his hand and pulled him away.

I got to my feet and wandered outside toward the back deck. No sooner had I stepped onto it than I saw Lashanna, Mia, and Bethany talking to a bunch of the other girls from the soccer team.

"*He-ey*, guys!" I called. I had the urge to throw my arms around them the way Stacy and Emma always greeted me. "You know," I said, walking over to them, "I think I understand the cheerleaders a lot more now. It's like they're on a constant infusion of cherry-infused vodka."

The girls looked at me, then burst out laughing. "Oh my God, you are *wasted*," Mia observed. "What have you been drinking?"

I held up the nearly empty bottle I'd stolen from Jake. "*This!*" I announced dramatically.

Bethany tasted it. "Holy shit!" she cried. "That is deadly."

I grabbed the bottle from her and hugged it protectively

against my chest. "It's not." I stroked the bottle lovingly, as if it were a small animal. "Don't insult my cherry-infused vodka."

From a distant room I could hear music start to play, something loud and techno-y. Lashanna took me and Mia by the hand. "Come on. Let's dance." I grabbed Bethany's hand as Lashanna pulled a line of us along the deck, then down a flight of steps, onto the lawn, and through a set of sliding glass doors. *First we're outside*, I sang in my head. *Then we're inside.*

It was lovely to let Lashanna lead me around. This house was so *big*! It was the hugest house I'd ever been in, almost like a hotel. Lashanna pushed open another door, and we were inside a crowded, dimly lit room with an actual disco ball and insanely loud music pounding away.

Mia shouted something, but I shook my head. I couldn't hear a word. She leaned toward me and cupped her hand around my ear. "It's like an orgy in here."

I looked around. It was too dark to identify anyone who wasn't within a few inches of your face, but you didn't have to recognize faces to see that people everywhere were grinding away to the throbbing music.

"Wow," I said to no one in particular.

We started dancing. At first it felt good to move my body to music again, but it didn't take long for me to discover that techno and cherry-infused vodka were an *extremely* bad combination. The pounding bass line was starting to feel like a spike being driven directly into my brain.

I tapped Mia on the shoulder. "I've gotta get some air," I yelled.

Her arms were up over her head and her eyes were closed. "What?" she yelled back, opening them.

I pointed at the ceiling. "Air!"

She nodded. "Do you want me to come with?"

I shook my head and made my way out of the room, heading out a different door from the one we'd come through. It was much, much quieter as soon as I shut the door, and I followed a long hallway to a floating staircase. I tripped a little when I got to the top step, and a guy I didn't know who was sitting on the floor said, "Careful," but I kept walking. Finally, I found what I was looking for, and I slipped into a bathroom and closed the door.

It was bright enough outside for me to see without turning on the light, and I went over to the window and looked out at the lawn, which glittered with moonlight. Then I looked up at the sky, which was cloudy. Lawn: moonlight. Sky: no moon. Finally I realized that the Wilsons had lights on their property that *looked* like moonlight.

Weird.

I placed the bottle carefully on a shelf, then sat down on the edge of the tub, the porcelain cool through my skirt. The party seemed to be happening far, far away, the sounds I was hearing coming from a gathering on a distant planet. *Everything* felt far away, even my own body. The cold of the tub could have been chilling someone else's thighs. I put my elbows on my knees and sort of flopped my face into my hands. I was floating, saying good-bye to the kids at Wamasset, to the bathroom I was sitting in, to my body. I was just thoughts, just air. There was nothingness all around me.

Was this what it was like to be dead? When you died, did you still sense everything going on around you, only it was happening so far away that you didn't care about it? You were floating through space and time, and nothing that happened to you mattered because nothing *could* really happen to you because you didn't exist?

I stood up, swaying unsteadily, and crossed to the sink. I splashed some water on my face, then stared at my reflection in the dim light. "You are not dead," I said out loud. "You are not dead. No one is dead." What I'd just said didn't even make any sense. My reflection and I stared at each other for a little while longer; then I headed out of the bathroom, leaving the bottle behind.

I thought I might have trouble finding my way back to Lashanna and Mia, but all I had to do was follow the music, which now seemed to be rocking the house to its foundation. When I opened the door to the room where the dancing was, a blast of sound hit me, and I was immediately sucked into the underwater world of Mack Wilson's homemade dance club.

It was even more crowded than it had been when I left, and it was impossible to spot Mia or Lashanna or Bethany among the writhing bodies. As I moved through the room, half looking for them, half just moving to the music, I bumped into someone, and when I checked to see who it was, I found myself looking at Calvin.

He was dancing with one of the Bailor twins, who was draped over him like a toga. He and I made eye contact in the dim light, and as we stared at each other, I saw him slip the girl's arms from around his neck and shift his body so he was facing me. Without exchanging a word, we started dancing together.

Calvin was wearing a tight dark T-shirt, maybe blue or black; it was impossible to tell. He had on a pair of jeans, and his hair was damp with sweat. I was surprised by what a good dancer he was, how he moved his body so comfortably and easily to the music. He wasn't grinding his hips in a gross way; he flowed, liquid, into the beat. I liked it. It made me want to be a part of his movement, and I put my hands on his hips, slipping my index fingers through his beltless belt loops.

If he was surprised, he didn't show it. He moved a little closer to me and put his hands on my hips, and now we were definitely dancing together, not touching except for our hands on each other's bodies, but moving in sync, as if my hands were guiding his legs and his hands were guiding mine. I gave myself over to it, and soon every few steps our legs were brushing against one another, and then it was like the music was inside me and it was inside Calvin and it was winding us together, pulling us into each other with every step. There was nothing in the world, just me and Calvin and the music. I slid closer to him until our bodies were moving together, and then I ran my hands up his back, and then all I wanted was for everyone around us to disappear so we could be alone.

As if he'd read my mind, Calvin took his hands off my hips, and without saying a word, he pulled me by the hand and toward yet another door. For a second I felt the cool air of outside on my face, and then he was opening *another* door and we were back inside and then, without either of us saying a word, we were making out.

Making out with Calvin Taylor was like one of those car ads: zero to ninety in sixty seconds. I wanted everything, his skin, his lips, his body. Still not having spoken a word, I pulled his shirt out of his jeans and yanked it off over his head. He groaned softly, in the back of his throat, and he dug his hands into my hair. It all felt so good. I'd never experienced anything that felt this good.

"Zoe," he whispered quietly, kissing my jaw right where it met my ear. I shivered. "Zoe."

"Shhh," I whispered. I didn't want to talk. I didn't want to think. I just wanted to keep doing this. I ran my hands up his chest. With our lips pressed together, we stumbled across the room, and then the back of my legs hit something and we were falling and then we landed and I realized we were lying on a bed.

A bed! This was so what I wanted, to be lying on a bed with Calvin Taylor.

We rolled over so Calvin was underneath me. My whole body was on fire. I pressed myself hard against him, and he pressed himself against me. I could imagine how good this would feel without my shirt and his jeans and my skirt in the way. I sat up, straddling him, and he reached for me.

"I just have too much clothes on," I explained. "I mean, too much clothing. I have too much clothing on." I started to unbutton my shirt, realizing after I'd undone two buttons that what I was doing didn't make any sense. "They're decorative," I explained. I lowered my voice, as if I were letting him in on a major secret. "I have to take it off over my head." It was really hard. As I tried to remove it, the sheer fabric seemed to grow tentacles that grabbed at me. And every second I spent struggling with it was time I *wasn't* touching and kissing Calvin.

I gave up and lay back down on top of him. It felt so good. Fuck the shirt. I'd take his jeans off instead.

I reached between our bodies and started to unbutton his jeans. Before I'd gotten the first button open, Calvin took my hand. "Zoe?"

Oh my God, this was fucking *impossible*. Why did people wear clothes?

"Take off your pants," I said. Then I giggled. "I order you to take off your pants."

I sat up, arching my back and running my free hand through my hair. Everything just felt so good. Looking around me, I saw that we were in some kind of mini house—on the other side of the room was a shiny-looking kitchen. There were two walls of French doors leading outside. Through one set of doors I could see the synthetic moonlight shimmering on the covered pool.

"That's not real moonlight, you know?" I announced. I looked down at Calvin, who was still holding my right hand. "Oh my God, you are so *hot.*" I slipped my hand out of his and ran it across his shoulders, then leaned forward and started kissing his neck.

His body strained up to meet mine, and then we were kissing and it was just so fucking hot that when he pulled away from me I knew he was going to unbutton his own jeans, and I reached behind me to unzip my skirt, but instead he said, "Zoe, are you drunk?"

"A little," I admitted. Then I bent forward and kissed my way down his chest, down, down, down until I was level with his jeans.

"Oh God." He breathed in deeply, his stomach retreating slightly from my lips.

I reached for the top button. Now that I could see what I was doing, I could totally get his pants unbuttoned. But before I even started, Calvin put his hand between us. "Wait." He was breathing heavily, almost panting.

"What?" I asked. I was breathing heavily too. His stopping me from doing what we both wanted me to do was seriously annoying.

"Listen." He pulled me by the hand until I was lying beside him. I started kissing him again, and at first he kissed me back, but right in the middle of our hottest, most delicious kiss, he carefully pulled away. "No. Wait. Zoe. Listen." He put his weight on one elbow and laid one hand on my face so gently it was beautiful.

"What?" I whispered.

"I really want to be here with you. But I feel like you're pretty drunk. Are you?"

"As a matter of fact . . ." I started to giggle. "I am. I'm pretty drunk."

"Oh." He let go of my face and dropped back onto the bed. "How drunk are you?" His voice was flat.

"God, I don't even know." I rolled toward him and put my hand on his stomach. "Not too drunk to fuck, that's for sure." Then I couldn't stop myself. I started giggling again. I'd barely even been to first base on that one date with Jackson, but I was about to hit a home run. I knew Calvin liked sports, but before I could share my astonishing baseball metaphor with him, he'd moved my hand away and sat up.

"Jesus, Zoe, how much did you have to drink?"

"A *lot!*" I said, pointing my finger at him. "I had *a lot* to drink." I put my arms around his neck and leaned toward him. "And let me tell you that *plenty* of guys would be *extremely* psyched to fool around with a very drunk girl. So I don't know what *your* problem is." I kissed the side of his face once. Twice. Three times.

"Wow," said Calvin, "when you put it that way, I can't believe what an asshole I'm being." He peeled my arms off his neck and stood up. The fake moonlight shone on his torso. He was like something chiseled out of marble. I reached for him, but he stepped back. "I think I should take you home."

I stood up, which was really hard because my legs were suddenly difficult to find. "Oh, okay. *Dad,*" I said. Then I started giggling again.

He bent over and picked up his shirt. "You're hilarious," he said, pulling it over his head.

"*That's* right," I sang, throwing my arms wide. "I'm the funny one." I took a step toward him and placed my finger in the center of his chest. "Hey, here's a joke. Why don't you. Go. Fuck yourself?"

Still laughing, I turned and marched out the door.

~ 19 ~

I didn't so much wake up as I fell out of unconsciousness and into what can only be described as a vortex of agony. My stomach was raw and active; I pictured a swirling sea of acids just looking for an excuse to emerge from my mouth. My phone was ringing. That's what had woken me. I crawled on all fours over to my bag, which was on my desk chair.

"Hello?" My tongue felt thick and furry.

"Zoe?"

"Oh my God, Livvie." I curled into a ball on the floor, one arm wrapped protectively over my head.

"Are you okay?"

"I'm okay. I'm okay," I assured her. "Wait! You're calling me. You're . . . you're better?"

"Yeah," she said, sounding tired but okay. "Wow. It must have been some party."

"Um, it was all right." I heaved myself up into a sitting position. Something inside my head shifted dangerously before righting itself. "What time is it?"

Livvie laughed. "It's eleven. Are you hungover or something?"

"I think I am. Maybe. A little."

"Well, get over here and tell me all about it."

The night came rushing over me in a tsunami of horribleness. *Oh God. Oh my God.*

What had I done?

"Are you . . ." I cleared my throat. "Are you sure it's okay? Are you sure you're up to it?"

Livvie snorted. "You sound like my mom. Yes, it's okay. Yes, I'm up to it. The question is are *you* up to it?"

"I'm fine." I forced myself to my feet. My stomach rose up briefly, then dropped back down. "Really. I just need a shower and some coffee. Just . . . give me half an hour, okay?"

"Definitely." Livvie laughed. "God, you really sound bad, Zoe. I can't wait to hear all the juicy details."

"Right," I said. "Sure. I mean, of course I'll tell you everything."

"See you soon," she said. "Love you."

"Yeah," I said. "Love you too."

◆ ◆ ◆

200

Of course I *had* to tell Olivia what had happened at the party last night.

That was how Livvie and I operated. Shit happened, we told each other about it. Full disclosure.

But this wasn't just *any* shit. This was, like, *serious* shit.

Which was all the more reason to tell her.

Luke let me in. Livvie was upstairs in her room, and she looked fine, more like she had before the car wash than after it. She was wearing a yellow T-shirt, and she had a soft-looking, pale blue felt hat on instead of her wig.

"It itched," she explained, even though I hadn't asked. "So I'm taking a break from my wig." She turned to her mom, who was putting some laundry away. "Why don't *you* take a break, Mom?"

"I think you mean, why don't I take a hint?" Her mom was like a different person than she'd been the day before. She kissed Olivia lightly on the cheek and left the room.

"Okay, spill it!" Livvie sat forward, eyes glowing with anticipation.

I sat in a chair someone had put next to the bed. "You didn't have to go to the ER. That's so great." My enthusiasm sounded forced, but Olivia didn't comment on it.

"Dr. Maxwell said it had to get really bad before they'd want me in the ER because the odds of my getting an infection were so much higher in the ER anyway." Impatient with her own answer, she waved it away with her hand. "Tell me about

201

the party. How'd you get so drunk?"

"It was *totally* your brother's fault," I said quickly. "He was drinking this cherry vodka and he didn't warn me about how deadly it was."

Livvie laughed. "I heard him come home. He was *wasted*. My parents were so mad. You know he was supposed to be the designated driver."

I was shocked. "He drove *home?* Livvie, that's like . . . impossible. He could barely walk."

She shook her head. "He only drove there. Calvin drove him home."

I dropped my eyes and toyed with the edge of her comforter.

"Okay," she continued eagerly, "so you got drunk. And . . ."

"Well, there was dancing." I wrinkled my face as if trying to remember the exact sequence of events. *It was the funniest thing. One second I was dancing and the next I was trying to get Calvin Taylor to have sex with me in Mack Wilson's pool house.*

"And what?" Livvie tossed a small throw pillow at me. "I'm *dying* here. Not literally," she added quickly.

"Ha-ha."

"Now, tell!"

I looked at her. With her blue cap and her wide green eyes, she looked like a Renaissance painting of an angel. She *was* an angel. If anyone would understand what I'd done, it would be Livvie.

But how could I ask that of her? *Livs, I know you have cancer and you're losing a year of your life and you're taking this medication that makes you really sick. So if it's okay, I'd just like to ask you to deal with one more thing. . . .*

"Come on," said Olivia, mocking impatience but also clearly impatient. "Tell me. I have to live vicariously through you, so I hope you did something awesome."

It was impossible. Maybe if she'd been healthy, I could have told her. But if she'd been healthy, I never would have been at the party alone last night. I never would have gotten drunk and fooled around with Calvin in the first place. In fact, if she'd been healthy, maybe *she* would have been the one fooling around with Calvin last night.

The thought made my blood run cold.

I shrugged and gave a little laugh, then looked back down at the blanket scrunched up in my hand. "There's nothing to tell."

"Oh." She looked disappointed.

"It was just because you weren't there," I promised, finally making eye contact with her. "The next time we go to a party, it will be way more exciting."

The look she gave me was definitely puzzled, but whatever answers she was seeking in my face, she didn't find them. "Yeah," she said finally. "Okay."

"Okay," I echoed. "Great. Now." I slapped my hands on my thighs. "Enough about the stupid party. Tell me about *you*. When did your fever break?"

"Well," Olivia began, "it was crazy, really, because my mom was totally freaking out. . . ."

The whole time she talked, I kept almost interrupting her, almost telling her the truth about what had happened with Calvin. But each time, instead of saying something, I just squeezed my lips together until the urge passed. Even when every cell in my body screamed, *Now! Tell her now!*, I didn't.

I couldn't.

Somehow, it felt as if my decision to stick with it was as inevitable as the choice I'd made to lie.

∾ 20 ᳱ

Mind over matter.

That is something you learn when you study dance. Your feet are cracked and bleeding and your legs ache and you're so tired you feel you can't take another step, and then the curtain goes up and the music starts and you put a smile on your face and you *dance*.

I danced around what had happened all day, and by Sunday evening I found I wasn't working nearly as hard as I had been not to think about Calvin. The party took on a vague quality, something I might have imagined or dreamed or made up.

Besides, there were more important things to think about. Dr. Maxwell had said that if Olivia's fever didn't come back, she could still go to school Monday. The only conditions were that she had to stay away from people who were sick and she had to agree to wear a surgical mask indoors at all times. Livvie said she wasn't even sure she wanted to go to school at all since she'd look like such a freak in her wig and surgical mask. This, of course, thrilled her mom, who was adamantly against the whole plan and would have been happy to have her daughter in isolation until she started chemo again next week. But I kept promising Livvie it was going to be okay, that nobody would care, that everybody just wanted her to be there with them, and Sunday night, as we picked out clothes for her to wear, Livvie started getting excited.

"You realize you're getting excited to go to Wamasset, right? I mean, it's not like you're spending the week in Paris."

Livvie laughed. She'd been laughing all evening. The tiniest, stupidest joke could make her crack up.

"This is the dark side of cancer," she said, making her voice serious and taking me by the shoulders. "Even the dullest existence feels fantastic by contrast."

When Jake and Olivia pulled up in front of my house Monday morning, my mom and my dad were actually standing with me on the front porch, as if the day were as big a deal for me as it was for Olivia, and I hugged them both, then dashed down the steps to the driveway. Livvie cracked up when she saw me.

"What?" I asked, pressing my face with its surgical mask on it up against the car window.

She shook her head, still laughing, and when I slipped into

the backseat, she got on her knees, turned around, and hugged me hard. "I love you, Zoe," she said. "I just love you."

When we pulled up to the school, the first thing Livvie saw was five cheerleaders standing on the front steps wearing surgical masks.

"Oh. My. God," she said. She studied the scene for a long minute, then turned to Jake. "Did you organize this?"

Jake raised his hands to show he was innocent—"Don't look at me!"—but then he reached into his pocket and pulled out a surgical mask of his own. "I just do what I'm told."

Slowly, Olivia turned to face me. "This was your idea, wasn't it?"

I shrugged. "I might have mentioned it to Stacy. But, I mean, who can ever know *what's* registering in that cotton-candy brain of hers."

She didn't say anything. I leaned forward. "Are you crying?"

"Only a tiny bit," she said, sniffling.

I hugged her, my arms embracing the seat as well as her body. "It's okay," I said. "I'm crying a little bit too."

The entire school wasn't wearing surgical masks, but a *lot* of people were. It was so crazy. These people didn't even know Olivia, not really.

"This is the power of the cheer squad," I announced.

"Underestimate it at your own risk," Mia agreed.

We were walking to lunch together. I'd tried to get out of

history early to meet Olivia at her class on the other side of the building from mine and walk to lunch with her, but Ms. George was having exactly none of that.

"I know people came to the car wash, but everyone looked *hot* at the car wash, you know?" I said. "People don't mind doing things if they look hot. People look dumb in surgical masks." Talking to Mia in her surgical mask as we walked down the hallway together made me feel a little like a doctor on some medical show.

We turned the final corner before the cafeteria. Standing by their lockers were Jake and Delford.

And Calvin.

I stopped so abruptly that Mia walked into me. "Hey," she objected.

It is one thing to pretend something didn't happen when there is no evidence that it happened. It is another thing to pretend something didn't happen when the person it happened with is staring you in the face. Calvin and I made eye contact, but neither of us spoke, and then the current of people flowing through the hallway carried me and Mia away from the guys and toward the cafeteria.

Mia gave a brief whistle. "O-*kay*. You want to tell me what that was all about?"

"What *what* was all about?" My heart was beating extremely fast. I sounded breathless.

Mia glanced back over her shoulder, then looked at me.

"That Olympic stare you and resident hottie Calvin Taylor just exchanged."

I forced a laugh. "Wow, Mia, way to have a vivid imagination."

"Oh my God, you are so *totally* gaslighting me!" Mia cried, putting her hand on my arm.

"I don't even know what that is," I told her. I used my hip to open the cafeteria door. "Come on. Let's find Olivia."

∽ part 2 ∾

Winter

∾ 21 ∾

One week later, Olivia went back into the hospital for her second round of chemo. I'd thought I was prepared for it, but as I watched them slip on her plastic bracelet, settle her into bed, and set her up with her IV, it felt like I was letting my best friend be kidnapped. The walls of the hallways were decorated with paper turkeys and Pilgrims, and even though I knew the people who had put them up had meant well, it still made me mad. What exactly did people on a pediatric oncology ward have to be thankful for?

Olivia wanted to talk about the dance class, and since it seemed to be taking her mind off what was going on around her, I just let her float her insane theory that I was doing a fantastic job as her coteacher.

"While I'm in the hospital, you should keep trying to

choreograph something challenging with them for the recital. Those girls will work hard for you." The nurse said everything looked good and told us to ring him if there were any problems. When he left, Livvie sighed and stretched out on her bed. Her mom had gone to get her a ginger ale, and her dad was at work, so it was just the two of us in her room.

"I don't know," I said, tucking my legs up under me. "When you're not there, they don't really take the class that seriously."

"That's so not true!" Olivia objected. "They worked really hard on Saturday. They all learned that sequence."

"Yes, because *you were there*," I said, reminding her of the obvious. "Skyping the class equals your being there."

"Trust me," said Olivia, ignoring what I said. "They love you."

I snorted, but instead of responding to my doubt, Livvie folded her hands on her chest. Then she turned her head to look at me. "This is what I'll look like dead."

"Will you *stop*!" I slapped her arm. "Jesus."

She stared at the ceiling, eyes wide. "I cannot believe I have to start all over again."

"Dr. Maxwell said it's going to be *much* easier this time," I said quickly.

"*Might*. She said it *might* be easier this time."

"You're such a stickler for details." But now that she'd said it, I remembered. Dr. Maxwell *had* said might.

Eyes on the ceiling, Livvie asked, "What are we doing for your birthday?"

"For my birthday?" I shrugged. "I don't know. It's still a month away." The fact that my birthday was coming up had crossed my mind a couple of times recently, but given everything that was going on, I hadn't been able to get especially psyched, not even about the fact that I'd finally get my driver's license. Besides passing my road test, I didn't have too many big-ticket items on my birthday list this year. Maybe because *All I want for my birthday is for my friend to be in remission* doesn't exactly have a festive ring to it.

"I want you to plan something," said Livvie. "Something great."

I stared at her. "You want me to plan something for my birthday?"

Still looking at the ceiling, she nodded.

"Like, a party?" I asked. For my sixteenth birthday, I'd had a bunch of people over. It was hardly the elaborate sweet sixteen that a lot of girls at Wamasset had, but it had been a fun night. Even though seventeen's not a special birthday (outside of the whole driver's license thing), if I played the my-best-friend-has-cancer card, my parents probably would have thrown me another party.

Livvie made a face. "I don't think I'll be able to be around a lot of people then."

I did the math. In four weeks, when I turned seventeen, Livvie would be out of the hospital, but she would still be immunosuppressed. "God, right," I said. "Sorry."

"But I want it to be something really special." She sat up abruptly, the tube of her IV swinging. "Something fantastic. Something I can look forward to while I'm surrounded by this." She gestured around the hospital room.

I thought for a minute, chewing on the inside of my cheek as I did. "Okay," I said finally. "Let me get this straight. You want me to plan a spectacular celebration that doesn't involve a lot of people, won't tire you out, and that your mom won't veto the *second* she hears about it."

"Exactly," said Livvie. When I didn't respond right away, she added, "I'll just take your silence as a sign that you're already busy thinking of something."

What was I going to say—no?

"Of course," I assured her. "I'm on it."

I didn't call my parents to pick me up from the station, deciding maybe the birthday celebration idea that hadn't come to me on the train would come to me in the brisk evening air. But even the streetlights popping on around me didn't inspire a *eureka!* moment. The truth was, I wasn't very good at planning birthday stuff in general; Livvie had always been much better at it than I was. Even my sixteenth birthday party had been her idea. But I had the feeling my telling her to come up with something fantastic wouldn't exactly satisfy her need to look forward to some big birthday surprise.

When I got home, my mom and dad were sitting in the

living room. I assumed they were going to ask how Olivia's return to the hospital had gone, and they did, but it quickly became clear that wasn't why they were waiting for me.

"We need to talk," said my dad, and he patted the couch next to him. Livvie and I were always joking that my parents were trapped in a tragic 1970s vortex. They both drove Priuses, and they belonged to an organic food co-op, and they were obsessed with recycling. But the most obvious proof of their love for the 1970s was our living room. The couch my dad wanted me to sit next to him on was brown corduroy, and his feet rested on a multicolored shag rug. I sat down.

"Honey, did you know that you're getting a C in history?" asked my mom. She slid a yellow slip of paper onto my lap. It was something called an academic notice, and it informed my parents that my average in history was more than ten points lower than it had been at this time last year.

"Really?" Actually, I had no idea how I was doing in history. Or in any of my classes, for that matter. At the bottom of my paper on the Thirty Years' War, Ms. George had written, *This could have used a little more thought.* Then she'd given me a grade. B? Or had it been a B-minus? I hadn't paid much attention. The truth was, I didn't have any more thought in me. The only thing I thought about was Olivia.

"We know there's a lot going on for you right now," said my dad, his voice serious. "This is an unimaginably hard time. And of course you're going to be distracted. But you're a junior

217

in high school. You have to think about your future."

"College," my mom explained.

"Thanks, Mom. I get that when Dad says 'future' he means college. And that when he says 'college' he means Yale." Actually, my dad didn't say *Yale*. He said *New Haven*, as in *When I was a student in New Haven* . . . Both my parents went to Yale, though they didn't know each other there and my mom wasn't nearly as obsessed with it as my dad was.

"Don't get testy," said my dad. "Your mom and I were very supportive when you were dancing. We never pressured you to make different choices from the ones you wanted to make. As long as you kept your grades up, we let you dance."

"But now that I'm *not* dancing, who's going to want me?" I refolded the letter and dropped it onto the glass coffee table in front of me. "That's your point, right?"

He held up his hand. "I never said that. But you don't want to make decisions now that are going to limit your options in the future."

This was unbelievable! "Well, maybe I have been a little distracted lately. Perhaps you remember that my best friend has *cancer*," I reminded them.

There was a brief silence. Then my mom said, "Olivia's illness is a tragedy, Zoe. Don't turn it into a petty excuse."

My parents limited my hospital visits to three days a week. Theoretically I was spending more time on my work, and I guess technically I *was* spending more time on my work, but I was also spending a lot of time trying to figure out what amazing thing Olivia and I were going to do for my birthday, which, like helping with the dance class, was proving to be a bigger pain in the ass than I'd anticipated.

Clearly we were going to have to go out. My birthday was on a Thursday. On Saturday I'd take my road test, and if I passed, I could drive us somewhere.

But where?

Two weeks later, with less than two weeks left before I turned seventeen, I was no closer to an idea than I had been when I'd promised Olivia I was on it. After a dance class that wasn't as bad as the last one had been but wasn't exactly productive, I even asked the girls what they thought Olivia would want to do, but the only thing they could all agree on was "go to Disney World!"

I promised to give their suggestion some serious consideration.

"There's always Deco's," suggested Lashanna. Despite the calendar's saying there should have been an autumnal chill in the air, Mia and Lashanna and I were sitting on the lawn outside eating sandwiches. It was so warm we weren't even wearing coats.

Deco's was a fancy restaurant in downtown Wamasset

where a lot of people went on special occasions, but it was small and crowded. Mrs. Greco would never agree to Olivia's sitting there in the middle of flu season.

"What about going into the city?" said Mia. She wiped some mustard off her lip with a napkin.

"Yeah, but then our parents or someone would have to drive us." Right there, in my opinion, was the difference between the city and the New Jersey suburbs: You might be a cool driver at seventeen in NJ, but you weren't cool enough to sit behind the wheel on the other side of the bridge until you were eighteen. "Olivia's mom makes her totally batshit, and my parents wouldn't understand why they couldn't just come to the restaurant with us."

"Could Olivia's dad drive you?" Bethany asked.

"Possibly." Mr. Greco was definitely the most likely candidate to support an extravaganza. And I meant that literally. Even if I could (miraculously) think of some *amazing* celebration, how was I going to pay for it? And even if I could figure out how to pay for it, how was I going to get Mrs. Greco to let Olivia go? Now that Olivia's chemo was over and it was just a matter of waiting for her counts to come up so she could come home from the hospital, Livvie's mom was already talking about "when this is over" and "as soon as Olivia's had her last round of chemo." This was not a woman who was going to be eager to let her daughter do *anything* risky. I crumpled up the wrapping from my sandwich and stuffed it into my bag.

"If he said it was okay for us to do something," I said, speaking the idea as I had it, "Olivia's mom would have to go along with it." I remembered how he'd gotten her mom to back off the surgical mask thing on the day of the car wash.

"How very 1955," observed Mia. She shoved her bag under her head and lay down, closing her eyes against the sun.

I toyed with the strap of my backpack. "Maybe I should go call him now," I mused out loud.

"What if you guys went out for dinner someplace swanky, only you went *really* early so it wouldn't be crowded," Lashanna suggested as I got to my feet.

"Early bird special," Mia said. "Way to celebrate."

Lashanna flipped Mia the bird.

"Yeah, I'm going to go call him," I announced. I said bye and headed inside. I was nervous about calling Mr. Greco, and I didn't want to do it with Lashanna and Mia watching. It wasn't like he wasn't perfectly polite, but he always made me feel that I was wasting his time.

Olivia said that was because he functioned in billable hours.

The lobby was deserted. Most people who weren't in the cafeteria or in class were outside on the lawn. I googled the number of Mr. Greco's firm and dialed it, but as I put my phone to my ear, I saw two guys walking down the hallway toward me. I was about to duck into the alcove where the school's only pay phone was located, but then I saw that one of the guys was Calvin.

I froze, my cell pressed to my ear.

Ever since the party, I'd been successfully avoiding him. We passed each other in the hallways sometimes, but there were always tons of people around, and he never said anything to me and I never said anything to him. The few times we'd both been in the Grecos' house at the same time, I'd always managed to slip out the door without having to talk to him.

It was extremely helpful that Olivia's house had two staircases.

But there was no staircase in the Wamasset lobby. Calvin saw me, hesitated, then said something to the guy he was walking with. Whoever it was turned down the science corridor.

Alone, Calvin walked down the hallway toward me.

"Thompson, Miller, Greco and Stein." The woman's voice was chipper and professional.

I hung up without saying a word.

"Hi," he said when he was just a few feet away. He was wearing an old white oxford that was partially untucked. I forced my eyes away from where the shirt met his jeans.

"Hi," I said.

Silence.

"So I just hung up on Mr. Greco's office." My voice was pitched about an octave higher than normal.

Calvin didn't say anything, and I continued, speaking very quickly. "I'm calling him because Olivia wants to do something special for my birthday, and I can't figure out what to do. I thought maybe we'd go out for dinner, but it would have to be really early to avoid the crowds. Mia was like, 'Early bird special, way to celebrate.'"

Nothing.

I traced my thumb over the screen of my phone. "I don't even know if Livvie wants to go out for dinner. Maybe—"

"So are we ever going to acknowledge what happened at Mack's party?" Calvin interrupted me.

I forced a laugh. "Um, is no an option?"

Calvin snapped his fingers and made a disappointed face. "Oh, too late. I already wrote about it in my diary."

"Ha-ha."

Another pause.

"I don't get it," he said. "Were you just drunk? Was that it?"

Say yes.

Say, "Yes as a matter of fact, I was just drunk."

His eyes bored into mine. I looked away and studied the shelf of trophies set into the wall next to me as if I really gave a shit that we'd been the 2012 regional fencing champions.

"No," I said finally. Reluctantly. "I wasn't just drunk."

"Then why—" He turned away, slapped his leg in frustration, and turned back. "Why are you fucking with me?"

"I'm not fucking with you," I snapped, taking my eyes off the trophy case and looking at him. "What does that even mean, 'Why are you fucking with me?' That's like—that doesn't make any sense."

"Yes it does. Fucking with someone is"—he started enumerating his points on his fingers—"flirting with that person—"

"I never *flirted* with you!" I corrected him.

"And thanks for letting me finish. It's *dancing* with someone." He counted the second point off on a finger. "It's making *out* with someone." He looked at me as if waiting for me to object, and when I didn't, he made his last point. "And then *ignoring* that person."

"You ignored me, too!" I reminded him.

"Zoe, the last words you spoke to me were 'Go fuck yourself!' I'm sorry, what exactly is the appropriate follow-up to that?"

"What am I supposed to say, Calvin?" I dropped my hands to my sides. "I had a lot to drink, okay? I'm sorry. Is that what you want to hear? I'm sorry."

He stared at me. "I know you're going through a tough time," he said finally. "I don't need an apology."

"So what do you *want* from me?" I threw my arms wide to show how exasperated I was.

"Uh-uh." He shook his head and wagged his index finger back and forth. "The question is: What do *you* want from *me*?"

I gave a little laugh, as if what he'd just said was the stupidest thing in the world.

Calvin waited for me to do more than laugh at him, and when I didn't, he shrugged. "Well, when you're ready to tell me, I'm ready to hear it."

Just as he finished talking, the bell rang. It was like he'd *timed* it or something. People started spilling out of classrooms and into the building through the front door. I only needed a minute to figure out some amazing, clever, brilliant retort, but before I could come up with one, he was gone.

✎ 22 ✎

When I called him after school, Mr. Greco instantly understood what I wanted from him.

"You need me to help you pull it off," he said as soon as I told him that I was calling because Olivia had asked me to plan something special the two of us could do for my birthday.

"Exactly," I said, relieved that this was going more smoothly than I'd hoped.

"We're going to have to finesse it with Adriana. She'll be nervous about letting Olivia go out."

"Right." I was walking home. I'd been too thrown by my exchange with Calvin to try and call Mr. Greco again until now.

"We'll need Dr. Maxwell's approval, of course. What are you planning?"

I looked around me. The neighborhood Olivia and I lived in wasn't one of those awful developments where every house is identical, but it was definitely suburban. There was nothing cool for us to do here. "Something in Manhattan," I said.

There was the slightest pause, and then Mr. Greco said, "Sounds a bit vague."

"I realize that."

Was I crazy or did this moment call for a *sir*?

In the background, I could hear his other line ringing. "I can't go to Adriana and Dr. Maxwell with 'something in Manhattan.'"

"No, of course not," I said quickly.

"Well, you think of a specific plan and get back to me," he said briskly. "I'll help you in any way I can." He hung up.

"And *that's* why I always feel like an asshole when I talk to you!" I shouted into my phone.

Well, at least he hadn't said no. And he was willing to help.

Still, even if he would drive us and pay for stuff, the central question remained:

What the hell were we going to do?

Three days before my birthday, I still hadn't come up with a plan. When I came downstairs, I sat across the table from my dad, eating a bowl of cereal and staring at the back of the *New York Times*, which he was holding in front of him.

"Way to be social, Dad." I didn't know why I was criticizing him for not talking, since I didn't feel like making conversation either. All I wanted was to figure out what the hell I was going to do with Olivia Saturday afternoon. She'd asked me about my plans almost daily, and I'd kept assuring her things were shaping up nicely. I'd implied the wow factor was going to be *pretty sweet*. I might even have used those exact words: pretty sweet.

Oh, did I say pretty sweet? *I meant, pretty* lame.

My dad slid the sections of the *Times* that he wasn't reading down the table toward me. "Here," he said. "Educate yourself."

I didn't bother to pick up the paper, just kept staring at the back of the page he was reading in a kind of zoned-out way. There was a full-page ad for NYBC's *Nutcracker*.

God, Livvie and I had loved dancing *The Nutcracker*. It was exhausting and crazy and by the last performance we never wanted to hear the word *snowflake* for as long as we lived, but still. You got to be *onstage*. You got to *dance onstage*. Every year, our parents and grandparents would come, and after the show they would come backstage bearing elaborate bouquets. We'd started dancing our very first year with NYBC. Last year had been our first year not doing a performance.

I banged my head against the table. "Ugh. Ugh. Ugh."

"I know," my dad said. "The world is going to hell in a handbasket. Luckily, it's the Christmas season. We can all celebrate peace on earth and goodwill toward men. Except for all the war zones out there."

It was my dad's saying the word *celebrate* that gave me the first inkling of an idea. Slowly, I lifted my head off the table and stared at the ad, which featured a woman's leg from the knee down, her toe shoe tightly laced up her calf. Next to her foot, miniature mice and children danced around a Christmas tree.

Olivia would love to see *The Nutcracker* again. Our moms had taken us every year from the time we were three. We'd only stopped seeing it when we'd started dancing in it.

Of course, it would be impossible for her to go. The company performed to packed theaters. Nothing would be more dangerous to Olivia than a confined space with hundreds of people in it. And it wasn't as if I was in a position to make an audience of theatergoers put on surgical masks.

Unless.

There *were* a handful of performances that weren't going to be sold out. That would be empty, in fact. Or nearly empty.

But for us to get to watch one of them, I would have to make another phone call, one to a man far scarier than Mr. Greco.

❧ 23 ❧

"Are we going to sit here all day? Because that's not so much a celebration as it is, you know, incredibly boring."

"All in good time, my dear," I assured Livvie. "All in good time."

It was Saturday afternoon and we were sitting in the Grecos' living room with her parents, her grandparents, Jake, and the twins. My nervousness about pulling off this escapade had made my road test (which I'd passed) a breeze, and I'd been so distracted by the details of my plan that it had been hard to feign excitement about the new phone my parents had gotten me. All I'd thought about for almost a week was whether or not Livvie was going to like what I'd planned. Livvie wasn't one to ask for something lightly. In fact, looking back over more than a decade of friendship, I couldn't think of one other major thing she'd asked me to do for her.

So I'd figured this had better be good.

As per my request, Livvie was dressed up, wearing a dark blue dress she'd bought for the last NYBC gala we'd attended. Mrs. Greco felt "young girls" shouldn't wear black, so almost every time Livvie and I went shopping for a fancy dress for her, she ended up with a dress in the darkest blue she could find. The one she was wearing now was taffeta, about ten shades darker than navy, and it had a scoop neck and a three-quarter-length skirt.

Maybe because I'd gotten used to it, Livvie's wig looked more natural to me. I tried to imagine how she would look to a stranger, and I couldn't see how anyone who didn't already know would guess she was sick. And right now she wasn't *that* sick. I'd been there two days ago when Dr. Maxwell had come to say good-bye, and she'd sounded really optimistic about how well Olivia was doing.

"Your numbers are excellent," Dr. Maxwell had said. "Your counts are coming back up beautifully. We'll do some more blood work next week."

"What are you looking at when you do blood work?" I'd asked from the radiator where I was sitting and admiring the gorgeous view of the river. If UH had had apartments instead of hospital rooms, they would have sold for a fortune. "If her counts are basically back to normal, what are you checking for?"

"Minimal residual disease," answered Dr. Maxwell. "All it takes for leukemia to come back is one leukemia cell. We want no detectable leukemia, and with modern technology, we can find one cancerous cell in a million. We want to *not* find those cells."

"If they find them," Olivia explained, "they have to change my treatment. I might get different medicine." She toyed with the strap of her overnight bag, which was packed and sitting on the bed next to her. "Or I might need a bone marrow transplant." The last sentence was spoken in a near whisper.

"You're not going to need a bone marrow transplant," I said, getting up from the radiator and going to stand next to her. "So let's . . . we don't have to think about it. I'm sorry I even asked." There was silence again.

Gently, Dr. Maxwell asked Livvie, "You okay?"

"Yeah," she said. "Totally." She looked up at Dr. Maxwell and changed the subject. "So, you going to tell me all about this amazing afternoon Zoe's planned for me? I know she had to get your permission."

Dr. Maxwell smiled like the *Mona Lisa*. "I'm sure the experience will be quite . . . satisfactory," she promised Livvie. Then she said good-bye to both of us and left the room.

Now I saw Mr. Greco, who'd been watching the street, suddenly nod at something beyond the window and say, "It's time, girls." He stood up and walked out of the house.

I got to my feet. I was wearing a magenta wraparound silk

dress and a pair of heels. The combination of Livvie's whole family sitting around in the living room waiting to see us off and our both being so dressed up made me feel like we were going to the prom.

"What's going *on?*" Livvie demanded as she accepted the coat Jake was holding out for her. She was trying to sound frustrated, but it was obvious how excited she was.

Just as I went to open the door, Mrs. Greco cried, "Wait!" Then she threw an extra scarf around Livvie's neck. "You take it very, *very* easy, okay? I don't want you overdoing it."

"Yes, Mom," said Olivia, hugging her mother. Despite her thick hat, scarf, and coat, she looked beautiful. Mrs. Greco hugged me, also.

"Take care of her, okay? Don't let her get tired out."

"I won't," I promised. I pushed open the front door and stepped onto the porch. Mr. Greco was in the driveway, standing next to a black Mercedes-Benz and talking to a man in a chauffeur's uniform.

"Holy cannoli!" Livvie whispered at my side. Her eyes were enormous with amazement.

"A limo seemed tacky," I explained, relieved that the first part of my birthday extravaganza seemed to be having the desired effect. "Black Mercedes says, 'I'm important. But don't notice me.'"

We were both giggling as we headed to the car.

◆ ◆ ◆

The lobby of the NYBC theater was nearly empty. As we walked through the echoing marble-and-glass space, I forced myself not to think of all the dozens of times we'd seen performances here. *Been* in performances here. Livvie clutched my arm. Her face glowed with excitement, but then she turned to me and asked with concern, "Is this killing you? Being here?"

I shook my head. The last thing she needed was to be worried about me. "It's nice to be back," I lied. Or sort of lied.

As we stepped into the theater, the velvet seats and carpet muffling our steps, I had a sudden memory, so sharp it made me gasp. Livvie turned to me, concerned.

"You okay?"

"Yeah," I said quickly, not wanting to get into it. "I'm fine."

There were a few people sitting together almost exactly in the middle of the theater, but otherwise, it was empty. Lots of dance companies let people watch dress rehearsals—some even sell tickets to them—but Martin Hicks, the director of NYBC, was a total fascist about anyone attending his dress rehearsals. He didn't even let members of the company attend unless they were his special pets. In fact, that was how you often found out who was in Mr. Hicks's favor: someone let you know he or she had been invited to sit with him at a dress rehearsal.

As the door to the lobby slowly swung shut behind us, a single figure got up from the group in the center and headed toward us.

It was Martin Hicks.

In all my years with the company, he and I had never spoken. The hardest thing about putting today together had been the phone call I'd had to make to him. It had taken me a whole day just to work up the courage to dial the number. And now here he was, standing beside me, gripping my shoulder as if we were old friends.

"Zoe," he said. "And Olivia." He looked into our eyes as he said our names. "I'm so glad you could come watch today." He was wearing his signature outfit: a black turtleneck and a pair of Levi's 501s. I always forgot this, but he was almost exactly my height.

In my memory, he was seven feet tall.

"It was so nice of you to let us come," I said. I'd played the cancer card *hard* with Mr. Hicks. He hadn't even returned my first two calls.

"It was an honor to be asked." He put his hand to his chest gently, as if indicating we had literally touched his heart.

I knew for a fact he had basically no idea who we were, but he acted so moved that it was impossible not to believe he was sincere.

A voice from up near the stage called, "Martin!" and he excused himself. Olivia was still smiling a phony smile when she turned to me.

"Okay," she said through her teeth, "he still terrifies me."

"Duh. He terrifies everyone."

"How did you pull it off?" she asked after we'd chosen our seats. "I've always dreamed of going to a dress rehearsal."

I took Livvie's hand and looked into her eyes. "Honestly?" I asked.

"Honestly," she said.

"I told him you were dying," I said. Immediately we both burst out laughing. The conversation that had been going on in the middle of the theater broke off, and I could feel several pair of eyes glaring at us. Livvie and I both slid down low in our seats, still giggling.

"Okay," announced Mr. Hicks. "Let's get this started."

For a couple of minutes there was silence, and then the sounds of *The Nutcracker's* overture—bright staccato notes jabbing the air—filled the theater. Something in my throat got tight as the music played. It had been less than two years since I'd heard it, yet so much had happened since the last time Olivia and I had danced *The Nutcracker* that this tune seemed to come at me from a different universe.

The curtain rose on the party scene, Clara and Fritz and all their friends playing in the Stahlbaum living room, the beautiful tree shimmering stage right. Neither Olivia nor I had ever played Clara, but we had danced in this scene. In the darkness I felt Livvie's hand wrap around my own, and I remembered how before we'd gone on, we'd often held hands—damp, sweaty palm against damp, sweaty palm—barely able to make out anything in the chaos of backstage except each other.

I'd picked the restaurant because of its roof deck. Even though it was only five thirty, I was afraid that the restaurant would be crowded and Olivia would end up sitting next to someone incubating a cold. As long as we could sit outside, we were safe. The hostess I'd spoken to had assured me that the heating lamps would make it perfectly warm, and though Olivia shivered slightly as we made our way to our table, as soon as we sat down, she took off her coat in the toastiness of the giant lamps above us. Good for energy conservation? No. Good for a friend with a compromised immune system? Yes.

"This view is amazing," said Olivia.

I'd been so focused on the health benefits of the outdoor seating that I hadn't paid attention to much else, but Olivia was right: the view was incredible. All of Manhattan was stretched out at our feet, fifty stories below us.

The waiter came and took our drink order, and as we sat sipping the virgin whiskey sours that he'd brought us, Livvie demanded, "Okay, be honest. Was it torture?"

I shook my head and put my drink down. "You know what I remembered?"

"What?"

"My mantra." I twirled my maraschino cherry through the foam at the top of my drink, unable to meet Livvie's eyes.

"You had a *mantra?*" she shrieked. A woman at the next table glanced over at us, and Livvie lowered her voice. "Why didn't you ever tell me that?"

Instead of answering her question, I asked my own. "Do you want to know what it was?"

"Sure," she said, my tone making her slightly less enthusiastic.

"It was . . ." I looked at a spot just above her head and recited in a robotic voice: "Let me be good enough. Let me be good enough. Let me be good enough."

"Oh," said Livvie quietly. When I finally looked her in the eye, the expression on her face showed we were thinking the same thing.

"I know," I said, even though she hadn't said anything. "It *is* depressing."

Livvie reached across the table and gently placed her hand on my arm. "No, it's not—"

"No, it *is*," I interrupted her. "It's awful." Hearing my own mantra, forgotten all this time, had conjured for me all the other things I'd forgotten about those last months and even years of dancing—how frightened I'd been all the time, how desperate to prove I deserved to stay in the company, how insecure and pathetic I'd felt.

"It was stressful," Livvie said gently. "We were *all* stressed out."

There was a pause, and then I said, "I hated it."

"No you didn't," Livvie said automatically.

But I stared across the table at her, and she didn't argue anymore.

"I don't get it," said Livvie finally. "If you hated it so much, why didn't you quit?"

"Grrr." I dropped my head into my hands and yanked on my hair. "I don't *know*. I don't think I realized that I hated it. I mean, I thought I just hated myself for not being good enough. I hated that I wasn't a better dancer."

"You were a beautiful dancer," said Livvie.

"Thanks."

I raised my head, and when our eyes met, hers were sad. "What?" I asked.

She shrugged. "I feel bad. I didn't know you were so unhappy. I'm your best friend. How could I not have known?"

"I don't think *I* knew," I said after a pause. "I don't think I knew until just now."

A few tables away a couple laughed.

"I understand," said Olivia. She dropped her chin into her hand. "I don't know if I *hated* it, exactly. But it definitely stopped being fun. Except when we were messing around in your basement, I don't think I liked dancing much by the end." Cocking her head to the side, she asked, "Why did it stop being fun?"

"For me . . ." I looked at the Empire State Building, sparkling in the distance. "I think it stopped being fun when I started wanting to be the best."

I turned back to her. Livvie's eyes were bright. "Sometimes I wish we were still little again," she said. "Just dancing at

Madame Durand's. Getting all excited for those stupid recitals."

Neither of us said anything about Livvie's being sick, but we were both thinking about it. "Me too," I said, my eyes stinging.

Olivia sniffled, but she didn't cry. "You know," she said after a minute, "it's dumb to be sad. I mean, we can still have the awesome apartment in Manhattan."

"Snazzy jobs." I snapped my fingers and did a little dance with my shoulders to emphasize the point. "Sexy boyfriends. Weekends in the Hamptons."

"Day-into-evening wear," she added. When we were younger, we read this article in some magazine about how every woman should have day-into-evening wear, and we'd thought it was the most hilarious concept ever. For months, it was pretty much the punch line of every joke we made. I'd be sitting in her den in sweats and a T-shirt and I'd go, *Hey, do you think this qualifies as day-into-evening wear?* And she'd go, *Oh, totally.*

"Day-into-evening wear," I repeated.

"It's going to be amazing," she said, taking my hand across the white tablecloth and holding it tightly. "We're not going to be dancers, but one day our lives are going to be amazing, Zoe. *Totally* amazing."

I pictured the two of us sitting here in five years, ten years. Twenty years from now, we would still be less than forty years old. There was so much time for things to happen to us. Fabulous things. Things we'd never dreamed of because we were so busy dreaming of being ballerinas.

"Hey," I said suddenly, "we have to start planning *your* birthday now."

"It's not until June," Olivia pointed out, as if I'd somehow forgotten when her birthday was. "I think we have a little time."

"Okay," I said. "But we've got to plan something really *really* great."

She looked around, taking in the view and the restaurant, then looking across the table at me. "It's going to be hard to beat today."

"Yeah," I said, "today was pretty fun, wasn't it?"

"It was better than pretty fun, Zoe. It was perfect." She squeezed my fingers. "Except for one thing."

Damn. I locked my hands together and closed my eyes. "Okay," I said. "I'm ready. Break it to me gently. What did I screw up?" Livvie kicked me under the table. "Ouch!" My eyes snapped open. "I thought you're supposed to be all weak and shit."

She laughed. "It's not something *you* messed up. It's something *I* messed up. It's your present. By the time I figured out what I wanted to give you, I didn't have time to make it."

"You're *making* me something?"

"Maybe," said Livvie, holding her hands palms up and shrugging mysteriously. "Or maybe I didn't have enough time to make it *happen*." She gave me a meaningful look and then cracked up.

For some reason, her saying that made my eyes fill with tears. Only I didn't want Livvie to see that I was about to cry, so I just said, "You're a terrible liar, you know that?"

"Well, you can't have everything," Livvie said. "Looks. Brains. Great sense of humor. Tragic cancer story. I'll trade being a good liar for all of those."

"It's a good trade," I agreed, my voice husky. And I think I would definitely have started bawling if right then the waiter hadn't come over carrying menus, which he placed on the table in front of us.

"Would you like to hear the specials now?"

I sniffled and wiped at the corners of my eyes with my knuckles. It was stupid to cry. Livvie was right. Everything—from her birthday to the rest of our lives—was going to be awesome.

Totally awesome.

"Sure," I said, smiling up at him. "I think we're ready."

～ 24 ～

I was a little surprised that Mrs. Greco said yes when Jake asked if he could have some people over to the house for his birthday, the last day of Christmas vacation. Olivia was scheduled to go back to the hospital for her third round of chemotherapy at the end of the following week, and the lead item in the news recently had been how bad the flu was this year. If Olivia had any sort of illness—even a cold—they wouldn't start the chemo until she got better, and now that we were at the halfway mark of her treatment, Mrs. Greco was getting impatient to have it all over with. And not just Mrs. Greco. Olivia, too. We'd spent a lot of the vacation driving around in my dad's car just the two of us, listening to cheesy music while coming up with destinations that would give us an excuse to keep driving: *Let's rent a movie! Let's get Pop-Tarts at the Kwik Mart! Let's go to Weehawken and look at the skyline.* As we'd driven and talked, I'd noticed how Livvie had started saying, *When I'm better we'll . . .* or *After this is over I'll . . .* It was like the cancer was already in her rearview mirror.

But between the small guest list and his promise that everyone would wear surgical masks if they were in the same room with Livvie, Jake managed to convince his mom that it was okay for him to have a few friends over. So the Sunday before we went back to school, about twenty people gathered at the Grecos' to celebrate Jake.

Most of the guys were hanging out in the den playing Xbox, though not Calvin, who was still skiing with his family. Olivia and I had made our camp in the den with Lashanna and Mia.

I was sitting on the floor near Livvie's chair, and even though she was the only one in the room wearing a sweater, it seemed to me that she looked totally normal. Or as normal as any of us, considering we were all wearing surgical masks.

Mia's parents were freaking because her PSAT scores had been way lower than they'd anticipated. "It's so dumb," Mia said, scooping a handful of chips out of the silver bowl on the coffee table. "UCLA doesn't even care about SAT scores. They care about the brilliant documentary I'll be sending them."

"Is that the thing you're making about the rec center?" My PSAT scores had been the opposite of Mia's—way higher than my parents expected. When they'd arrived, my dad had practically gone online to book a hotel for Yale's parents' weekend two years hence.

"Not exactly," Mia started. "That's more of a promotional thing. I'm also working on a film about how—"

"Hel-*lo*!" sang Stacy, coming into the living room. She was with Emma and Hailey. All three of them had their hair up in high ponytails, and they were all wearing tight low-rider jeans and tiny T-shirts in near-neon colors. They looked to me like slutty American Girl dolls. "How are we feeling today?"

Emma and Hailey were carrying their surgical masks, but they put them on before plopping down on the couch. Stacy left hers off as she stood by the archway between the living room and the foyer to make an announcement. "You guys, this is so *fun*! And I just want to tell you that Jake's having this party has *totally* inspired me and Emma to have a Valentine's party. The theme is: Great Couples in History!" She gave a little squeal of joy, then put on her mask and came into the room.

"Like Beyoncé and Jay-Z," translated Hailey, in case any of us didn't know what great couples in history meant.

"Brad and Angelina," added Emma.

"Bogart and Bacall," suggested Mia.

"Who?" asked Stacy, but she didn't wait for Mia to answer. Instead, she continued with her plans for the party. "Costumes, of course. And dancing. But not like, you know, fuck-dancing à la some people at Mack Wilson's party." She gave me a little wave as she quickly added, "I mean, no offense." Then she and Hailey started laughing, and so did everyone else in the room, me included.

If you put a lobster in warm water and turn up the heat slowly, the lobster will have no idea it is being boiled to death until it is actually dead. That was what it was like for me while Stacy was talking. I listened to her talk about fuck-dancing. I listened to her say "no offense." I listened to her laugh. I laughed. And the whole time, I failed to see that I was being boiled to death.

"Wait, Zoe, is she talking about you?" Livvie's voice was incredulous, and she was still laughing a little. "Were you seriously, you know, grinding?"

My heart was beating way too fast. "God, I don't even . . . I mean, I hardly remember that night."

Hailey laughed again. "That room was like the *orgy* room! I swear, people should have been wearing condoms."

"It was *so* not that bad," said Lashanna, stretching out over the back of the couch. "Please. I was there. People were just dancing."

"*Some* people were just dancing," said Stacy, and she started laughing again. "*Some* people"—she swirled her finger before pointing it at me—"were fuck-dancing."

You could tell Stacy really thought this was completely hilarious. And that almost made it worse. Like, if she'd known what she was doing—if she'd *wanted* to blow some big

246

secret—I could have hated her. But she was just gossiping. She could have been talking about anyone and anything.

The only person I had to hate in this scenario was myself.

I was still smiling behind my mask. "Whatever," I said in a way I hoped ended the conversation. "It was just a stupid party."

"Oh my God!" said Livvie. "Who were you dancing with?"

Behind my surgical mask, my smile was frozen on my face. I literally could not speak.

"It was so dark," said Mia. I had no idea if she sensed what was happening to me and was trying to help or if she was just describing the scene as she remembered it. "I don't see how you could see who was dancing with anyone."

"Wait," Livvie interrupted. She leaned forward slightly to where I was sitting by her feet. "Who were you dancing with at the party?"

"Can I just say that I thought Margaret was going to rip your *eyes* out when you and Calvin walked off the dance floor together," said Hailey. She made her hands into claws, hissed, then started cracking up.

"That girl is *crazy*!" Stacy said. "Did you hear about what happened with her and Sean?"

"What?" Emma demanded, sounding hurt. "I didn't hear anything."

"Oh my God, are you serious?" asked Stacy. "Well . . ."

Hailey and Emma moved over to Stacy. Even Lashanna

and Mia turned in her direction to hear the story.

Olivia and I stayed where we were. Her jaw was making funny movements, as if she had something to say but hadn't learned how to form words. "Did you . . ." She wrinkled her forehead and shook her head, then gave a tiny laugh. "Did you fool around with Calvin Taylor at that party?"

"Livvie . . . ," I started.

"Did you?" she repeated, her voice harsher.

"Livvie, I can explain," I whispered. She was staring at me, with a look in her eyes I had never seen before.

"Oh my God." She said it so quietly it was almost like she was talking to herself. A second later she was on her feet, racing toward the stairs.

I leaped up. "Olivia!" I called.

I could sense all the girls on the couch staring at us, but I didn't care. I just called her name, louder this time. "Olivia!"

She was halfway up the stairs. I barely managed to get across the foyer before I heard the door to her room slam.

I was sure she would have locked her door, but when I tried the knob, it turned, and then I was in her room. She was standing by the far wall, her back to me.

"Liv, I—"

"I really don't want to talk to you right now," she said, not even bothering to turn around.

"I know, but if you'll just let me explain. It was a horrible mistake." I was panting from my sprint up the stairs. "I told you how drunk I was. It didn't mean *anything*. I swear."

"Maybe it didn't mean anything to *you*, but it means something to *me*." Her voice was shaking.

"I'm so, so sorry, Livs." I took a tentative step toward her. "I know you like him and—"

She spun around. "You think this is because I *like* him?" Her eyes blazed with fury. "I don't even—I had a *tiny* crush on him, okay? The point is that you *lied* to me."

"Olivia, I—"

"And not just once. Not just when I asked you about what happened at the party. Constantly. You have this whole secret . . . thing with Calvin." She shook her head, amazed anew by what she'd just discovered.

"Okay, I do not have a *thing* with Calvin!" I shouted. Then I lowered my voice. "We fooled around. Once. When I was drunk."

"And you haven't spoken to him since? Is that what you're telling me?" She folded her arms across her chest.

"Olivia." I looked at her like, *Give me a break*, but when she didn't speak, I said, "We go to the same school. We see each other. I am not claiming that I haven't exchanged a single word with Calvin Taylor in the past two months."

"You are such a *liar*, you know that?" Glaring at me, she made her voice high-pitched and enthusiastic. "'Oh, Olivia, I love you so much. Oh, Olivia, I'd do anything for you. Oh, except tell you the truth.'"

I started to cry. "You know that isn't true. You know I've never lied to you."

"You lied to me every day. Every time you looked at me it was a lie." She was crying also.

"That is *so* not fair. What happened with Calvin was a mistake."

"You felt *sorry* for me. You pitied me."

"That is not true." I emphasized each word as I spoke it. "That is *not* fucking true."

She pressed the heel of her hand to her forehead. "I feel like such an idiot," she said quietly.

"Olivia, please." I took another step toward her. "You have to believe me. I'm so sorry. Please, Olivia." I was crying hard now, panicky tears that made it impossible for me to think straight.

Olivia's face was hard. "Get out of here."

"Please. Livvie." I held out my hand to her.

"I swear, Zoe, if you don't get out of my house this second I am going to call my father and he'll come upstairs and *make* you get out."

The thought of Mr. Greco throwing me out of his house on Olivia's orders was more than I could take. I was sobbing so hard I could barely breathe, but my tears had no effect on Olivia. She just kept watching me with the same cold stare. Finally she said through gritted teeth, "Get. Out. Of. My. House."

~ 25 ~

After I left I called Olivia's cell all afternoon, but she never picked up. Out of desperation I finally called the landline, but Mrs. Greco told me Olivia was sleeping. I couldn't tell from her voice if she was lying or not.

For two days, I kept trying to reach her and she kept not responding. I considered going over to her house, but imagining her mom blocking my entrance and saying Olivia wasn't *up for visitors* stopped me cold. On the third day, I forced myself to stop trying to contact her. What if my constant texting and emailing and calling was just making her madder?

Some song my dad likes has a line that goes, "The waiting is the hardest part." The guy who wrote that definitely knew what he was talking about because I would have seriously rather done just about anything than sit on my ass waiting for my phone to ring. But that's what I did for almost a week: I waited. I even started leaving my cell at home because it made me so crazy to sit in class staring at it all the time. I kept seeing Jake around school, and I thought about asking him how Olivia was doing, but I was embarrassed. If he didn't know Olivia and I were in a fight, my asking him how she was would definitely tell him. And once he knew we were fighting, he'd want to know why.

It was bad enough that Olivia knew what a lying sack of shit I was. Did the rest of the Grecos have to know also?

"Hey," said Mia, coming up to my locker Thursday after school. "What are you doing now?"

"Nothing," I answered. "Less than nothing." Because that was what waiting was starting to feel like—less than nothing.

"Perfect." She bent down and picked up my bag from the floor. "Come get a latte with me before I have to start editing?"

"Oh . . . no," I said. I turned and gave her an apologetic smile. "I mean, sorry. Thanks. But I can't."

"Yeah," said Mia, leaning against the locker next to mine. "I can see how doing nothing is better than getting a latte with your awesome friend Mia."

I looked at her. Mia seriously wanted to spend time with me. Why? Why would *anyone* want to spend time with me?

"Are you okay?" she asked, seeing the expression on my face.

"Yeah," I said, and immediately burst into tears.

⋆ ⋆ ⋆

The bleachers were empty, and sitting on the highest one we could see the entire campus spread out beneath us. It was amazing how getting just a few feet up made everything on the ground look so tiny.

"Wow," said Mia when I finished telling her what had happened. "That really sucks."

"Yeah." I leaned forward and wiped my nose on my jeans.

She dug into her bag and handed me a napkin. "Here. I think it's more or less clean."

"Thanks."

Mia surveyed the trees on the edge of the lawn. "Maybe . . . is it possible you just really like Calvin and that's why you fooled around with him? That doesn't have to have anything to do with you and Olivia, does it? I mean, obviously the timing sucks, but falling for a guy when your friend is sick doesn't make you a bad person."

"You left out the part about my falling for a guy my sick friend likes," I said, stuffing the dirty napkin in my pocket.

"Oh, come on, Zoe." Mia pursed her lips in disbelief. "She said herself she doesn't give a shit about him. She's mad because you lied to her. But she'll get over that."

"How can you be so sure?" I snapped. "Why can't she just be mad at me forever?"

"Zoe, you're a great friend, okay?" Mia said patiently. "I've seen what a good friend you are. And you're basically an honest person who just made a bad call."

"You don't know that." I shook my head frantically from side to side. "You don't know that I'm basically an honest person."

"Fine, you're a lying sack of shit. Feel better now?" She leaned back on her elbows.

I looked down at the empty football field below us. The white lines were faded, but in some places you could still make out ghostly numbers in the grass. "I lied to you."

"Oh yeah? What, you secretly bombed your PSATs?"

"No," I said sulkily. "But I told you I decided not to dance anymore. That's not what happened. I was cut. I wasn't good enough, and they asked me to leave the school." I turned to glare at her. "So there you go. Make your case for what an honest person I am now."

"I don't get it," said Mia, meeting my gaze. "You thought I'd like you better if you were a quitter than if you weren't good enough?"

I looked back at the field. "Something like that."

Mia laughed. "Jesus, give people a little credit, will you?" She stood up. "Look, I'm leaving because I've got to get to the editing room, not because I'm so horrified by what you've just told me that I can't stand to sit here with you anymore. I think it's too bad that you thought I'd judge you for getting kicked out of dancing school, but I can see why it would be embarrassing for you to tell someone you barely knew at the time what happened. I can only hope—and this conversation *gives* me hope—that if the same thing happened today, you would feel you could be honest with me.

"Now"—Mia leaned over and picked up her enormous black leather bag—"this fight with Olivia is awful. But I feel confident that you're going to work it out. Because while I have not known you nearly as long as Olivia has, and while you and I are not one one-thousandth of the friends you and Olivia are, I can promise you that I would forgive you for something like this because you are a really awesome person and a really awesome friend."

I could feel my eyes getting damp again. "Thanks," I said. I smiled up at her. "You are a really awesome friend too."

"I know," she said. "It's my superpower." She headed down the bleacher stairs, but before she got to the bottom, she turned back. "You should go home and do something you like to do," she called up to me. "Make yourself feel better."

"That's the problem with me," I yelled. "I don't like to do anything."

Mia put her hand on her hip. "I thought you liked to dance."

"I don't know," I said, shrugging one shoulder. "Maybe."

"Try it," she said, and she waved good-bye to me.

There was no call from Olivia when I got home. I practically wasn't even surprised not to hear from her anymore. After I walked Flavia, I tried doing homework, but it was pretty much impossible to focus on sines and cosines.

Our last year at NYBC, Livvie and I were friendly with a French girl whose parents had a super-swanky apartment near the UN. She'd invited us to one of their parties, and we'd gotten dressed at her place, listening to the French singer Serge Gainsbourg and dancing around her enormous bathroom, slathering heavy, dramatic makeup on our eyes and putting our hair into elaborate twists.

Now I plugged my phone into my speakers and put on the same song we'd played that afternoon. My parents weren't home, and I blasted it as loud as it would go. I started moving, not dancing so much as occupying the music. I remembered how we'd bopped around Nadia's bedroom that long-ago afternoon wearing nothing but our bras and underwear, so used to getting changed in front of one another that we barely noticed we were more or less naked. Everything had been so beautiful—the three of us dancing and laughing, Nadia singing along with Gainsbourg, me and Olivia pretending to sing along even though neither of us knew French.

I pressed my hands against my eyes, seeing in the blackness behind my palms the perfection of that day. Now, as I stood in my bedroom, the music was so loud it drowned out thought. Spinning around with my eyes closed and my ears throbbing, I could almost pretend that I wasn't dancing by myself.

26

Friday morning, as I was walking up the steps to school, I felt a hand tap my shoulder. I turned around and found myself staring at Calvin.

This was the closest we'd been to each other since the night we'd made out at Mack Wilson's party. It was so weird that he was at the center of this huge fight Olivia and I were having, and yet we barely knew each other. I hadn't even talked to him since before my birthday, that day when he'd asked me why I was fucking with him.

"Hey," he said. "Can I talk to you?" He seemed nervous.

I was suddenly weirdly nervous too. I thought about what Mia had said about my maybe really liking him.

Was it true? Did I like Calvin?

"Yeah," I said. "Sure." We were five minutes from the

warning bell, and pretty much every Wamasset student was heading into the building. Calvin turned into the crowd and, like a snowplow, pushed a path for me out past the main steps and gravel walkway and over to one of the stone benches that lined the lawn. When we got there, he didn't say anything, just sat down and stared at the pavement between his feet. I stood facing him. There was a puddle with a thin layer of ice, and he tapped it lightly with his heel until it cracked.

Eyes still on the ground, he asked, "Something's up with you and Olivia, isn't it?"

It was the last thing I'd expected him to say, and I definitely didn't know how to respond. Did he know that we were fighting? Did he know *why* we were fighting?

I kept my eyes on the puddle also. "What makes you ask?"

He laughed. "Zoe, I can count on one hand the number of times I've been over at the Grecos' without your being there. Suddenly I haven't run into you *once* in almost a week? Did you guys have a fight or something?"

"You could say that," I said cautiously. I glanced at him.

He was staring up at me, squinting into the sun behind my back. "Zoe, when's the last time you spoke to Olivia?"

"Why?" I was suddenly nervous, but now it wasn't because of Calvin. What was going on here?

He reached forward and took hold of my fingers, pulling me a couple of steps closer to him. "Zoe, I have to tell you something. About Olivia."

How could Calvin Taylor possibly know something about Olivia that I didn't? "What do you mean?"

"I . . . They . . . Shit." He let go of my hands and rubbed his thighs, gazing out over the lawn. "When they did her blood work, you know, those checks they do?"

"Yeah, I know." My heart was racing. Whatever he was about to tell me had nothing to do with my fight with Olivia.

His voice was quiet. "They found some leukemia cells. The results came back yesterday morning."

There was a long, long silence. I felt waves of panic crashing over me, and I dropped down on the bench next to Calvin. The important thing was to remain calm and focused.

"What . . ." I cleared my throat. "What does that mean, exactly?"

Calvin turned his head to look at me. "Dr. Maxwell met with the family yesterday afternoon. They're going to do a bone marrow transplant. Jake's a match for her. But I think you already know that."

"Oh my God," I whispered.

"Olivia went into the hospital last night. They're giving her chemo. It's what they do to try and get her into remission before the transplant."

"Oh God," I said again. I pressed my fingers hard against my lips to try to get them to stop quivering.

The warning bell rang, but neither of us made a move to leave. Calvin put his arm around me. I realized as he did that my whole body was shaking. "Work it out with her, Zoe," he said finally, his voice quiet. "Whatever it is, work it out."

By second period everyone knew that Olivia was going to have a bone marrow transplant. People kept asking me how Olivia was doing, and despite my conversation with Mia about the advantages of honesty, each time someone came up to me and asked about her, I just lied. "She's, you know, she's okay," I said. "She's doing as well as you would expect." Every time I opened my mouth I fucking loathed myself. If only I'd had the balls to tell people the truth. *I don't know how she's doing. She hates me, okay?*

It was halfway through lunch when Stacy and Emma came over to where I was sitting with Bethany, Lashanna, and Mia. They were both wearing their cheer uniforms, and Stacy put her arms around me and instantly started weeping.

"Oh my God, Zoe, I'm so scared for Olivia," she said. The enormous bow in her ponytail bobbed against my chin.

"And for Jake," Emma added. Her nails were long and square, and when she wiped at a tear on her cheek, I was surprised she didn't take out her own cornea. "They're going to take a *needle* and go into his *bone!*"

"Seriously?" asked Mia. She looked to me for confirmation, and I nodded. "Jesus."

"When are they doing it?" Lashanna asked me.

Of course she asked me. Why wouldn't I know? Why wouldn't I know all the details of my best friend's illness and treatment unless it was because I had totally betrayed her and she fucking loathed me?

Instead of answering, I mashed my straw wrapper into a ball.

"Next week. Tuesday morning," Stacy told Lashanna.

From across the cafeteria, a guy called, "Yo, Stacy!" and both Stacy and Emma looked up. Then Stacy answered, "Just a sec!"

She turned back to the table. "Olivia's going to get this *huge* dose of chemotherapy. More than she's ever had before. It's so *everything* gets killed."

Emma picked up the explanation. "Jake was telling us that after she gets his bone marrow, she'll have a whole new immune system. He said his cells are going to be like the American soldiers on the beach at Normandy."

"Wow," said Lashanna. "That's incredible."

"We'll see you later, 'kay?" Emma said. As she and Stacy walked away, Stacy called over her shoulder to me, "When you talk to Olivia, tell her I love her and I'll call her later."

Clearly she was one more person who had no idea that I probably wasn't *going* to talk to Olivia later.

"Are you okay?" asked Mia as soon as they were gone.

"Yeah," I said. "I mean no. I mean . . . I don't know." Suddenly I could not sit in that cafeteria for one more second. I stood up abruptly, sending my chair sliding over the smooth floor. "I've gotta go."

"Where are you going?" Lashanna asked.

"You want us to come with you?" asked Mia.

"You can't," I called out to them without turning around.

Then I left the cafeteria, walked down the hallway, crossed the lobby, and exited the building.

❧ 27 ❧

At home I showered off the school germs and got dressed. My mother was in upstate New York for a daylong site visit; there was no way she would cut that short to drive me to see Olivia. There was also no way Mrs. Greco (assuming she was with Olivia, which seemed like a safe assumption) would let me into Olivia's room after a germy train or subway ride to the hospital. I didn't know what a cab to Manhattan would cost, but it was definitely more than the thirteen dollars I had in my wallet.

Luckily, my dad was downtown meeting an editor for lunch. He'd walked to the station, then taken the train into the city.

Which meant his car was in the garage.

It was the car I'd learned to drive on, the car I'd passed my road test on, the car I now drove whenever I was allowed to take a car somewhere, the car Olivia and I had driven all over New Jersey during break.

Backing out of my driveway, I felt calm and clearheaded. This was nothing I hadn't done millions of times. As I headed toward the Holland Tunnel, I reminded myself that I wasn't technically breaking the law. Not yet. I merged into the E-ZPass lane, still a law-abiding citizen, then descended into the fluorescent world of the tunnel, keeping my eyes on the taillights of the car in front of me, my hands at ten and two on the wheel. Nothing happened when I crossed the line marking the division between New Jersey and New York—no sirens went off, no police car appeared in my rearview mirror. That's how laws are, I guess. Nothing actually happens when you break them unless you get caught.

As I drove along the West Side Highway, I found myself getting angry about the rule that seventeen-year-olds couldn't drive in New York. There was *no* difference between driving in Manhattan and driving in New Jersey. "You think you're so fucking *cool*, New York!" I yelled. "But you can kiss my fucking ass." I stopped for a red light, remembering that you can make a right on red in New Jersey but you can't in Manhattan.

"I guess that's just one more way New York City is better than the rest of the *fucking* world," I shouted, banging the steering wheel for emphasis.

As soon as I caught my first glimpse of UH, I had a

decision to make. There were a surprising number of empty spots on the street, but my parallel parking was for shit. Even with the little screen that told you what was behind the car, I could never figure out when to turn the wheel or when to stop backing up and move forward. Half the time when I parallel parked I was actually *on* the curb. That was the one thing I'd been sure I was going to screw up when I took my driving test, but I did a halfway decent job, the guy who administered the test wasn't too strict, and I managed to pass. Still, was I going to risk getting a parking ticket I'd have to explain to my parents?

I turned into the hospital lot. If my conversation with Olivia wasn't worth $9.95 for the first hour, nothing was.

I half expected to be stopped by hospital security. *You can't go up there; Olivia isn't speaking to you.* But they were as lax as ever, and I got my visitor's pass with Olivia's room number Sharpie'd on it no problem. The elevator swept me up to her floor, and then I was walking down the hallway and opening the door to her room.

She was lying on her bed, an IV in her arm, the TV on. Her mom was sitting on a chair (this one pale green instead of pale pink) next to her; her father was sitting by the window on his BlackBerry with his iPad on his lap. As I walked in, he was saying quietly, "Give me those numbers again."

Mrs. Greco smiled when she saw me. "Hello, Zoe. What a pleasant surprise."

265

Well, that answered my question. Apparently the Grecos *didn't* know their daughter thought I was a lying whore.

Olivia glanced at me, then turned back to the television. "What do you want, Zoe?" Her voice was lifeless.

"What do I *want*? I want you to forgive me." I stupidly stamped my foot for emphasis.

"Tough." Her eyes were still on the screen. A woman was running on the beach. "Comfort you can trust," said the announcer.

"Girls?" said a confused Mrs. Greco. "What's going on here?"

"Oh, give me a break." I walked over to the bed, grabbed the remote, and turned off the television.

"Hey!" Olivia objected loudly. Startled, Mr. Greco looked up from his iPad. Olivia reached for the remote, but I took a step back.

"You forgive me now," I said. I pointed the remote at her.

"You know, Zoe, maybe this isn't the best time for your visit," said Mrs. Greco, getting to her feet.

"What are you going to do, beat me into submission with a remote control?" Olivia demanded.

"Maybe!"

"I'm going to have to call you back," Mr. Greco said into his phone. Like his wife, he stood up. "Now, girls, what exactly is going on here?" Mr. Greco was wearing a serious power suit, and his voice was stern. It scared me.

Olivia rolled her eyes. "For heaven's sake, Zoe!"

"That is *no* way to talk," Mr. Greco snapped at Olivia. Then he turned to me. "Zoe, I don't know what's wrong between the two of you, but your visit is upsetting Olivia. I'm going to have to ask you to go."

"Dad, I can take care of myself!" Olivia yelled at him.

"Don't yell at your father!" yelled Olivia's mother.

"Don't tell me what to do!" Olivia yelled at her parents. "This is between me and Zoe!"

"I will not have you getting upset like this," said Mrs. Greco.

"Well, it's not *up* to you!" Olivia yelled. "Now get out of here! *Please!*"

But since none of us knew who she was talking to, we all stood there sort of shuffling around. "Mom! Dad!" she finally shouted.

"What is it, sweetheart?" asked her mother, placing her hand on Olivia's forehead.

"I want you to go," she said more quietly. "I want to talk to Zoe."

Even though I was scared to hear what she wanted to say, I felt relieved that it was her parents she was throwing out, not me.

"Honey, I don't think that's such a good idea," Mrs. Greco said. "Dr. Maxwell said you're supposed to take it easy."

"I want. To talk. To Zoe," Olivia repeated.

Mr. and Mrs. Greco looked at each other. "Should we let her?" asked Mrs. Greco quietly.

"She's right *here*." Olivia slapped the bed with frustration. "She's right here and she wants you to go."

I couldn't read the look that passed between the Grecos, but the next thing I knew, they were heading to the door.

"We'll be right outside" were her dad's parting words.

"Zoe, please Purell your hands," said her mom.

And then they were in the hallway and the door was slowly closing behind them.

When we were finally alone, Olivia said, "They're driving me crazy." She looked over to make sure the door was shut all the way. "I'm telling you, my dad's going to be on his BlackBerry at my funeral."

"I'm sure he'll at least turn it to vibrate," I assured her.

A small smile flirted with the corners of Livvie's mouth, and I watched her force it away. "I cannot *believe* you lied to me."

"I know," I said quietly. "I'm sorry."

"It makes me feel like I'm just this . . . patient." She threw her arms out in front of her. "This *thing*. This messed-up blood and these symptoms. It's like I don't even *exist*." She glared at me.

"You exist." It sounded so lame, and yet I said it twice. "Of course you exist."

"I mean, I understand my parents treating me like a baby,

but you're my *friend*. How could you do that to me?" She started to cry.

I started to cry also. "Livvie, please." I took a step toward the bed. "Tell me what I can do to make it up to you."

"Maybe I'd even be happy for you," she said, crying hard enough that it was difficult to understand her words. "If you had a boyfriend or, you know"—she swiped at her face with her sheet—"whatever." Catching her breath, she added, "At least it would be something to talk about besides how I'm *feeling*."

"I should have told you."

She glared at me, but it was somehow a self-conscious glare, a glare that she had to work at. "You should have trusted me."

I wiped my cheek. "I didn't want to hurt you."

"In other words, I'm so delicate I couldn't have handled your making out with some guy I had a tiny crush on." She turned to face the window. A huge tanker was being pulled by a tugboat, but I couldn't tell if she was watching it or just staring at the glass. "What did you think would happen—did you think I'd die of *grief* or something?"

"No," I said quickly. I pushed my hair off my forehead as I tried to reconstruct my own logic. "It's . . . I thought, 'Oh, God, I did this thing, this stupid thing that's going to hurt Olivia.' And I didn't want to be the person who did something to hurt you, because I love you, and when I realized—when I *thought*—I'd done something that might hurt you, I felt terrible and so I lied about it. I'm very, very sorry."

The boat passed out of our line of vision, and Livvie turned back to face me. "If you like him, you should tell me."

I looked at her. She looked back at me, unflinching.

She was right. If I liked him, I should tell her.

I took a breath. "I like him," I said, admitting it to myself as much as to her.

She nodded, as if it was the answer she'd expected. "Have you told him?"

I shook my head.

"Well," she said, rubbing her thumb over her collar bone, "if you like him, you should tell him. Because you never know what can happen." She swirled her hand around the room. Suddenly her shoulders started shaking, and at first I thought she was laughing, but then I realized she was crying. "You never know what can happen," she repeated, sobbing this time. "So you . . . you really shouldn't wait, okay?"

"Livvie." I dashed my hands under the Purell dispenser, then crossed the room in a couple of steps and put my arms around her.

She buried her face in my shoulder. "They *nuked* me. They *nuked* me twice. And it came back. How are they . . ." She raised her head and leaned back against the pillows. "How are they going to get rid of it?"

"Dr. Maxwell is . . . I mean, she's the *best*." Gently I tucked the blanket around her. "She's going to cure you."

Livvie swiped at her cheeks with her fingertips.

"Really, Livs. And a bone marrow transplant. I mean you won't even have your blood anymore. You'll have Jake's blood. You'll have all-new blood! Without leukemia in it." Just saying it made Olivia's leukemia feel like something in the past tense.

She studied her hands on the blanket. "People die from bone marrow transplants."

My body went cold all over, but I managed to make my voice firm. "You're not going to die."

"I guess." I thought she was going to argue with me, but after a pause she wiggled her fingers for the remote. "Gimme." I handed it to her. "I just want to watch TV," she said. "Is that okay? I just don't want to think about anything anymore." I was about to tell her I'd go and let her watch when she said, "Will you stay?"

"Of course," I said, relief at her asking washing over me.

She pointed at the dresser against the opposite wall. "Get a surgical mask. They're in the top drawer. My mom will freak if she comes back and you're not wearing one. She thinks the school is a petri dish."

"Sure." I went over to the dresser, took out a surgical mask, and hooked the elastic over my ears. Then I pulled the chair closer to Olivia's bed and faced it toward the screen. Two women were sitting in a suburban kitchen drinking tea.

I looked over at Livvie. "Are we okay?"

"We're okay," she said, her eyes on the screen. Then she

turned and looked at me. "Seriously."

"Okay," I said.

One of the women was saying, ". . . and I know Todd called his brother before he left."

"What are we watching?" I asked, though the truth was, I couldn't have cared less.

Livvie shrugged. "I have no idea."

"Perfect," I said, "I love that show." Livvie smiled, then turned up the volume. We both settled back to watch.

❦ 28 ❧

I wouldn't have hit the car if I hadn't been so focused on the cement pole.

Everything should have gone smoothly. Livvie and I both got totally into the soap opera we were watching, and when Mrs. Greco came back into the room she got into it too, and even though we never quite managed to get a handle on the plot, we watched, rapt, for the rest of the hour while Mr. Greco conducted business from his BlackBerry. Right before I left, Mrs. Greco went to get a cup of coffee. After making sure her dad was on a call, I told Livvie about having driven into the city by myself.

Her eyes went wide. "No you did *not*."

I nodded. "That's why I have to go," I whispered. "I have to bring the car back before my parents see." I reached down to hug her, and she hugged me back hard.

"I'm sorry," she whispered into my shoulder. "I'm so sorry we had that fight."

"Me too, Livs," I whispered back. "I'm so sorry about everything."

Sitting in the car, I didn't realize my hands were shaking until I went to start the engine. The keys rattled against the dashboard, and I had to stop trying to insert them, take a deep breath, and wait a couple of minutes before I tried again.

"You're okay," I said out loud to myself. "Everything is okay. You just did this drive two hours ago." I got the key into the ignition, put the car in drive instead of in reverse, turned to look over my shoulder, hit the gas, and nearly drove into the wall.

"*Fuck!*"

I dropped my head against the steering wheel and took a deep breath. "Okay. Okay. I can do this." My hands were slippery with sweat, but this time I remembered to put the car in reverse. I checked behind me. No one there. The car was now dangerously close to a cement pole, and as I slowly backed out, I kept my eyes glued to the right front bumper, biting my lip and talking to myself as I slid slowly backward.

That's when I hit the car.

There was the sound of breaking glass and the screech of rubber on cement as the other driver and I both slammed on our brakes, and the next thing I knew, I was standing outside my car and looking at my dad's smashed taillight.

Oh my fucking God, I am so dead.

"Are you *crazy?*" demanded the driver. He climbed out of his enormous Lincoln and came around the front of it to study the damage. The damage that had been done to *my* car, by the way. As far as I could tell, his was fine.

"I'm sorry," I said. I was in a full-on panic. He was going to ask to exchange licenses and registrations. Insurance information.

I was never, never going to be allowed to get behind the wheel of a car again.

"You're *sorry?*" He was wearing a sweater-vest with a button-down shirt and a bow tie. I could picture his ancestors giving Native Americans blankets infected with smallpox. "Young lady, do you realize if someone had been walking behind you that person could have been *killed?*"

Behind his, a line of cars was forming. He looked at my dad's taillight. "That is going to cost a pretty penny to fix. I don't know if they teach you about insurance in driver's education, young lady, but in New York State, the person in *drive* has the right of way, not the person in reverse. My insurance company is *not* going to pay for that to be repaired."

"Zoe?" I swung around to see who was calling my name. In the line of cars was Jake's. He was leaning out his open window and waving at me. I could see Calvin sitting in the passenger seat.

Why Calvin? Why *now*?

"Are you okay?" asked Jake.

"Yeah." I gave a small wave back. "I'm fine."

The man cleared his throat, impatient for me to say something.

"Well, I guess if it's my car that's damaged and I'm going to have to pay to repair it, then it doesn't make sense for us to exchange insurance information, does it?" I hoped I sounded less rabid than I felt.

Out of the corner of my eye, I could see Jake still leaning out of his car. Someone a few cars behind his honked.

The man was watching me suspiciously, arms folded across his belly. "And what am I supposed to do if it turns out there's something wrong with my car that is *invisible to the naked eye?*"

For almost a full minute, the only sound was the blasting of horns as the line of cars grew.

"I'm sorry," I said finally. "I honestly have no idea what to say to that." I couldn't believe this was how I was going down—car damage invisible to the naked eye.

"Well"—the man wagged a finger in my direction—"you're lucky I'm in a rush, young lady." He turned and headed back to his car. "Next time, look where you're going." He opened his car door and screeched off.

"Thanks," I called to his retreating bumper. "I'll keep that in mind."

Jake and Calvin pulled into the space next to mine. Jake glanced into my car, clearly expecting to find one of my parents sitting in the driver's seat. When he didn't, he looked at me. Then he looked back at the car. "Zoe," he said slowly, "who drove you here?"

"My invisible chauffeur." I stared at the shattered taillight. "Shit. Shit. Shit. Shit."

Calvin and Jake came closer to see what I was looking at. "Damn, girl," said Jake. "What are you doing driving into the city by yourself?"

"A cop will pull you over for that," said Calvin. "It's against the law to drive with one of your taillights out."

"Great." I walked around to the passenger side of the car and stood there being furious with myself. "This is just *fucking* great." I was going to have to call my parents. There was no way around it.

"I can drive you home later," offered Jake. "After I see Livvie."

"Thanks," I said, so grateful to him I could have cried. "Really, Jake, thank you. But even if you drove, my dad would be pissed at me for taking the car. I've just gotta call him and . . ." I reached into my bag and got out my phone, then put my head against the cool of the car's roof and stood there for a minute, gathering the courage to make the call. My dad was already in the city, so he'd be the one to have to come get me, which meant I should call him first. But he was also the one who was more likely to be furious about what I'd done. If I called my mom and had *her* call him, it was possible she'd manage to calm him down, sparing me the worst of his anger. But that was assuming she wasn't totally pissed off also.

If I told her about Olivia's having relapsed, would my parents understand why I'd had to drive myself into Manhattan?

I heard what my mom had said to me that afternoon in our living room. *Olivia's illness is a tragedy. Don't make it into a petty excuse.*

Okay, they were *so* not going to understand.

"Here," said Calvin abruptly. "Give me your keys."

I rotated my head to look at him, keeping my forehead pressed against the cold metal of the car. "You're joking."

"I'm not joking." He put his hand out. "Give me the keys."

Tempting as it was, I could not let him do this. "You didn't come into the city to drive me home."

"It's fine," he said. "I was just keeping Jake company for the ride. Then I was going to take the train home."

"Seriously?" I asked. "That's . . . that's really nice." I remembered Calvin's saying my packing Olivia's suitcase was a Zoe-Olivia thing. Was driving into Manhattan only to take the train home again a guy thing, or was it a Calvin-Jake thing?

"What can I say?" Calvin turned his palms up to the ceiling. "I'm a nice guy."

"It's not like a cop won't pull *you* over for a broken taillight," I pointed out.

"But it's not against the law for me to be driving in this county." Without waiting for me to accept his offer, Calvin extended his fist toward Jake. "See you later, man."

Jake bumped his fist against Calvin's. "Yeah, man, see you later. Thanks for the company."

"Anytime." Calvin walked around and opened the driver's door. He looked at me over the roof of the car. "You getting in?"

"Yeah," I said. "I mean . . . thanks." Everything was moving so fast. One second I was getting ready to confess everything to my parents, the next I was all get-out-of-jail free. (Well, except for the whole, Sorry-I-broke-your-car's-taillight-Dad thing. But surely I could come up with an explanation for the damage I'd done that did not make mention of my having committed a crime.)

"Here," said Calvin. "Throw." I tossed him the keys, got into the car, and buckled my seat belt. Calvin slid into the driver's seat, backed the car the rest of the way out of the space, and drove us out of the parking lot and into the darkening Manhattan evening.

29

We drove in silence for what seemed like a long time. On the way into the city, I'd been so juiced up by the audacity of what I was doing that I hadn't had time to think about why I was doing it. Sitting passively in the driver's seat, I was overwhelmed by the reality of what was happening. How had Olivia's leukemia come back so quickly? It wasn't *possible*.

We were stopped at a red light. "I just don't get it," I said. The thought had been in my head for so long I felt almost as if I'd already spoken it. "Olivia's had two rounds of chemotherapy since September. How can her body already be making new leukemia cells?"

"Jake said that Dr. Maxwell said that Olivia's leukemia is very aggressive." The light changed, and Calvin put his foot on the gas. "Apparently they knew that from the beginning, but then she responded well to the first round of chemo, so everyone got their hopes up."

I looked out the window. The few trees we passed were brown and leafless, and the Hudson River—normally so luminous and rich—did nothing but reflect the slate-gray winter sky back at itself. Everything seemed cold and dead and hopeless. I bit down on my lower lip.

"I'm sorry I've been such a bitch to you." I glanced over at Calvin, but he was focusing on navigating the traffic merging to enter the tunnel. "Anyway," I continued when he didn't respond, "I appreciate your helping me today."

We slipped into a lane behind a bright red Subaru. "It's no problem," he said. Looking at Calvin in profile, I could see the bump where he'd broken his nose. Weirdly, it made him look more handsome, not less.

I watched the cars ahead of us merge. There were so many of them trying to get to the same place, you would have expected an accident to happen every two seconds. But somehow it all worked out. People honked a lot, but for the most part everyone just waited patiently for their turn to move forward. "You're a good guy, Calvin. You really are."

"Zoe, you don't have to do some big song and dance just because I'm driving you home." He glanced at me, then turned his eyes back to the road. "It's really no big deal. I don't mind." We slipped into a lane and picked up speed, and suddenly we were encased by an artificial night.

I felt very aware of being inside a tunnel, of traveling through a tube of concrete and metal that had millions of gallons of water pressing down on every square inch of it. I thought about what Olivia had said. *If you like him, you should tell him. Because you never know what can happen.*

But how was I supposed to tell him? Just come right out with it—*Calvin, I like you?*

I licked my dry lips. Then I pressed them into a line. There was no way that sentence was coming out of my mouth.

Calvin had one hand on the wheel. The other one was resting on his leg.

Without saying a word, I reached over and put my hand on top of his.

My heart was pounding so hard and so fast I was having trouble catching my breath. I kept my eyes straight ahead, glued to the taillights of the car in front of us, as if I were the one who was driving.

Calvin didn't say anything, and he didn't move. It was almost like he hadn't noticed.

And then, just as I was about to open the car door and leap out to avoid the humiliation of ever having to face him again, Calvin laced his fingers through mine. He lifted our intertwined hands to his face and gently kissed the back of my hand.

I felt the electricity of his lips through my whole body.

✦ ✦ ✦

The next time either of us spoke was when Calvin pulled into my driveway. He turned off the ignition. We were still holding hands.

"Thanks," I said. I looked at the house instead of at him. The porch lights weren't on yet, which meant I'd beaten my parents home.

"Anytime," he said.

"I think . . ." I kept my eyes straight ahead of me. "I think I might really like you."

"You *think?*" Calvin asked, and I didn't have to see his face to know he was smiling.

I curled my leg up under me and shifted in my seat so I could look at him. He was looking out his window, and I reached over and turned his face toward me. It was dark enough out now that he was hard to see.

"I feel like I'm on this . . ."—I groped for the right words—"this roller coaster. I know that's a pretty bad cliché," I added quickly, "but it's really how I feel. Like I'm up on this roller coaster, and you're down on the ground, and you're watching me and going, 'Come down! Come down from there.' And I can't. I can't come down until Olivia's okay." My voice got squeaky on the last words, and I knew I was about to cry.

"You're not alone," he said softly. "Everyone who loves Olivia is on that roller coaster."

"I know."

It was so quiet in the car I could hear us breathing. Calvin leaned forward and pressed his forehead against mine.

"But I get what you're saying," he whispered.

And then he moved a little and I moved a little and suddenly we were kissing. At first the kiss was so soft, like our lips were just brushing against each other accidentally. Then we were kissing harder, almost fiercely. The more we kissed, the more I wanted to kiss, as if kissing were a food that made me hungry. I put my hands on the back of his neck and pulled him toward me as he grabbed me by the shoulders so tightly it almost hurt.

"I should drive you home," I said when we finally came up for air. We were both breathing hard, and the windows of the car were all fogged up.

"I'd rather walk," he said, and then we were kissing again.

"This is complicated," I whispered into his lips.

"That doesn't mean it's bad," he whispered back.

I have no idea how long we sat in my driveway kissing, but eventually I said, "It's not going to help me make my broken taillight case sympathetic if my parents find me sitting here making out with you." I was lying across Calvin's lap, my arms around his neck. He kissed me lightly and I shivered. "I can't believe I used to think you were an asshole."

I'd thought my feelings about him had been pretty obvious, but Calvin looked hurt. "You thought I was an asshole?"

"Well, I mean . . ." Okay, this was awkward—I hadn't expected to have to explain myself. "You were so mean to me.

Remember? When I went out with Jackson that time."

Now Calvin seemed embarrassed. He toyed with a lock of my hair, but he wouldn't meet my eyes. "Yeah, about that. I think . . . I think I kind of had a crush on you."

I sat up. "You *what?*"

"Jesus, Zoe, is that really such a shocker? I liked you. And I thought you might like me. But then you went out with Jackson, and I was jealous, and so I was . . ." He laughed and shook his head. "Yeah, I guess I was kind of an asshole."

I stared at him. So it wouldn't have been Olivia with Calvin at Mack Wilson's party. Not even if she'd been healthy.

"What?" he asked, finally turning to face me. "Is this, like, seriously rocking your world or something?"

"Kind of," I admitted. But even though he gave me a searching look, I didn't answer his unasked question. It felt too private to tell him about Olivia's crush, like that would have somehow been an even bigger betrayal than the one I'd already committed.

I opened the door and stepped out of the car. The cold air was a shock—the temperature had dropped with the sun, and I'd left my coat at school. Calvin walked me up to the porch.

"So what happens now?" he asked.

I put my foot on the first step. "They harvest the marrow from Jake on Tuesday and then they give it to Olivia and hope it starts making healthy cells."

"Sorry, I meant with us," Calvin clarified. He was standing on the ground and I was standing on the step, so when I turned to face him, we were exactly the same height. I put my arms around him, and he put his arms around me. Standing pressed against him felt as good as it had the last time, and I felt the urge to bring him upstairs and take off all our clothes and just forget about everything but our bodies.

"I don't know," I said, my face inches from his. "I feel like I have to be there for Olivia. And I've got to get the girls in the dance class ready for their recital—I seriously didn't think about it all vacation. And I'm, like, failing half my classes. I—"

Calvin pressed his lips to mine, and when he pulled away, it was hard for me to catch my breath. "I get it," he said softly. "I get it." He kissed me one last time, then turned and headed down the driveway.

"What do you get?" I asked his retreating back. When he didn't answer, I yelled again, "What do you get?" He still didn't answer, and now I wondered if he was too far away to even hear me. But that didn't stop me from yelling one last question at him. "Will you explain it to me, please?"

∽ 30 ∾

It was even harder than usual to focus on my classes Tuesday morning. I kept looking at the clock, wondering if they were done harvesting bone marrow from Jake. Harvesting. The word made me think of Pilgrims and wheat, not blood cells. They should have called it something else.

Livvie had told her parents she wanted me to be there when she got the transplant, and they hadn't argued with her. At least as far as I knew. But it seemed unlikely that they had. I couldn't imagine anyone arguing with Olivia about anything right now. I'd visited her Monday night, and she was so knocked out from the chemo that she'd barely been able to talk. The whole time I was there, she didn't say anything except once, when her mom went to ask the nurse a question and left us alone together.

"Calvin gave you a ride home yesterday," she'd whispered, turning her head from the door her mom had just exited and staring at me with her bruised-looking eyes.

I nodded. We had to talk about what had happened with Calvin. I *knew* we had to talk about what had happened with Calvin. If I hadn't thought she was too tired, I would have brought it up myself. It should have been a relief that she'd brought the subject up, but now that she had, I felt nervous.

She gestured for my hand, and I gave it to her, not taking my eyes from hers.

"If you didn't tell him how you feel about him," she said, forming each word carefully and taking a breath after almost every one, "I'm going to be really mad." Her saying that almost made me cry, right up until she pinched the skin between my thumb and forefinger. Hard.

"Ouch!" I complained, jerking my hand away. "Jesus! I told him. Okay? So just . . . you know, pinch someone your own size."

She laughed and closed her eyes, then said something I couldn't make out.

"What?" I asked, torn between not wanting to force her to talk and not wanting to miss anything she said.

"I said . . ." She took a deep breath, and I put my hands on the bed and leaned closer to her, only slightly nervous that she was suddenly going to pinch me again. "Tell me you kissed him."

"I kissed him," I said. And now my eyes did fill with tears.

She smiled and walked her fingers over to mine. Then she fell asleep, still smiling.

Tuesday afternoon, my parents drove me to the hospital. They didn't come inside with me—Mrs. Greco had made it clear that there were to be no more visitors than were absolutely necessary. I was glad to be necessary, but I was also a little nervous. My mom and my dad both got out of the car and hugged me.

"We're just going to drive around," said my dad. "So as soon as you need us, text us and we'll meet you downstairs."

"But don't feel rushed," my mom added quickly, giving me another squeeze.

"Thanks," I said. I thought of how they'd sat with me watching *Law and Order* that night when I was freaking out about Olivia. How they were always worrying about whether or not I was okay. How they'd been mad about my having knocked out the taillight in the parking lot in downtown Wamasset (which was the story I'd told them about the accident), but they hadn't grounded me.

They were okay, my parents. They really were.

The guard at the visitor sign-in desk directed me to a different elevator bank from the one I'd used in the past. When I got off, I wasn't on the pediatric oncology ward; I was at the entrance to the bone marrow transplant unit. The second I stepped off the elevator, I was bombarded with warnings about infection, cleanliness, hand washing, sterilization. Before I could enter the unit, I had to Purell my hands, and then I passed through a set of double doors that advertised a stern warning: NOTE: YOU ARE ENTERING A FACILITY WITH PATIENTS WITH COMPROMISED IMMUNE SYSTEMS. IF YOU ARE (OR IF YOU SUSPECT YOU ARE) SICK OR HAVE BEEN EXPOSED TO ILLNESS, DO NOT ENTER. NO PLANTS OR FRESH FLOWERS. WASH HANDS THOROUGHLY BEFORE ENTERING A PATIENT'S ROOM.

I found myself missing the cheesy seasonal decorations in her old digs.

When I got to her room—after having Purelled my hands yet again, this time using the dispenser outside her door—Olivia was dozing on the bed. Her family was already there, even Jake. He was wearing a pair of sweatpants and a hoodie, and he was sitting in a wheelchair. "How'd it go?" I asked, putting my hand on his shoulder.

"Okay," he said, putting his hand on top of mine. "They got what they needed."

"That's good," I said. "You okay?"

"Yeah. Sore." He gestured at the wheelchair. "This is protocol."

"Got it," I said.

Livvie heard us talking and opened her eyes. She smiled at

me, and I waved. "Hey," she said sleepily.

"Hey."

The twins were squeezed together on the lounge chair, and Mrs. Greco was sitting with Olivia. Mr. Greco stood by the foot of the bed. I thought about what a beautiful family the Grecos were. They should have been posing for their annual Christmas card, not gathered around their daughter's bed wearing surgical masks. It made me so sad I almost started crying, which would have been *really* appreciated. I went over to the dresser and took a surgical mask out of the box, then put it on just as Dr. Maxwell walked in with a nurse.

"Hi," she said. "It's so nice that you're all here." For the first time ever, Dr. Maxwell's entering the room didn't ratchet up the anxiety level. Maybe we were all already so freaked out there was no way for us to be wound any tighter.

Everyone said hello, but that was it. Dr. Maxwell and the nurse went over to the IV pole next to Olivia's bed, and the nurse hung a small bag of reddish liquid from it. Then Dr. Maxwell slid the needle into Olivia's IV.

"Okay," she said quietly to Livvie. Then she looked up at the rest of us. "It's started."

"That's it?" I asked. "That's the bone marrow?" The liquid was reddish and murky, and the bag wasn't even that big.

"That's it," said Dr. Maxwell, her hand on Olivia's arm. "It's small, but it's powerful stuff."

How could that tiny bit of stuff save Livvie's life? It seemed impossible. I moved my eyes away from the bag, and for a second they caught Livvie's. As our eyes held, I thought I saw the same question I was thinking run through her head, and there was a look of fear in her eyes. Immediately, I smiled at her, then realized she couldn't see my smile behind my mask.

"I'd like to say a prayer," said Mr. Greco. I blushed. Talking about God always made me embarrassed. But Jake, the twins, and Mrs. Greco just lowered their heads and closed their eyes. Olivia didn't believe in God, and at first she didn't do anything, but when her mother put her hand on Olivia's head, she closed her eyes too.

I knew that Mr. Greco was praying for Olivia to get better, and I imagined his prayers being joined by Mrs. Greco's. Jake's. The twins'. Mr. Greco's parents. Mrs. Greco's parents. All of Olivia's aunts and uncles and cousins. Everyone at school. I dropped my head and closed my eyes, and I pictured all their prayers like a giant beam of light shooting up to God at the speed of thought. It would be impossible for any God to ignore that many prayers, that much love.

He would have to let her live.

～ 31 ～

There are two dangers for someone who's just had a bone marrow transplant. The first is graft-versus-host disease. Apparently the leukemia cells weren't the only thing Jake's blood cells were capable of fighting. His cells, released into Olivia's body, would think they were in their *own* body. Which would mean they could start attacking Olivia's body, thinking it was an invader, as foreign and dangerous as any cancer. Meanwhile, Olivia's body would think *Jake's* cells were invaders. To the extent that her diminished immune system was capable of launching an attack, it would launch that attack as vigorously as it could at the new bone marrow it had received.

But of course, Olivia's cells, while they were capable of attacking Jake's cells just enough to make her feel really shitty, weren't really capable of *defeating* invading cells, so she was just as vulnerable to infection as she had been with chemotherapy—maybe more so, since this last round of chemo had been so much more lethal than all the others. That was the second danger. Her cells weren't (as Emma had claimed) well-trained American soldiers. They were crazed terrorists with no allegiance to any country or cause, desperate only for their own survival.

I hated them.

Livvie couldn't eat fresh fruits or vegetables, both of which could carry bacteria. She had to brush her teeth gently so her gums wouldn't bleed, and she was showering twice a day with antibacterial soap. Infections were everywhere—not just outside Olivia but in her own body. Mrs. Greco told me about how the antibiotics Olivia was taking to fight infection could make normal bacteria in her body grow out of control and give her fungal infections. Livvie's mom watched everyone who visited Olivia like a hawk, making sure we didn't touch our faces or our mouths without washing our hands. Mine were red and raw from all the Purell and soap and water I was using.

As the days passed, Olivia looked worse and worse. She was shaky and nauseous. Her mouth was sore, and it was hard for her to talk. She had diarrhea. Almost every other day, when I called to see if I could visit, Mrs. Greco said Livvie was just too tired.

Meanwhile, we were waiting. Like pandas flown to a zoo

in the hopes that they'll mate, Jake's bone marrow cells had been injected into Olivia's body to *engraft*, which meant to grow and make new blood cells, but that could take anywhere from ten to thirty days. And while we waited for engraftment, all we could do was hope none of the things happening in her body—the graft-versus-host disease, the bacteria growing everywhere, the fevers and the diarrhea and the vomiting— would be enough to kill her.

When I visited, I always wore a pair of latex gloves and a surgical mask. There was a cart loaded with them outside Livvie's room. Even though Dr. Maxwell had said that the most important thing was that people not visit if they were sick, Mrs. Greco wanted everyone who came into the room to wear the gloves and the mask. I'd gotten so used to wearing protective clothing around Olivia that it would have felt weird not to—like driving without a seat belt.

Time passed. I went to school. I had lunch with people— mostly Mia and Lashanna and Bethany, but sometimes other people too. I went over to Mia's house a couple of times. But I couldn't really focus on anything I was doing—not my classes, not my friends. Wherever I was, I'd just fiddle with my phone, waiting for a call or a text from Livvie. It was like I was there but I wasn't there. The only time I felt like I was actually able to get caught up in the moment was when I was with Calvin. And not just with Calvin but *making out with* Calvin. Sometimes I'd text him from a class, and we'd meet in the parking lot and just fool around in his car, and for a few minutes the fact that Livvie was so sick would just disappear, erased by Calvin's lips and hands and body. None of my teachers ever yelled at me for cutting out of class. Unlike my parents, they seemed unwilling to remind me that Livvie's illness was a tragedy and not an excuse.

We counted the days. Literally. The day of the transplant was day zero. On day ten, there was no sign of engraftment, and Livvie felt terrible. On day fourteen, there was still no sign of engraftment, but when I pushed open the door of her room after school, she was sitting up in bed, and her cheeks were pink. "Hey," I said. "You look really good." It was all so relative. For the way she'd looked before she got sick, she looked like shit. For the way she'd looked the last time I'd seen her, she looked amazing.

"I got a transfusion this morning."

"Vampire." I sat in the chair Mrs. Greco was usually sitting in. "Where's your mom?"

"She thought she might be getting a cold," said Livvie. "Dr. Maxwell said she should stay home for a couple of days. Could you get me an ice pop?" Even if Livvie looked okay, she still sounded pretty tired.

"Of course," I said. I went out into the hallway and got one of the ice pops the nurses stored in a freezer. When Livvie's mouth and throat hurt, they were the only things she could eat.

"Thanks," she said when I came back with the pop. She peeled the paper off it, and I gestured for her to hand it to me so I could throw it out. The nurse had given me a pop also, and we sat eating them in silence.

"It's so weird how there's weather out there," Olivia said finally, watching the icy rain spatter against the window. She looked around the room. "It's like, what does that have to do with me? I haven't been outside in weeks."

"It's not so great," I assured her. "It's a snowless blizzard out there. It sucks."

"Mmmm." Livvie slurped on her ice pop. I put a box of tissues on her lap. "Thanks." She took one out and wrapped it around the wooden stick.

It was quiet.

Too quiet. I didn't like the silence, and so I filled it.

"So," I said, sitting back down in Mrs. Greco's chair, "I tried what you said, you know, with showing the girls some harder steps. It didn't work out that well. They were like . . ." I rolled my eyes to try to communicate how unenthusiastic they'd been. "Anyway. Then I tried improvising, like we'd talked about. I played them some Tchaikovsky, hoping, you know, just that they'd like it or something . . . but *that* was pretty much a fucking disaster." I laughed a little at the memory of how not into Tchaikovsky the girls had been. Or fake laughed.

"Oh," said Livvie dully. "That's too bad."

"You know, you'll be outside soon," I promised, pulling my

chair closer to the bed. My voice was chipper. "As soon as this is over. And then you won't even have to go through chemo again! That's the good thing about your leukemia coming back and your needing a bone marrow transplant and everything. You get to be cured with no more chemo."

"Who knows," said Olivia, affectless. "I mean . . ." She shrugged. "Maybe I won't be cured. Maybe I'll die."

"Of *course* you won't *die*," I said, rolling my eyes and reaching forward and fussing with her blanket. "You're doing *great*, Livvie."

"Did you know that the kind of leukemia I have has a thirty percent survival rate?" Her voice was accusatory, as if I'd known and been hiding the information from her. "I found that on the internet. Dr. Maxwell kept telling me not to go online. Well, now I know why."

The number made me feel sick. Thirty percent? With all the chemo and the bone marrow transplants they could do, how could seventy percent of people with the kind of leukemia Livvie had die?

I racked my brain for a reassuring explanation of the statistic she'd quoted, and miraculously, one came to me. "Livvie, it's an old-man disease, right? So they probably can't tolerate the drugs as well as you've been able to." I snapped my fingers as I thought of another idea. "And some people don't even get good treatment. I mean, seriously, what percentage of people with AML actually get to have bone marrow transplants from matched donors at a place like UH?"

She shrugged. "I don't know. Some."

"But Livvie—"

"Could you just please not fucking 'but Livvie' me?" she cried. "You sound like my fucking mother." To emphasize her point, she pointed her ice pop vigorously in my direction, and it flew off the stick and across the room, smashing into the far wall.

I could not think of a time in the history of our friendship that Olivia had used the word *fuck* once, much less twice.

"Um, I'll get that." I took the box of tissues from her lap and used a couple to pick up the melting ice pop. Then I brought the lumpy, dripping mess over to the garbage can and tossed both that and my own pop. "Do you want me to get you another one?"

Livvie shook her head. Visitors weren't supposed to use her bathroom, so I used the Purell dispenser to wet a tissue, then started cleaning the wall. The pale red line running down it looked like blood.

"I'm just saying there's a really good chance I could die, and I fucking wish I could talk to someone about it."

I was on my knees wiping up the floor. When I lifted my head and turned to look at Livvie, she was looking at me. Her eyes were huge and green, and as I thought about how many thousands of times I'd looked into them all I wanted to say was, *You are not going to die.* Because the alternative was unthinkable.

But Olivia didn't want me to promise her she wasn't going to die. She wanted something else.

I wrapped a clean tissue around the dirty ones and dumped the whole bundle in the garbage. Then I Purelled my hands and went over to stand by her bed.

"Okay," I said.

"Okay what?"

I spread my hands out in front of me, palms up. "Okay. Let's talk."

"Okay," she said. Then she laughed awkwardly. "I don't even know what I want to talk about, exactly." There was a tear on her cheek, and she wiped it away. She looked at me. "What do *you* think happens when you die?"

I remembered being in the bathroom at Mack Wilson's party. That lonely, disconnected sensation that had felt almost like a premonition.

Which it wasn't. It was a stupid drunken theory. In driver's ed, the teacher had made fun of people who claimed to drive better when they were drunk. How much dumber was it to claim to understand the universe when you were chock-full of cherry-infused vodka?

"I don't know what happens," I admitted, sitting back down. "But there has to be *something*." My mind groped for something I could offer up. "What about being a spirit? There are so many stories of that happening. All those people who say their loved ones came back after they died can't just be crazy."

Livvie gave me a look. "Of course they can."

We were both quiet. What would the opposite of the sensation I'd had at Mack Wilson's party be? Something warm and beautiful and comforting.

"There could be a heaven," I offered.

Livvie snorted. "Clouds and angels? I mean, seriously. What am I doing all day? Learning to play the harp?"

"No!" I shook my head emphatically. "It doesn't have to be all that crap. It could be something totally different. Something amazing. Like . . ." I started to get excited by the idea and leaned forward in my chair. "Like imagine the most amazing moment of your life. Only multiply it by a million. And imagine it goes on forever. It's the most incredible feeling, only we can't even imagine what it's like because we're still alive. Trying to imagine heaven could be like . . . trying to picture the fourth dimension. We can't do it. But that doesn't mean it's not there."

"Maybe," said Livvie. She seemed okay with my idea, but then suddenly her face crumpled. "But I feel like I'd just be so lonely there."

I wanted to say something reassuring, but the thought of Livvie being lonely and dead somewhere was so sad I couldn't catch my breath. I started to cry, and then I leaned forward and squeezed her hand, crying too hard to say anything. We just sat like that, holding hands and crying for what felt like a long time. Finally, I reached into the box and gave each of us a tissue. While Livvie blew her nose, I stood up and went outside to the little cart by her door. Below the piles of gloves and surgical masks were paper smocks that we didn't normally bother to put on. But now I wrapped myself in one.

"Nice dress," said Livvie as I reentered her room.

"Thanks," I said. I tied the plastic belt, slipped my shoes off, and lay down on the bed next to her. She rested her head on my shoulder. "I don't want to die," she said quietly.

Her voice was calm; she wasn't crying anymore. I wiped the tears that rolled down my face as surreptitiously as I could. "I don't *want* you to die." My voice was squeaky. It was so obvious that I was crying.

"That's a relief," she said. There was a pause, and then she gasped.

"What?" I asked, alarmed.

She put her hand over her eyes. "Do you realize I could die a virgin?"

"You are *not* going to die a virgin," I said firmly.

"I can't believe it. I might die a virgin." Her voice was soft with amazement.

"Livs, you're *not* going to die a virgin," I repeated.

She ignored me, slowly shaking her head. "I spent all that time having a gay boyfriend. I should have realized this might happen."

"You should have realized you could get *leukemia?*"

I was being sarcastic, but she nodded. "If you realize life

is short, you break up with your gay boyfriend and get a real boyfriend." She laughed.

So did I. "That's *exactly* the kind of thing you really wish they'd put on a greeting card but they never do."

"I know," she said, leaning back against the pillow and yawning. "My mom says God is love. She says God has a plan for all of us but we just can't understand it."

"That sounds nice," I said, patting her gently on the shoulder.

"Maybe." Her voice was fuzzy, and she yawned again. "If leukemia is love, who needs it?"

"Good point," I whispered.

Outside, the rain splattered against the window. Inside, Livvie had her head on my shoulder. After a minute, she began to breathe the slow, steady breath of sleep. I tried as hard as I could to believe in a God who was holding us—all of us—in his arms just like I was holding Livvie. I tried to imagine a God who would never let anything really awful happen to us for no reason.

A God who loved us too much to take us away from each other.

⨪ 32 ⨪

Jake's cells engrafted on day sixteen, and Dr. Maxwell said she wanted Olivia home no later than day twenty. Once upon a time, she explained, people who had bone marrow transplants would stay in the hospital for twice that long, but now, with all the hospital-borne antibiotic-resistant infections that existed, it was dangerous for Olivia to stay in the hospital any longer than was necessary.

I'd had some idea that Livvie would magically get better as soon as engraftment happened, but she seemed to feel just as crappy on day nineteen as she had on day twelve. By the morning of day twenty—when she was supposed to go home from the hospital—she'd developed some fluid in her gut, and they had to drain it. The day after the procedure she didn't feel any better. Or the day after that. Or the day after that.

"It's like they're *torturing* her," I said to Mia as I shoved my books into my locker after my last class of the week on Friday. "It's obscene."

"See you tomorrow at the rec center!" called Stacy, sailing by with the Bailor twins.

"Oh my fucking God, I can't believe I have to teach that fucking dance class again tomorrow." I fell back against my locker. "Those girls hate me. I'm serious."

Mia laughed. "What's happening?"

I closed my eyes. "They just don't care about the class when I'm teaching it."

"So, they hate you or you hate them?" asked Mia.

I opened one eye. "They're children. You can't hate children."

"Mmm-hmmm," said Mia, clearly not convinced.

"No. Really. I don't hate them. I just don't know how to *talk* to them. I get all jolly and fake with them, and they don't listen to me. Plus, we're making zero progress on our dance for the recital. Livvie said last year they'd choreographed half the dance by now."

"What's the dance?"

"That's the thing. There *is* no dance. I wanted it to come from them and their ideas, but every time I ask them what they want to do, they just say, 'We don't know.' And when I try to teach them steps that I've worked on, they get all . . . squirrelly and distracted." I closed my eyes again. "You're right.

I do hate them."

"Maybe you just have to show them who's the alpha dog," Mia suggested. "Maybe they're waiting for you to take control of the class."

"But I don't want them to hate me!"

"I don't think that can be your priority," said Mia. "You have to get them to take you seriously, and if they hate you . . . well, too bad."

I thought about that. Maybe I *was* being too easy on the girls. I kept asking them what they wanted to do. Letting them goof off. When Olivia ran the class, she didn't do that. She was firm with them. Maybe that was what I needed: to be firm with them. I turned around, shut my locker, and jammed the lock onto it.

"Okay," I said to Mia. "No more Mr. Nice Guy."

Saturday morning, I was like a drill sergeant, and the girls seemed to be responding. When I told them to line up, they lined up. When they started giggling about something, I told them to stop it *immediately*, and they did. Twenty minutes into class, we'd gotten through more than we normally got through in the whole hour. I made a promise to myself: today, they'd either learn the steps I'd come up with or they'd come up with their own. No excuses.

Just as I had that thought, Charlotte ran into the room. She was often late, but she'd never been *this* late before.

"Why are you late?" I demanded.

"It's not my fault," she said. "The bus was late."

I thought about Mia's saying the class needed an alpha dog. Maybe accepting Charlotte's lame excuses for her lateness was just one more way I'd been too easy on everyone.

"Look, Charlotte," I said, giving her my hardest stare, "you need to leave your house earlier. Because the bus being late is not an acceptable excuse for *you* being late."

Charlotte looked at me for a long minute. I waited for her to say something snotty or defensive or mean, so I could show her that I wasn't going to take that kind of talk anymore. But she didn't say a word. Instead, she did the one thing I never in a million years would have expected.

She turned and ran out of the dance studio.

When Mrs. Jones called me into her office as I was walking out of the building, I'd actually forgotten all about what had happened with Charlotte. I figured the director wanted to know how Olivia was doing, so that was the first thing I told her about when she closed the door behind me.

"Olivia's supposed to come home tomorrow, but I don't know if it's really going to happen. It's like something always goes wrong."

"Yes." She settled into her chair and gestured for me to sit in one of the chairs facing her desk. "I spoke to Olivia's mother earlier this week. I understand the bone marrow transplant has been a very frightening procedure."

"Oh," I said, sitting down, "I didn't realize you were in touch with her."

"Yes, I am," Mrs. Jones said. "I actually called you in here on another matter entirely today." She folded her hands on the desk in front of her

"Okay," I said. I still wasn't worried. After Charlotte had left, we'd actually had a really productive class. Maybe not the happiest dance class in the history of the world, but a productive one.

"How much do you know about Charlotte Bradley?" asked Mrs. Jones quietly.

"Charlotte Bradley?" When she said the name, I had no idea who she was talking about at first. Then I realized. "Oh, Charlotte. I don't . . . I didn't know that was her last name."

"Mmm-hmmm." Mrs. Jones made a tent with her fingers and rested her chin on them. "I spoke to Charlotte earlier today as she was leaving the building. I gather she was late to your class and you chastised her?"

"That's right." I leaned forward. I felt bad about how Charlotte had run off, but I wanted Mrs. Jones to understand that it wasn't like she'd been late once and *bam!* I'd come down on her like a ton of bricks. "I didn't mean to frighten her away from class or anything like that, but she's late a lot, and, I mean, I think it's important for the girls to be on time. I'm trying to get things a little more . . . organized."

"I see," said Mrs. Jones. Her tone didn't indicate whether she thought my plan to get organized was a good one. "Did you know Charlotte is nine years old?"

"*Nine?*" I couldn't believe it. She was taller than the twins. "I thought she was at least . . . I don't know, twelve or thirteen."

"No, she's nine, all right." Mrs. Jones's expression didn't change. We could have been talking about the weather. "She's nine years old, and she's got two younger sisters. Two sisters who she's often made to babysit."

"You can't babysit when you're nine," I informed Mrs. Jones. "That's, like, not even legal. Once, when I was ten and I was sick, my dad wanted to go out and get me juice, but he said he couldn't leave me alone, so he waited until my mother got home."

Mrs. Jones was giving me a certain look. At first I wasn't able to place it, but then I realized she was looking at me the way I generally looked at Stacy Shaw. She was looking at me like, *You are the stupidest person in the entire world.*

"Look, Zoe," Mrs. Jones said, leaning back in her chair, "that is a beautiful story about your parents, whose every waking moment is no doubt given over to your happiness and comfort. But Charlotte's mother does not see the world that way. She does not particularly see herself as *obligated* to look after her daughters, do you understand what I am saying? She drinks too much and she smokes too much and it is my firm belief that before too much more time passes, those three beautiful little girls are going to be taken away from their mother, which, it is sad to say, is no doubt going to be the best thing that could happen to them, and that is definitely not saying much.

"But that little Charlotte is so strong and so brave that every Saturday morning she manages to get here to come to your dance class." Mrs. Jones got to her feet and walked slowly around the desk. "She takes the bus *by herself*. And sometimes she first has to find someone to leave her sisters with, because she feels more of an obligation to those little girls than anyone has ever felt for her. And she comes because she has made a commitment to this class." She was standing directly in front of me, and she put her hands on the arms of my chair. "So when you complain about her being *late*, why don't you take a minute and think about what it takes for her to get here *at all?*"

There was a pause. Then, without my responding, Mrs. Jones stood back up. "Now, I know you are feeling bad about what I've just told you, and I'm sorry for that. Sometimes it's hard to hear when we've done something wrong. But we can learn from our mistakes. And I sincerely hope you will learn from this one." She'd made her way back to the other side of her desk. "You may go now."

I slid the chair back, then headed out of the office and down the hall. I was already crying by the time I hit the parking lot.

❦ 33 ❧

Olivia did come home from the hospital on Sunday. But her homecoming was nothing like it had been the day she came home from her two rounds of chemotherapy.

First of all, she was still weak. Like, seriously weak. She could sit up for brief periods of time, and she could walk to and from the bathroom, but that was all. As her mom settled her into bed, I thought of how Livvie and I had shaved her head the first time she'd come home from chemo. It was almost impossible to imagine her doing all the things she'd done that day. I doubted she could even sit on a stool for a minute now, much less for all the time it had taken to cut and shave her hair. When Mrs. Greco said it was time for me to leave, I didn't even bother to object. You didn't have to be Olivia's mother to know she needed her rest.

As I pulled open the front door, I literally walked into Jake, who was coming in. Calvin was standing right behind him.

"Hey, Zoe," said Jake.

"Hey." He hugged me, and I hugged him back, hard. Ever since the bone marrow transplant, I felt this intense gratitude to Jake. Without him, Olivia wouldn't even be alive.

"It's freezing out. You want a ride?" he asked. He was carrying a plastic bag from Driscoll's Pharmacy. It was overflowing with the small white paper bags that prescriptions come in, and I thought of Livvie struggling to swallow all the pills in them.

I shook my head. "I feel like walking."

Jake slipped inside as I held the storm door open for him. "You going in?" I asked Calvin. His cheeks were bright with cold.

"I could walk you home," he offered.

I let the door close behind me. It was cold and silent outside, and I pulled him out of the light that spilled onto the front porch from the foyer and pressed him up against the side of the house. For a second his lips were cold, and then they warmed up. His tongue was gentle, but it was still enough to make me dizzy. I grabbed hold of his shoulders, squeezing his body through the soft material of his down jacket.

"We're not walking," he whispered, breaking away from a kiss.

"We're not?" He had his hands buried in my hair, and I

tried to kiss him again, but he nodded toward the house. "Jake said she's feeling pretty rocky."

The streetlight flicked on, throwing my shadow over Calvin's chest. "It's okay," I assured him. "She's going to be okay." I kissed him again, hard, and he kissed me back.

But for the first time, his kiss wasn't quite enough to shut out what was happening in the house we were leaning against.

∽ part 3 ∽

Spring

∽ 34 ∽

As we neared day sixty, Olivia started getting noticeably stronger. Her hair began to grow in, a soft blond fuzz that made her look like a baby chick. And her face, which had been so gaunt and pale—almost as if it were made of wax—filled out a little, the old, healthy Olivia showing through ever so slightly, just like her hair.

On Thursday after school—day fifty-eight—I came in and found her sitting at the kitchen table. She was wearing a long-sleeved blue T-shirt with white piping at the neck and wrists. Thin as she was, she could have been a healthy girl hanging out in her kitchen and talking on her cell. If you'd put her in one of Mia's black ensembles, the buzz cut wouldn't even have been out of place. She just would have looked like a *serious* badass.

She gestured for me to sit down at the table with her. "Right. . . . Great. . . . Yeah, I think that would be totally possible. . . . You too. . . . Thanks."

"That was Mrs. Jones," she said after she'd hung up. "She asked if I thought I'd be up for teaching the dance class again next year. I said I had to talk to you about it."

I burst out laughing. "What, you think I'm going to want to keep it for myself?"

"I don't know." Livvie gave me a wicked smile. "I thought we could do it together."

I raised my eyebrows at her. "Um, why do I feel like I've had this conversation before?"

"You've done an *amazing* job without me. Just imagine how great it—"

"Olivia, I have *not* done an amazing job without you." I put my feet up on the chair next to hers. "I've done a mediocre-to-crappy job without you. A nine-year-old girl *dropped out* because I was so mean to her." It was true. After Charlotte had left, she'd never come back. Mrs. Jones had tried to reach her, but with no luck. And while I was definitely getting the girls to march to my tune as we learned the steps to a dance for the recital, the dance class, which I had the feeling had once been the high point of their week, had begun to feel like something we *all* dreaded.

"Look, you don't have to answer now," said Olivia. She picked up her spoon and dipped it into the bowl of rice pudding

318

in front of her. "I just told Mrs. Jones that I would probably do it." She took a bite and swallowed. "But I would really, *really* rather we do it together, okay? So, you know"—she pointed her spoon at me—"think about it." She stretched luxuriously and then laughed. "I feel so not bad today."

"Is not bad the same as good?" I asked.

"It's close enough," she said.

Calvin wasn't with Jake when he pulled into my driveway Saturday morning, so it was just me and Jake in the car. We ended up getting into an argument about this really lame rap he was listening to. Or at least *I* thought it was lame. He thought it was awesome.

"It sucks, Jake," I told him. "Seriously. It's just noise."

"Oh, is that your professional opinion?" he demanded, laughing.

"It is. Now . . ." I took out my phone and looked for a song to play for him. "Aha!" I said when I got to "Pauvre Lola," the song Nadia and Olivia and I had danced to years ago. "*This* is a good song." I connected my phone to the car stereo. "It makes you want to move. It's *music*." As soon as the song came on, I grew antsy. It was impossible to sit still while that beat grabbed your body and moved through it.

Jake rolled his eyes, but by the time the chorus came on for the second time, he was tapping the steering wheel to the beat. We pulled into the parking lot, and I saw Calvin's car by the door. It made me feel good to know that even if I wasn't with him, at least he was close. Jake put his arm around my shoulders, and together we walked toward the building.

Suddenly Jake started laughing. "Damn you, Zoe. Now I can't get that song out of my head."

"Really?" I asked. In lieu of an answer, Jake did a dance move somewhere between a moonwalk and an electric slide. "Dude," I said, "that is just sad."

"It's a miracle!" Jake cried, jumping up and down. "A white guy can dance! A white guy can dance!"

And that's when I got my idea.

After we did our warm-up, I made the announcement. "We're going to play a game," I said.

"What game?" asked Aaliyah. Her voice was suspicious, like she couldn't actually believe I was going to do something as fun as an actual game.

"It doesn't have a name yet. I just made it up."

"Really?" asked Imani. She giggled. So did a few of the other girls. Then they suddenly looked nervous—like maybe I was going to yell at them—and stopped.

This was what I'd done: made dance class a place where you got in trouble for laughing.

"Really," I said. I walked to the center of the room. "Here's how it's going to go. I'm going to do a move. Then I'm going to call someone's name, and that person is going to do the same move. Then she'll call someone *else's* name, and that person will do the move. The trick is to do the move and call someone's name as fast as you can *without* being sloppy about your form."

"It's like hot potato," said a girl named Desiree. I couldn't remember Desiree ever speaking before. My mnemonic for her was *Desiree does not desire to discourse*.

"Exactly!" I agreed. "It's just like hot potato."

I plugged my phone into the speaker and hit play. Serge Gainsbourg filled the room. "What's this?" asked Imani.

"Like it?" I asked. The song popped and rolled. I could see a couple of the girls start moving their hips.

"What is it?" asked Lourdes, still suspicious.

"Oh my God, will you just dance?" I laughed and turned the music up really loud so they couldn't ask any more questions.

"Plié," I called out, and then I did one and yelled, "Lourdes."

Lourdes panicked and stared at me. "Plié!" I repeated, doing another one. Quickly she dropped her knees. "Who's next?" I prompted her.

"Oh. Imani!" she said.

"Louder!" I urged her.

"Imani!" she shouted.

Imani did a plié and threw it to Anna who threw it to Rashad who threw it back to Lourdes who threw it to Mirabelle. When every girl in the room had gone at least once, I yelled, "Two chaînés." Then I quickly did the turns, holding first position briefly when I was finished.

321

"No fair! That's too hard!" Lourdes said.

"I can't hear you," I lied. "Lourdes, two chaînés."

The turns she did weren't great, but she did them. When she finished, she held her position as I had and called to Rashad.

You could feel the energy in the room, the girls nervous and excited, holding themselves still as they waited for their names to be called but also moving a little, the energy of the music impossible to resist. I knew how they felt. Each time it was my turn to call a move, I got excited, my body spinning and leaping with a pleasure I hadn't felt since before Ms. Daniels had called me into her office at NYBC and brought my life crashing to an end.

No. It had been longer than that. As I moved and spun and leaped, it seemed to me that I hadn't enjoyed a dance class this much since before NYBC had accepted me.

When the class was finished, everyone was flushed. There was an unfamiliar energetic buzz in the room.

"That was *awesome*!" I told them. I clapped, and a few of the girls clapped too. I'd actually gone over by about five minutes—the music must have been too loud for me to hear the bell. "You guys, I'm really sorry, but it's time to go."

Aaliyah did a line of jetés from where she was standing to where I was standing. Then she hugged me. She only came up to my waist, so her ear was pressed against my belly button. "You're a great teacher, Zoe," she said. "I love dance class!"

322

I knelt down so I could hug her back. "Seriously?" I asked.

"Yeah," she said, laughing. "You look so surprised."

"I guess I am," I admitted. I sat on the floor and looked up at her. "I thought I was too mean to be a good teacher."

"Well, you're *kind* of mean," Aaliyah admitted. "But you're kind of nice, too."

Now it was my turn to laugh. "I appreciate your honesty, Aaliyah."

"Okay," she said. "See you next week."

"See you next week," I said.

Everyone, as they left, said, "See you next week."

And they all seemed happy about saying it.

❧ 35 ❧

I went home and showered and changed. It was such a habit now. I had the feeling that in a few weeks, when Olivia wasn't immunosuppressed anymore, it would be weird *not* to have to try to make myself sterile before going over to her house. My mom and dad were on their way to some lecture, and they gave me a ride to Livvie's.

As I strolled up Olivia's front walk, I considered how I might use what we'd done in class today for the recital. We could do something where one or two girls at a time did a move and then maybe that move was picked up by other girls until everybody was doing a move in unison. Maybe we'd plan out some of the routine and some of it we'd improvise so the performance would have a little of the energy of today's class. I could still feel the buzz, still see the top of Aaliyah's head as she put her arms around my waist. The girls had worked hard, but they'd had fun, too. It had actually been *fun*. I was glad that in the fall Olivia and I would be teaching it again. It would be weird to never see any of those girls again.

It would be sad.

As I rang the bell, I found myself thinking, *I've missed dancing*. Not NYBC dancing. Not will-Martin-Hicks-think-I'm-good-enough dancing.

Listening-to-music-and-moving-my-body dancing. Dancing-for-fun dancing. Dancing because it felt good.

Just dancing.

But maybe I didn't have to miss it. Maybe I could still—

The door opened, and I found myself looking at Mr. Greco. He was wearing a pair of khakis and a blue oxford under a wine-colored sweater, which was about as casual as Mr. Greco believed in getting.

His answering the door gave me a sudden flicker of anxiety. If you'd asked me why, I don't think I could have put my finger on what it was exactly. But Mr. Greco's answering the door was . . . *wrong*. It was just wrong. He pretty much never answered the door unless the Grecos were having a party. Certainly he'd never answered the door for me.

"Hi," I said, and it was then that I noticed that—behind his glasses—his eyes were bloodshot.

"Hi, Zoe." He put his hand on my shoulder, and a tear rolled down his cheek.

Olivia's father was crying.

Olivia's father was standing in the front hallway of his house and he was crying.

I felt what I can only describe as terror, a terror darker and blacker than anything I had ever felt before.

"What is it?" I asked. It was hard to get my tongue around the words. As I spoke them, I realized there was only one answer: Olivia had to have gotten some kind of infection. That was the only explanation. She'd gotten some horrible, life-threatening infection.

Mr. Greco swallowed, and he took a deep breath. "Zoe, we got some terrible news this morning." Over his shoulder, I could see Mrs. Greco and Jake sitting on a couch in the living room. Across from them, on the other couch, sat Olivia and the twins. No one was speaking. Luke had his head in Olivia's lap.

Olivia didn't look like she had a terrible infection. She didn't look any different than she'd looked any day for the past week. "What is it?" I repeated, my voice a whisper.

He put his hand over his eyes, his voice breaking as he spoke. "The most recent blood test showed that the leukemia has come back."

"Does that mean . . ." The thought was too horrible to utter, but I forced myself to say it. "Does that mean she has to have another bone marrow transplant?"

"They can't do another bone marrow transplant," said

Mr. Greco, and now his voice was calm, almost like Olivia's had been when she'd first told me about her diagnosis. "She wouldn't survive it."

"I don't understand," I said, even though somewhere in my brain a warning bell was ringing loudly. "If they can't do another bone marrow transplant, what can they do?"

"I don't know," said Mr. Greco, and I realized as he said it that I had never, in all the years I'd known him, heard Mr. Greco say those words.

We drove to the city in Mr. Greco's car: me, Olivia, Mr. and Mrs. Greco, and Jake. Mrs. Greco's sister had taken the twins to her house. When Olivia had said she wanted me to come with them to meet with Dr. Maxwell, neither of her parents had objected. I sat in the backseat, with Olivia between me and her mother. Mr. Greco and Jake sat in the front.

Nobody talked.

We went into a different building of UH, one that seemed more like a regular office tower than a hospital. When we got off the elevator on the eighth floor, we headed down a corridor that was surprisingly cluttered; there were carts with boxes on them and, up against one wall, several old computers piled on a sagging office chair. Instead of holidays, the walls advertised upcoming lectures with complicated titles. We wound left and then right, and I began to feel like I was in one of those terrible dreams where you have to get somewhere and you know something awful is going to happen to you if you don't get there but you can't find your way. Olivia was squeezing my hand, her grip so tight it was almost painful.

She was going to be okay. No one who could hold on that tightly was going to die.

Mr. Greco knocked on room 818, and an unfamiliar male voice called, "Come in."

He pushed open the door to a small office. There was brown carpeting on the floor. Sitting at a table with half a dozen chairs around it was a balding man with a beard who was wearing jeans and a gray sweater. Dr. Maxwell was leaning against a cluttered desk. It was strange not to see her in her white lab coat, and for a second I didn't recognize her. Her hair was in a ponytail, and she had on a pair of running shoes. Like the man, she had on jeans and a gray sweater, as if that were the uniform for doctors who weren't on the floor of a hospital. As soon as we entered the room, both Dr. Maxwell and the unfamiliar man stood up. He was astonishingly tall, maybe six and a half feet or taller. He was the tallest person I'd ever seen who wasn't on television playing basketball. Dr. Maxwell came over and hugged Olivia, then took Mr. and Mrs. Greco's hands in hers.

"This is difficult news," she said. "I'm so terribly sorry." She gestured for us to sit down, and as I walked by her, she squeezed me lightly on the shoulder. "This is Dr. Gold," she said.

The tall man nodded. "Hi, Olivia," he said. "I'm sorry to be meeting all of you under these circumstances." Mr. Greco reached across the table, and the two men shook hands. Then we all sat down. There weren't enough seats for everyone, so Dr. Maxwell and Dr. Gold remained standing. Olivia had not let go of my hand.

"Olivia's leukemia is aggressive," Dr. Maxwell began. "AML is rare in teens, and as we discussed, the genetic profile of Olivia's leukemia has always been worrisome. We suspect that's why it came back after the second round of chemo."

Olivia, Jake, and their parents nodded. I couldn't move.

"She responded beautifully to the bone marrow transplant," said Dr. Maxwell. She smiled at Olivia. "But at this point, our options are limited."

"But we do have options," said Mrs. Greco, her voice slightly breathless.

"We do, yes," said Dr. Maxwell. She glanced at Dr. Gold.

He clasped his hands together. "Dr. Maxwell asked me to be here today because I am running a clinical study that I could get Olivia into. It's a drug that has had limited success with patients who relapse after a BMT."

"How limited?" asked Mr. Greco.

"Limited," admitted Dr. Gold. "And because Olivia's relapse happened very quickly after her transplant, in all honesty I'm less optimistic about possible outcomes than I would be otherwise."

I could hear the quiet whir of a motor coming from another room, and then it shut off. The silence in the room seemed to pound against my ears.

"I still don't understand why we can't do another bone marrow transplant," said Jake. His voice was strong; he sounded almost angry. "I could give her more bone marrow. Dr. Maxwell told me it only takes a few days for marrow to regenerate."

Mrs. Greco reached over and took his hand. I watched her knuckles turn white as she squeezed it.

"Given how recently she had one, Olivia would not survive another bone marrow transplant," said Dr. Maxwell. "Her system is simply too weak."

Again, there was silence.

"And what are the other options?" asked Mr. Greco.

Dr. Gold stroked his beard. Dr. Maxwell shifted slightly. "The other option," she said, "would be palliative care."

"What's palliative care?" asked Olivia. Her voice was hoarse. I realized neither of us had spoken in over an hour.

"Palliative care is medication to make you feel better," explained Dr. Maxwell. "Things like pain medication."

"You mean so I can die more easily," said Olivia, and suddenly she began to cry. Mrs. Greco also started crying. Dr. Maxwell reached behind her for a box of tissues and placed them on the table, but nobody took any.

"Yes," said Dr. Maxwell gently. "So you can die more easily."

"The drug in your clinical trial," said Mr. Greco, his voice sharp. "You said you think it won't help Olivia, but you don't know that for sure."

"That's correct," said Dr. Gold. "I don't know that for sure."

"How sick will the drug make me?" asked Olivia, her voice small. Now she reached to the middle of the table and took a tissue.

"It would be like the first time you had chemo," said Dr. Maxwell. "You would have flu-like symptoms. Some nausea." Again she glanced at Dr. Gold.

"There have been some severe side effects associated with this drug, including liver damage," he said. "But the biggest concern for Olivia at this point would be cardiac toxicity."

"Cardiac toxicity," Olivia echoed. Her eyes were wide. "You mean my heart would be toxic?"

"Not exactly," explained Dr. Gold, smiling. "It's the drug that is toxic to the heart. It weakens the heart and makes it unable to pump blood through the body as well as it needs to. You can't get enough oxygen."

He didn't add *and you die*. He didn't need to.

Jake toyed with the box of tissues, knocking gently at one corner, then at another.

"What would you do?" Mr. Greco asked Dr. Gold. "If it were your child, what would you do now?"

"Every family is different," said Dr. Gold slowly. "What's right for one family isn't—"

"Okay, cut the crap," snapped Mr. Greco, and everybody at the table jumped slightly. I'd never heard Mr. Greco sound quite so angry, but I wasn't surprised by it. It was like all the years I'd known him, this was why I'd been just a little afraid.

"Carlo," said Mrs. Greco.

But Mr. Greco didn't seem to have heard her. He leaned forward, almost across the table, and stared at Dr. Gold. If Dr. Gold was horrified by what Mr. Greco had just said to him, he didn't show it. His face remained calm, and he continued stroking his beard.

"If it were my daughter, I would leave no stone unturned," he said finally.

"Fine." Mr. Greco sat back. And then, as if we'd just been negotiating a contract or a major merger or anything, really, except his only daughter's life, he folded his arms across his chest and looked around the table with a determined expression on his face. "We'll try the new drug."

Mrs. Greco sat on the bed with her hand on Olivia's forehead after Dr. Maxwell inserted the needle into Olivia's IV. Outside, it was getting darker and a light rain was falling. I remembered Livvie's saying how weird it was that there was weather outside when she was stuck in the hospital all the time.

"I'll come back and check on Olivia in a little while," Dr. Maxwell said. "We'll be watching her very carefully over the next few hours to make sure she can tolerate the medication."

The moment was anticlimactic, nothing like the bone marrow transplant. Mrs. Greco said, "Thank you," but there were no lowered heads and no prayers. Maybe we were beyond prayer by now. Eventually Olivia fell asleep and Mr. Greco and Jake went to get something to eat.

"It's funny," said Mrs. Greco. Her voice startled me. I was sitting on the radiator, watching the river, and she'd been so quiet I'd assumed she was dozing too. "This whole time I've wanted to trust Dr. Maxwell. But I've been thinking this afternoon about how often doctors are wrong and how it's just as likely that Dr. Maxwell and Dr. Gold *don't* know. I've been hoping that, really. That they'll be surprised by how well Olivia responds to this medication."

"I know," I said. I looked at Olivia sleeping on the bed. I'd gotten so used to seeing her with her duckling fuzz that she didn't even look strange to me anymore. "I've been thinking about how *somebody* has to be the five or ten percent that responds well to an experimental drug. Why shouldn't it be Olivia?"

Mrs. Greco had one hand on Olivia's arm, and she gestured toward me with the other. I walked around the bed until I was standing by her side. She took my hand in hers and looked up at me. "What a good friend you are. Olivia is so lucky to have you. We all are."

I'd made it through everything that had happened today

without crying, but as soon as Mrs. Greco said that, I started to weep.

"I'm sorry," I mumbled, wiping my cheeks and nose with my free hand.

But Mrs. Greco didn't seem to mind. "A person's whole life, she's lucky to have one or two *real* friends. Friends who are like family." She smiled. "You and Olivia are like family."

Now I was crying so hard I couldn't even talk. Mrs. Greco put her arm around my waist and patted me gently. "I know," she murmured. "I know. But it's going to be okay." She kept patting me, and I saw her other hand was also patting Olivia. "You'll see." She almost sang the words, like a quiet lullaby. "You'll see."

I don't know how much time had passed when Olivia woke up complaining that she was having trouble breathing. Jake and his dad still weren't back. I buzzed for the nurse while Mrs. Greco propped pillows behind her to help her sit up. When no one answered my buzz, Mrs. Greco told me to go find someone, and I ran out into the hallway, almost crashing into the nurse who was racing into the room.

Livvie was panting now, and she looked frightened. "I can't . . . ," she started to say. "I can't breathe."

I stood, frozen, by the door. *This is it,* I thought. *This is how Olivia is going to die.*

The nurse ripped some tubing out of a drawer, put it

into Olivia's nose, and pushed a button on the wall. "This is oxygen, honey," she said. "It's going to make it easier for you to breathe."

"Paging Dr. Maxwell. Dr. Maxwell to room 1225." The announcement came over the loudspeaker. Had the nurse made it? She seemed totally focused on Olivia. It couldn't have been more than a minute later that Dr. Maxwell burst into the room. She said something to the nurse, who ran out. Olivia was still breathing rapidly. I stood at the foot of her bed as Dr. Maxwell spoke quietly to her. The nurse ran back in, pushing a cart that had a computer on it, and Dr. Maxwell grabbed a white stick attached to a long cord, slathered some clear gel on it, and ripped Livvie's hospital gown open. She watched the screen for a minute, then said to the nurse, "Page Dr. Gold and Dr. Connor."

I went over to the side of the bed. Livvie's eyes were wide with fear, and Mrs. Greco was holding her hand. Dr. Maxwell was still moving the wand-like thing over Olivia's chest. When Dr. Gold and another man came into the room, we all looked at them, but they only had eyes for the computer screen. A long piece of paper came out of the side of the computer, and the three of them stepped back from the bed and studied it, Dr. Gold tracing something along it as Dr. Maxwell held the end up.

Dr. Gold asked Dr. Maxwell a question, and she shook her head, and then they both looked at the other man—I guess

Dr. Connor—and he said yes, loud enough for us to hear.

Finally, Dr. Gold, Dr. Maxwell, and Dr. Connor stepped away from the computer screen and came to stand next to Olivia's bed.

"What just happened?" asked Mrs. Greco. Her face was very pale.

"Olivia's heart is overwhelmed by the medication," explained Dr. Gold. For the first time, he was speaking without stroking his beard. "As we feared, the drugs are simply too toxic for her to tolerate. Her blood is becoming oxygen poor." He looked at Olivia. "That's why you have the sensation of not being able to breathe. Your heart's not pumping enough oxygenated blood through your body. It's clear from the echocardiogram, the machine we were just using. It shows us pictures of your heart."

"What are you saying?" Mrs. Greco demanded. She looked frantically from Dr. Maxwell to Dr. Gold to Dr. Connor.

Dr. Maxwell had been talking to the nurse, but now she came over to stand by Mrs. Greco.

"He's saying that we have to stop the medication, Adriana. It's too dangerous for Olivia. She won't survive the complete course. We can't give it to her anymore."

"Oh my God," Mrs. Greco whispered, pressing her knuckles against her lips. "Oh my God." She clutched at Dr. Maxwell, who let Olivia's mother stand there, grabbing on to her. "Oh my God," she cried, and she cried it again and again and again, and even when Mr. Greco and Jake came into the room, she didn't stop crying those three words over and over, as if eventually God would hear her and he would have to show some pity.

⌐ 36 ⌐

I had some idea that you have to die in a hospital, but it turns out I was wrong.

That night, when Olivia had recovered from the medication that had been supposed to save her life but that had almost killed her, Dr. Gold and Dr. Maxwell approved Olivia's discharge for the following morning. At first, they'd thought she'd have to stay on oxygen when she went home, but within a few hours of their stopping the new medication, Olivia was breathing on her own again.

Right before I left the hospital, I ran into Dr. Maxwell, who was walking out of another patient's room across from the elevator. I touched her sleeve lightly, and together we stepped to the side of the hall.

"How long . . ." I took a deep breath. "How long do you

think Olivia will . . . how long do you think she has?"

Dr. Maxwell shook her head and leaned against the wall. "There's no way to know, Zoe."

It felt coy, her saying that, and it made me angry. "I don't mean I need an *exact* number. I mean *approximately*."

"I think that you could have as long as a few weeks," she said. Her voice was calm. I could see the distorted reflection of my face in her glasses. "But I don't want you to count on that."

I leaned against the wall also, and I closed my eyes. "As long as a few weeks," I repeated. Like a few weeks was long. Like a few weeks was *anything*.

"These are precious days," said Dr. Maxwell. I opened my eyes and looked into hers.

"What do you mean?"

"Just what I said." She slipped her hands into her pockets without taking her eyes off mine. "These are precious days. Don't squander them."

When the Grecos' car pulled into the driveway the next morning, Jake said, "They're here." He and Luke and Tommy and I had been sitting and watching one of the Harry Potter movies, and I realized I'd actually gotten caught up in the plot. Maybe everyone else had too and that was why nobody was talking.

We turned off the television and went into the foyer. Mr. and Mrs. Greco senior, who'd been waiting in the kitchen, were already there. Jake opened the door. Olivia was leaning on her dad's arm, her mom walking slightly behind them, holding a small suitcase. I stood at the door next to Luke, watching them make their slow progress up the front steps. I did not make eye contact with any of the Grecos.

Upstairs, Olivia's mom and I helped her into a pair of pajamas. Livvie was rail thin, her spine protruding from her back like a thick rope. We propped up some pillows under her head, and then her mom headed downstairs to get her a protein shake. Apparently it was what the doctors had suggested she drink to keep her strength up.

"Hey," she said.

"Yeah?"

I went over to the bed, and she patted the blanket next to her. I sat down carefully, not wanting to shift the bed too much. "Do you think your mom will let you stay over tonight?"

Frankly, even if my mom had a problem with it, if Olivia wanted me to stay, I was staying. But Mrs. Greco was going to be trouble. There were about a million people staying at the Grecos'. Mr. Greco's parents were there already. Mrs. Greco's parents were arriving that evening, and her brother was flying in from California the next day. Mrs. Greco had never liked what she referred to as *a crowded house*. "Your mom's never going to say yes," I said.

Livvie rolled her eyes. "I'm dying, Zoe. She *has* to let you stay over."

∽ 37 ∾

Time does not care how precious it is, how hard you are working not to squander it.

Time passes.

"What do you think people did before television?" I asked. We were lying on Olivia's bed, her mom's laptop propped up in front of us. I'd gone downstairs to get Olivia the bowl of sorbet she was currently eating.

It was hour six of our *Glee* marathon.

"You mean in general?" Olivia asked. "Or just when they were dying?"

"I was thinking about dying," I admitted, taking a bite of my own sorbet.

Olivia dipped her spoon into the glass bowl and took a small bite as she considered my question. Then she swallowed.

"I bet they read the Bible a lot," she said.

She took another bite, and I pressed play.

At school one day, Stacy told me they were talking about canceling the prom. "It's hard, though," Stacy explained. "Because, you know, Olivia's not a senior."

"Yeah," I said. "I can see how that would be a tough call."

The relatives arrived. Cousins of Mr. and Mrs. Greco's. Mr. Greco's sister. Sometimes when I walked into the house, it felt almost like a party was going on, and in what I guess was a Pavlovian response to seeing a huge group of people gathered together, I got excited for an instant before I remembered why they were all there.

Jake got into Rutgers. Calvin got into Middlebury, and he said something about how Vermont wasn't that far from New Jersey, and I realized he was thinking about us and next year and I realized I was supposed to be glad, but I just didn't feel anything. Not even when I kissed him.

I went over to Olivia's after school one afternoon, and when I pushed open the door of her room, she was sitting on her desk chair, just kind of staring at the air in front of her. Normally she was surrounded by people, but today she was alone.

"Hey," I said.

"You know what I was just thinking?" she asked.

I walked into the room and shut the door. "Tell me," I said.

Slowly, she swiveled her chair around in a circle. "I was thinking I'm never going to live in Manhattan."

My eyes stung, and I bit my lip to keep from crying.

Olivia continued to turn the chair in slow circles, her head back so she was staring at the ceiling. "And I'm never going to go to Paris. And I'm never going to get married." She hesitated briefly, then pushed off on her foot and gently turned a quarter of the way around so that she was facing me. "And just for the record, I was right. I'm going to die a virgin."

I nodded and swallowed hard so I could speak. "I know," I said.

She closed her eyes. "I feel like there are all these things I should be doing, and all I can do is sit here and think about them." She got to her feet and slowly made her way over to the bed. "And even that tires me out."

Together, we helped her get settled under the covers. In a few minutes, she was asleep.

A hospice nurse came every morning and checked Olivia's vital signs and helped Olivia take a bath and get dressed. That was just life now. It was weird, sure. But if you're getting dressed and taking a bath—even if you need *help* to do those things— then you're still alive. There was a lot of talk of morphine. *When she needs morphine. If she's uncomfortable, we'll start her on morphine.* Nobody told me this, but slowly I realized that morphine would mean Olivia was dying.

But she wasn't taking morphine now, and morphine could be, for all we knew, a long way away.

At lunch one day, there were artichoke hearts in the salad bar. Mia was pissed. Because of budget cuts, the community service coordinator's contract wasn't being renewed, and Mia had been working on a film about how much good the community service requirement did for the student body. "Right there." She pointed at the salads Lashanna and I had made. "Right there is your community service budget."

Lashanna and I looked at each other. Then I said to Mia, "It's a really good salad."

"Seriously, Mia," said Lashanna, holding out an artichoke heart on her fork. "You should try it."

Because even though Olivia was dying, we still ate lunch.

My mom let me take the car to school so I could visit with Olivia during my free periods and make it back for class. One day when I went to visit, Livvie was sleeping. I told Mrs. Greco I'd come again later, and I drove back to school and then sat in my car in the parking lot. I started crying. I heard Jake and Calvin and Sean walk by, but I thought they didn't see me because I was hunched over the steering wheel. A few minutes later, the passenger door opened, and Calvin got in. I was still crying. He took my hand.

"Let me help," Calvin said quietly.

I thought about all the times I'd made out with him so I could forget about Olivia's being sick.

Then I thought about Olivia lying in her room knowing she was going to die.

"Zoe?"

I managed to take a few long, deep breaths. "The thing is . . ." I was about to start crying again, but I swallowed and stared hard at the steering wheel, tracing its pocked pattern rather than thinking about what I was about to say. "The thing is," I repeated, clearing my throat, "I can't . . . I can't do this anymore." Gently I extracted my hand from his.

He didn't respond. When I couldn't stand it, I filled in the silence. "I'm sorry, Calvin. I'm really sorry."

"Don't do this," he said. His voice was low but firm. "Please."

I turned to face him. His eyes bored into mine, and I couldn't meet his stare for more than about a second before I had to look back at the steering wheel. "I'm sorry," I said again.

"Zoe . . ." Out of the corner of my eye, I saw him tracing the edge of the seat with his index finger.

It wasn't enough to *look* away—remembering what his hands felt like on my body made me need to *get* away. So even though it was my car, I opened the door and stepped out. Calvin started to say something, but I shut the door before I could hear what it was.

When I went to my locker after school, there was an envelope taped to it with my name on it. Inside were my car keys.

There was no note.

Later that same afternoon, I arrived at the house as the hospice nurse was leaving. We met on the sidewalk.

"Hi, Zoe," she said.

"Hi," I said. I couldn't remember her name. She was an Asian woman, so slender and graceful that she could have been a ballerina.

"How are you doing?" she asked. She put her hand on my arm. The hospice nurses were always touching you. I didn't mind it, actually.

"I don't know. Okay, I guess. How is she today?"

That was the question I always asked when I first got to the house. *How is she today?* And Mr. or Mrs. Greco or the nurse or one of Olivia's grandparents would say, *She's a little tired this morning* or *She had a rough night* or maybe just *She's doing fine.*

"She's doing fine," said the nurse.

I glanced up at the house. It looked like it always looked. Then I looked back at the nurse. "Do you . . . I was just wondering if . . ." I took a deep breath. "Do you know how much longer she has?"

"Oh, honey." The nurse looked deep into my eyes. "That's the thing about dying. Nobody knows how long it takes."

"Right," I said. I'd been on the verge of crying, but I swallowed my tears. I thanked the nurse, and I watched her get into her car and drive away.

I thought about what she'd said as I made my way up the walk. *Nobody knows.* Even Dr. Maxwell didn't know. She'd said it could be weeks. If it could be weeks, why couldn't it be months?

And if it could be months, why couldn't it be years?

"I'm having the weirdest thought," said Olivia. It was nineteen days after she'd come home from the hospital, and I was sleeping over, lying on the trundle bed right next to her bed. She'd been dozing for a lot of the day, but we'd watched some more *Glee* and then a few *Law and Order* episodes.

I got up on my elbow, facing her. The shades weren't down all the way, and just enough light from the streetlamp came into the room for me to make out Olivia in the darkness. "What?" I asked.

"I'm thinking . . ." Her mouth was dry, and I could tell it was hard for her to swallow. "I'm thinking maybe if we went somewhere else, I'd be okay. Like, what if in New Jersey I'm dying of leukemia, but in Alaska I'm fine."

In my head, I pictured Alaska as miles and miles of white. Endless white. I could almost feel the burn of the cold on my cheeks. We could hide out there. Leukemia would never find her there.

"Let's go," I said quietly. "We could get in the car and go."

"Road trip!" she whispered. And then, even more quietly, "I wish we could really go."

I started to cry. "Me too," I said. "I wish we could really go too." In the dark, she reached over and took my hand.

I leaned across the space between our beds and wiped at her cheeks, but her tears were coming too fast for my fingers, and I had to let them fall. A few minutes later, still holding my hand, she fell asleep.

～ 38 ～

When I woke up in the morning, Olivia was restless and out of it. She was sort of tossing her head, and she moaned quietly once. Then it seemed like she was trying to tell me something, but I couldn't understand what she was saying, not even when she clutched me by the hand and said, "I have it. It's in the closet, Zoe. It's in the . . ." The last word was all muddled. She seemed agitated, so I went to the closet and opened the door, but that didn't calm her down. I looked around, thinking she wanted me to find something for her, but there was nothing besides her clothes. I went to get her mom, who called the hospice nurse, who said she'd be right over.

I did *not* want to leave Olivia to go teach dance class. The week before, I'd gotten Stacy to cover for me, but Olivia had been irritated with me for doing that, and I knew when she was feeling better later in the day she'd be mad if I told her I'd skipped again. When Jake and I pulled out of the driveway, the hospice nurse had just arrived, and I watched her walk out of her car and up the front steps. The nurses were always so calm. She would know what to do to make Olivia more comfortable.

The dance studio was empty. I hadn't realized how early Jake and I had left the house, but there were at least ten minutes before class was scheduled to start. I put on some music. I'd gotten used to warming up with the girls, and as I did a few pliés, I could feel how much easier even the most basic moves felt now than they had a few weeks ago. I'd lifted my leg onto the barre and was leaning over it, stretching my back out, when I heard the door open. I looked behind me.

Charlotte had just come into the dance studio.

"Oh my God," I said, dropping my leg and turning around.

"What?" she asked. Her voice was defensive, but I noticed how her eyes skittered nervously around the room.

"I wasn't expecting to see you here," I said honestly. "Where have you been? Mrs. Jones tried to reach you." I heard the accusation in my own voice and quickly added, "We were worried about you."

"Yeah?" Charlotte asked, and then she shrugged. "I was staying with my grandmother for a few weeks. My mom was sick."

I remembered what Mrs. Jones had said about Charlotte's

mother, how she drank and smoked and maybe did other things. Was that what Charlotte meant by *sick*? "Is your mom better now?"

"Kind of," said Charlotte. She had her bag pressed tightly against her side. "My grandma's staying with us. Just for a little while."

"Well, that's good."

Charlotte shrugged. "I don't know. She's kind of strict. I have a bedtime now and stuff."

"Oh," I said. "I can see how that would be kind of a drag. But, I mean, maybe it's for the best."

"Maybe." Charlotte didn't sound convinced.

"I've been meaning . . ." I took a couple of steps toward her. "I felt bad about what happened last time you were here. I shouldn't have yelled at you for being late."

She shrugged again. "I don't care."

If she wasn't going to accept it, I kind of wished she would tell me I could take my apology and shove it up my ass, but considering she was only nine, that seemed unlikely.

"Well, *I* care." I tucked my hair behind my ears, realizing as I did how long it was getting, how much time had passed since I'd gotten it hacked off at Hair Today Gone Tomorrow. I looked directly at Charlotte. "I realize now what a serious commitment you made to this class. I'm sorry I didn't appreciate it sooner. I feel very bad about how I behaved, Charlotte."

"Well, sorry, but I can't control how you feel," said Charlotte. "Because, you know, it's a free country."

I started to laugh. I couldn't help it. I laughed so hard I had trouble catching my breath.

"What?" asked Charlotte. And when I didn't answer, she kept asking. "What is it? What's so funny?"

Finally, I wiped my eyes and caught my breath. "Oh God," I said. "I'm sorry. I thought . . ." Was I seriously going to say, *I thought you would fall into my arms weeping with gratitude and understanding?* I shook my head. "I think I've been watching too many movies."

"My grandma says TV and movies rot your brain. She hardly lets us watch any."

"Yeah, well . . . your grandma's right." I went over to the wall and slipped off my sweatpants.

"Hey, you look all like a ballerina and stuff," said Charlotte, observing my pink tights and black leotard.

"We've been doing a lot of dancing while you were away. I had to be able to move."

"Okay," said Charlotte. She put her stuff down, took off her sneakers, and unzipped her bag. She took out her ballet shoes, which she sometimes forgot. "Got my shoes."

"That's great, Charlotte." I watched her slip them on her feet. "If you want, I can teach you what you missed before class starts."

Charlotte tilted her head and looked at me. "I guess," she

said. "That would be cool." Then, almost against her will, she added, "Thanks."

"No problem," I said.

I started showing Charlotte the moves, and she executed them gracefully, seemingly effortlessly. She was a born dancer, and I told her that.

"Thanks," she muttered, and even though she tried not to look like she cared, she couldn't completely hide her smile.

"You're welcome," I said.

When the other girls arrived, they helped demonstrate for Charlotte how we threw a move from one person to another. There was more to catch her up on than I would have thought; it ended up taking most of the class. We really had covered a lot of ground over the past few classes. I was glad to have something nice to tell Olivia. I knew she'd want to hear how well things were going.

But when I got to the Grecos' after class, Mr. Greco told me that after I'd left, Olivia had clearly been in a lot of pain. The hospice nurse had suggested starting her on morphine, which they had done. By the time I arrived, she'd already been on morphine for several hours.

Two days later, without ever regaining consciousness, she died.

❧ 39 ❧

Over a thousand people showed up for Olivia's funeral—kids from school, Olivia's family, neighbors, people Mrs. Greco knew from her charity work, people from Mr. Greco's law firm. The church was packed. People spilled out into the parish hall and the basement, and there they watched the speeches and listened to the music on a huge screen that had been set up for the occasion. Someone had told NYBC, and girls we'd used to dance with and even a few of our old teachers showed up. I barely spoke to anyone, keeping my head down, letting my mom guide me to and from a pew. At the cemetery, as they started lowering Olivia's casket into the ground, Mrs. Greco wailed the same way she had that day in the hospital room, and as she pulled at her clothes and hair, Mr. Greco held her fiercely in his arms, almost as if he was sure she might throw herself into the grave along with her daughter. It was only April, but it was brutally hot. A couple of old people fainted, and a few others had to be helped into the shade.

I wasn't hot.

I was cold.

Icy cold, as if I'd headed to Alaska without Olivia, lain down in the snowy landscape, and gone numb. Everyone went back to the house after the funeral, and I sat in the living room with my parents. A few people tried to talk to me, but I delivered monosyllabic responses that finally scared them away. Even Mia took the hint. Twice she approached me and twice I got rid of her. As my family was leaving, I saw Calvin coming down the stairs. I don't know if he saw me, but I managed to get out of the house with my parents before he could come over to us.

Days passed. At night, I dreamed about Olivia. I was at her house with a lot of other people. It was her funeral. Lonely, I went upstairs to her room, where I found Livvie sitting on her bed. She looked how she'd looked before she got sick, her hair long and thick. Sometimes she was wearing a leotard and tights, sometimes she was in a hospital gown, but no matter what she wore, the dialogue was always the same.

"Oh my God!" I said every time. "Livvie! I thought you were dead."

She laughed. "You did? That's so crazy."

"Livvie." I went over to her, feeling a sense of relief so

intense it was almost painful. "Livvie. I missed you so much. It was horrible."

"Don't cry," she said. "It was just a dream."

And I would wake up and I would be crying and Livvie wouldn't be there because it had just been a dream.

The girls in the ballet class had the idea to dedicate the recital to Olivia, and in the program that's what it said. *We dedicate our dance today to the memory of Olivia Greco.* When my mom saw it, she started crying. "It's so beautiful," she said. "That they dedicated it to Olivia is such a beautiful idea, isn't it?"

"Yeah," I said. "It is, I guess."

My mom gave me a concerned look.

"What?" I demanded. "You asked me if it was beautiful. I said yes. Why are you staring at me?"

My mom squeezed my shoulder. "No reason," she said.

My parents sat in the audience, but I watched the girls perform from the wings. They did a fantastic job. Thanks to Stacy, who'd gone to a florist that morning, I had a single rose to give every dancer, and they took their curtain calls holding them. They all hugged me after, even Charlotte, and I hugged every one of them back and told each one what an amazing job she'd done. Mrs. Jones told me how impressed she was by what the girls and I had accomplished, and she said that she was sure Olivia was proud of us also.

◆ ◆ ◆

Every morning at school Mia brought me a latte. She didn't say much besides, "Here." On Friday mornings, after she said "here," she said, "You want to come over and maybe watch a movie or something?"

Every day I thanked her for the latte. And every Friday I thanked her for the invitation. By the fourth time she asked, I told her she could stop asking. "I really appreciate your inviting me. But I'm not going to say yes."

"Look," said Mia. "I know you're not going to say yes for a long, long time. But one day, even if it's, you know, a year from now, you will. And when you do, we'll hang out and watch a movie."

The idea that one day I'd want to do anything—even watch a movie—would have been laughable if I could have imagined laughing.

Jake came back to school a couple of weeks after the funeral, and each time we saw each other, we hugged. I didn't know what to say to him. Maybe he didn't know what to say to me, either.

Why would he? I wasn't a person. I was an icicle.

The first week of June, Mrs. Jones asked me to come by the rec center. I suggested we could talk about whatever it was over the phone, but she wanted to talk in person. So I drove down to Newark and went to her office.

"It's a terrible thing when a young person dies," she said.

"Yes," I agreed. I hoped I hadn't driven all the way to Newark just to hear her say that. It had been a long drive.

"So," she said, placing her hands carefully on the desk in front of her, "I was wondering how you were planning to keep Olivia alive."

I laughed. "I'm sorry?" I said, shaking my head and blowing the air out of my mouth loudly in an attempt to get control of myself. "I really don't know what you mean."

Mrs. Jones didn't seem to mind that I was laughing at her. She pointed at the center of my chest. "You need to be true to the part of you that has Olivia inside of it. The part of you that did such a beautiful job with those girls at that recital. The part of you that helped Charlotte. In short, I'd like to see you teach the dance class again next fall."

So *that* was what this was about. Inwardly I rolled my eyes. "Mrs. Jones, I appreciate your saying all of those things. I really do. But I'm not Olivia."

"No one would want or expect you to be." She nodded as if she were agreeing with rather than contradicting me.

"Well, whatever." I toyed with the car keys in my lap. "The point is, the only reason I stuck with the class at all was because Olivia wanted me to."

Mrs. Jones nodded. "And now Olivia is gone."

"That would seem to be the case, yes."

"Well, Zoe . . ." She pressed her hands on her desk, straightening her arms and sitting back in her chair. "I think the important thing for you to decide is how you are going to honor her memory."

"With a gazebo."

She sat forward slightly. "I beg your pardon?"

I leaned in also, lowering my voice as if I were revealing a state secret. "With. A. Gazebo," I said slowly. "The Grecos donated a gazebo to Wamasset High. There's a ceremony at the school on what would have been her seventeenth birthday. That's how we're honoring Olivia's memory."

"That is a lovely thing," said Mrs. Jones. "But it wasn't exactly what I had in mind."

"I know it wasn't." I got to my feet. "But I'm afraid it's all I've got." I extended my hand to her. "I appreciate your confidence in me. I'm sorry not to be more deserving of it."

"Well, we'll see," she said after a pause. Then she too stood up, reached across her desk, and shook my hand. "Life is long."

"Not always," I reminded her, and I walked out of the office.

~ 40 ~

The day of the dedication of the gazebo dawned hot and cloudless, a beautiful June Saturday. Principal Handleman was going to speak. So was Mr. Greco. The Wamasset High orchestra was playing "selections from Tchaikovsky." Mrs. Greco had called and asked me if I wanted to speak, but I'd told her I didn't like talking in front of crowds, and she said okay. I suggested that Stacy Shaw would probably love to say some words. It was the only conversation we'd had since Olivia's death, and she must have called Stacy, because her name was on the program.

They'd put up the gazebo in record time. I'd watched the construction from my physics classroom, the intricate white wood structure emerging from the pile of lumber that had been delivered and dumped in a pile one afternoon. The spot they'd picked to erect it on was the only hill on campus, a small rise out beyond the fields near the woods that surrounded the school. Chairs had been set up in rows on Friday, and they were filled Saturday morning more than an hour before the ceremony started. Mrs. Greco had asked me to sit with the family, so I didn't have to fight my way to get a seat.

It was hot in the sun. Principal Handleman talked about how Olivia's illness had brought the school together. He used the word *tragedy* three or four times, and I found my mind wandering. A group of birds flew overhead, and I wondered if they were ducks or geese. It occurred to me that they were probably called a flock. Or were they? A flock of ducks? A group of ducks? A gaggle of ducks? It was tempting to take out my phone and google it.

When Principal Handleman finished, there was a pause while Stacy Shaw slowly made her way up the steps of the gazebo to the podium. She was wearing a tight black dress, black stockings, and black heels. She'd blown her hair straight.

It was as if she'd chosen her wardrobe by downloading a funeral attire app.

"My name is Stacy Shaw," she began. "A lot of you were at the car wash that the other cheerleaders and I organized. We hoped that it would be enough to keep Olivia alive, but we were wrong."

Flock of ducks. All birds were flocks. I was positive.

Reasonably positive.

". . . because during her illness, I really got to *know* Olivia Greco. She was an amazing friend. She was funny. She was smart. She was talented. Even when she was sick, she was always interested in other people. I emailed her every day, and when she responded, she always asked about *my* life. Even when she was in the hospital, she would want to know how I was feeling."

I snorted. Luke was sitting next to me, and he glanced over. I lowered my head.

"The important thing is that we should not cry for Olivia." Stacy's voice was bold. She could have been calling a cheer. "Olivia has gone to a better place. And though we miss her, we must picture her there. Dancing with the angels." Stacy's voice broke.

Dancing with the *angels?* Was she *fucking* kidding me?

And before I could stop myself, I looked around to roll my eyes at Olivia. Literally. I actually turned my head to the right and caught a glimpse of Mrs. Greco's tear-stained face before I thought, *Wait. Olivia's not here. Olivia is dead.*

Olivia is dead.

It was as if I had just gotten the news, as if it hadn't happened almost two months ago but had happened now, this instant. *Olivia is dead.* My lips began to tremble and my eyes filled. I wanted to tell Olivia what Stacy was saying about her, but I couldn't because Stacy was talking at Olivia's memorial service.

Just this one thing, I thought, but it was more of a prayer than a thought. *Please let me tell her this one thing. Just the thing about dancing with the angels.*

Her number was still programmed into my cell phone. Surely if I sent her a text she would get it. Surely in this modern world where everything is connected and wired and people can talk to China using satellites thousands of miles up in space, surely I can just send my dead friend one fucking text from her memorial service.

And suddenly I started to cry. Serious sobs, the kind where your stomach hurts and you can't breathe and there's snot running down your face. I was crying so hard I couldn't even mute the sounds I was making, and Luke put his hand on my back and I thought about how everyone would think that I was crying because of Stacy's fucking speech and I wanted to kill someone. I wanted to kill someone and I wanted to die and I wanted to run as far and as fast as I could because she was never coming back. She had fallen off the face of the earth and she was never coming back.

part 4

Summer

◦ 41 ◦

It is agony to thaw.

I'd failed to appreciate how the permafrost in which I was encased was protecting me, but now that it had melted, everything hurt. Sunlight. The walk to school. The cold metal of my lock as I jerked it open every morning. Lying in bed and watching the numbers on my alarm clock as they flipped, the minutes passing glacially as I failed to fall asleep for yet another night.

The astonishing thing, the truly shocking thing, was that life went on. There were finals. They didn't cancel the prom. Stacy told me (and I am completely not joking here) that to honor Olivia's memory, a lot of girls would be wearing black dresses that night. And then she told me (and I am *still* not joking) that she knew Calvin would want to go to the prom with me, and she suggested (still not joking) that it would be *good* for me to get out.

To give credit where credit is due, Calvin found me at the end of that same day and told me he was not going to the prom. He and Jake were going to go to Jake's house and just watch movies.

"Do you want to come?" he asked. "Not as . . . anything."

We were standing in the hallway. I'd avoided looking at him when he'd come over, but now I looked. He was leaning against the locker next to mine, and he'd gotten his hair cut. It looked good. Really good. I remembered how I'd told Olivia that the reason Calvin was irresistible was because he was a vampire.

That was how life was now—all roads led to Olivia.

"I can't, Calvin," I said, turning away from him. I shut my locker and slipped the lock through it, glad to have something to do with my hands and my eyes.

"Okay," he said. Then he said, "Zoe?"

"Yeah?" I could tell he was waiting for me to look at him, but I just studied the linoleum floor at my feet.

We stood there, not looking at each other and not talking, and then he finally said, "See you, Zoe."

By the time I looked up, he'd disappeared into the crowded hallway.

June ended and then it was summer and I would sit in my room and I would think, *A year ago, Olivia was alive. A year ago, we didn't even know Olivia was sick.* And then my mom or my dad would come upstairs to see if I was doing the work I was supposed to be doing because I'd taken incompletes in four of my six classes. And when they saw that I *wasn't* doing my work, that I wasn't doing anything for that matter, they would hug me and tell me it was going to be okay. About once a week, they'd ask if I wanted to talk to someone. And I would think, *Yes I want to talk to someone.*

They meant a therapist.

I meant Olivia.

And then, the first week of August, Mrs. Greco called and asked if I would come over to the house.

I didn't want to go, but you can't say no to something like that. You can't say, *I'm sorry, Mrs. Greco, but I can't handle coming to your house. The house my best friend used to live in. The house you have to wake up in every morning even though your only daughter is dead.*

I said what you have to say when something like that happens.

I said yes.

The last of Mrs. Greco's rosebushes were still in bloom on the afternoon that I made my way up the front walk. The lawn was the same perfect emerald green it always was. On the porch, the swing Olivia and I had never sat in even though we were always saying how it was a really nice swing and we should sit in it was still there.

Everything was completely unchanged.

Mrs. Greco answered the bell. She was unchanged also. It was a ridiculously hot day, but her hair shaped her face gracefully, as groomed as ever. She was wearing a crisp green linen dress and a pair of dark brown sandals. Her nails were polished a pale coral. You could never have imagined that the coiffed woman standing in front of me had, on the day of her daughter's funeral, clawed at her own suit so frantically she'd ripped the fabric.

She gave me a long, hard hug, and then I followed her into the kitchen.

"Would you like some water or lemonade?" she asked me.

It was her voice that gave her away. Even though she was only offering me something to drink, it shook ever so slightly, and I knew that no matter how polished she looked, inside she was still tearing at her clothing.

"Sure," I said. "Lemonade would be great." As soon as she took the carton out of the refrigerator, I saw that I'd made a mistake. Livvie's family always stocked this amazing pink lemonade that my mother refused to buy because it wasn't organic. For over a decade, I'd drunk it only at Olivia's house. Mrs. Greco brought me the glass and I thanked her, but I didn't so much as put my lips to it. One taste of the familiar drink would, I knew, push me over the edge.

"I called because . . ." Mrs. Greco went over to the table and took a sip of her iced coffee. "I think Jake might have told you that we've put the house on the market."

I shook my head. The things grown-ups think kids talk about shouldn't have surprised me, but it always did.

She stroked the side of the glass, almost as if she were cleaning the beads of water from it. "Yes. It's just . . . well, you can probably imagine."

"Not really," I admitted. "I mean, I can't imagine living here."

Her eyes met mine, and there was so much grief there that I could hardly bear to see it. "Neither can I."

We stood in silence. Mrs. Greco's nose got reddish, and she sniffled, but she didn't cry. "I have so much *stuff.*" Now she did begin to cry a little, but she kept talking. "There's so much stuff. My sister is going to help me pack it up and donate it, but before I do, I don't know if there's anything you want. Of Olivia's. I thought you could go upstairs and see."

It was yet another request I couldn't see refusing. "Um, sure," I said. I put my glass on the table, and even though the last place in the world I wanted to be was Olivia's room, I went upstairs anyway. I'd assumed Mrs. Greco would follow me, but she didn't.

Maybe she didn't want to be up there either.

Slowly I made my way up the Grecos' staircase. I had done this every day of my life, it seemed, sometimes several times a day. It was so familiar—the smooth banister under my hand, the creak of the loose step that we'd learned to hop when we were little so we could sneak downstairs for treats late at night when her parents thought we were asleep. I started to get butterflies in my stomach, and I actually ran the last few steps to Olivia's room. It wasn't until I pushed open her door that I realized why I'd been excited. It was like my dream all over again. Olivia should have been sitting on her bed. *I'm so glad to see you! I thought you were dead.*

I'm not dead, silly. I'm right here.

But of course she *was* dead. Which was why she wasn't in her room when I pushed open the door.

I looked around. Nothing, as far as I could see, had been touched. Her books were on the shelf. The photos of her were on the walls. Her bed was made with the comforter that had come home from the hospital with her; her bedside lamp sat on her bedside table. Even the schedule for the first day of school was still tacked to the corkboard. It fluttered slightly in the breeze from my opening the door.

What did Mrs. Greco think I was going to take? Olivia's clock radio? Her statue of an elephant that one of her cousins had sent her when he was in India? Her poster of the five ballet positions? How could I possibly take any of it? It was all Livvie's.

Still, I walked inside, my footsteps muffled by the plush carpet I'd helped Olivia pick. I didn't want to touch anything. I didn't want to change anything. I understood now why people created shrines to the dead, and I wished the Grecos wouldn't sell the house, that they would never sell the house, that I would be able—someday—to bring my daughter here so she could see Olivia's room exactly as it was now, exactly as it had been when she was alive. It would be a museum of Olivia, and whenever I wanted to, I could come back and be surrounded by her.

I pulled open her closet door, the light automatically going on when the little button was released. Was there one article of clothing in it I didn't recognize? I stroked the dress she'd worn the night we went out for my birthday. I could still see her sitting across the table from me. *One day our lives are going to be amazing, Zoe. Totally amazing.*

It was hard for me to see through my tears, but as I turned to walk out of her closet, I spotted, high up on a shelf, Olivia's memory box.

I stared up at it, studying its intricate geometric pattern. Inside was Olivia's whole history. The whole history of our life together. It was the closest thing to a shrine I was going to get, and I pulled her desk chair into the closet, climbed up on it, and grabbed the box.

Downstairs, Mrs. Greco said she was glad I'd found something to take. Then she hugged me tightly. "You'll always be a part of this family."

I nodded, but I didn't see how what she was saying could

be true. It seemed to me that what bound us together wasn't love or blood but a kind of infinite grief. Being together didn't soothe that grief for me; it intensified it, as if grief expanded exponentially. My grief alone was *almost* unbearable. My grief plus Mrs. Greco's *was* unbearable.

I was tempted to ask her if it helped to believe in God, but I kind of knew the answer already. Nothing helped. Not God. Not picturing Olivia in a better place. Not telling yourself you should be grateful for all the good times you had together.

There is nothing that makes the unbearable bearable.

Instead, I hugged her back and thanked her for letting me take the memory box. Then, though it was almost too big for me to get my arms all the way around it, I picked it up and headed out the door of Olivia's house for the very last time.

❧ 42 ❧

The tree branches hanging over my back deck made it shady and cool, and I sat at the picnic table going through Olivia's memory box all afternoon.

It was crazy the stuff that she'd kept. There must have been a hundred programs, one for every ballet we'd ever been to. Ticket stubs. Dried flowers from performances we'd given. Unlike Olivia's drawers, the box wasn't in any kind of order. Underneath the program from our eighth-grade graduation was a picture we'd ripped out of *Dwell* magazine freshman year. It was of a penthouse apartment in the West Village. The photographer had stood on the enormous roof deck and shot the apartment through a wall of windows. On the elegant white sofa in the middle of the stark living room, Olivia had drawn two stick figures. Above one she'd written *Zoe*, and above the other she'd written *Livvie*. Leaning against the sleek kitchen counter were two more stick figures, and above them I had written *Our hot boyfriends!!!*

I started to laugh. Next I came to a bright yellow Post-it that said, in Livvie's handwriting, *Definitely!* and below that, in mine, *Not!*

Definitely what? Definitely not what?

If she were alive, I could have called her.

If she were alive, I wouldn't have been sitting here alone going through the box of memories of our friendship.

I stopped laughing.

The Post-it was stuck to a shoe box, and I slipped that out of the bigger box, planning to open it. But when I lifted the shoe box, I found a thin box wrapped in pale gray tissue paper. Across the front, in blue pen, Olivia had written *Happy Birthday, Zoe.*

As if she were there, I saw Olivia sitting across the table from me at the restaurant the night of my birthday.

It's not something you messed up. It's something I messed up. It's your present. By the time I figured out what I wanted to give you, I didn't have time to make it.

You're making me something?

Maybe . . .

Hand shaking, I pulled the package from the bottom of the box and carefully unwrapped it. Inside, there was a layer of tissue paper, and when I moved it aside, I found myself looking at a framed collage composed of dozens of pictures of me and Livvie.

They stretched back to the beginning of our friendship. There was one of us from when we were about seven or eight, taken in front of the Wamasset movie theater before it had been closed and reopened as an American Apparel. There was one of us eating pizza at the place around the corner from NYBC where we'd gotten slices and club sodas at least four times a week for years. There was one of us at about eleven, squinting into the sun, sitting in the motorboat her dad had had for a couple of summers before he'd decided it was too much work and money and not enough payoff and he'd sold it.

In every single picture, we were wearing a variation on the exact same color scheme. In the one from the pizza parlor, I had on a blue tank top; Olivia had on a white one. In the one from the boat, I was wearing a white T-shirt with a blue collar and Olivia was wearing a dark blue dress with a thin white stripe. In the center of the collage was the photo of the two of us from the first day of school this year, both of us wearing blue-and-white T-shirts, both of us smiling into the camera, both of us blissfully unaware of the bomb that was about to explode our lives.

I ran my fingers over the photos, as if the joy we had felt when they were taken might be something I could touch.

"I love you, Livs," I whispered, brushing away the tears on

my cheeks before they could fall on the pictures. "I love you so much."

I put the collage down, and saw there was something still in the box. It was an envelope. There was nothing written on the front, but I slid the flap open and pulled out a card that had a photo of two girls in tutus on the front. One of the girls had blond hair and one had black. Each of them was holding a bouquet of roses almost as big as she was. They were facing each other and laughing, and they looked so much like me and Olivia that it hurt my heart to see them.

I flipped open the card.

Inside was a letter from Olivia.

Her handwriting—as familiar to me as her face—covered the shiny interior in slanting, neatly formed letters.

Dear Zoe,

My hands were shaking so much I could barely hold the card, and I had to set it down on the table to read what she'd written.

As you can see from these photos, for almost a decade we have been trapped in a tragic fashion Groundhog Day. Please promise me you won't wear white or blue (or white and blue) quite so regularly in the future.

I'm so grateful that I got to have thirteen amazing

years with you. And I'm sorry I won't be there to see your life, but I know it's going to be fantastic. Do not forget to have plenty of day-into-evening wear. Do not forget to have extra adventures since you will have to have them for me, too.

I've been thinking about what we said about heaven, and I think heaven would be a place where you could still somehow remember things that happened when you were alive. I wish I knew for sure, but I can't really imagine a place where I'd exist without remembering us.

I found this quote that I wanted to share with you. (No pressure or anything. I just thought you might find it interesting.) It's by Merce Cunningham.

"You have to love dancing to stick to it. It gives you nothing back, no manuscripts to store away, no paintings to show on walls and maybe hang in museums, no poems to be printed and sold, nothing but that single fleeting moment when you feel alive."

Whether you dance or not, I hope you feel alive your whole life, Zoe.

I love you.
Olivia

Taped to the card just beneath her signature and tied to each other with a thin red ribbon were two locks of hair. One was the one I had saved the day we'd shaved her head.

The other was mine. When the woman at Hair Today Gone Tomorrow had asked if I wanted to save a lock of my hair, I'd said no.

But Livvie had taken it.

I was crying so hard I couldn't even finish the letter at first. I just kept reading a word or two and sobbing and putting it down and catching my breath. Then I'd start reading again and the same thing would happen. It must have taken me half an hour to just get through the letter once. And then I had to read it over and over again. I read it so many times I almost memorized it. Flavia came over and sat beside me, and I just rubbed his head and cried and read Olivia's letter.

Finally I couldn't sit there crying anymore. I snapped on his leash, and we walked for a long, long time. I wished Olivia and I had had some special place that we'd used to go so I could take Flavia there, but we didn't. Except maybe the fortress, and I didn't want to go there. But I wanted to be with Olivia. I wanted to be someplace that was so much a part of me and Olivia that being there would make me feel like I was still with her. I missed her so much and I was never going to see her again.

And suddenly I had a sharp, bright picture of sitting across the table from Livvie the last time I'd seen her before she'd relapsed. She'd been talking on the phone with Mrs. Jones, and then she'd hung up and tried to get me to teach the dance class with her next year.

Was that where Livvie was? In dancing?

I remembered the first class I'd taught with her, back in the fall when she was still well enough to Skype, and how at the end of the class, I'd felt as if I'd spent an hour surrounded by ghosts.

Maybe being surrounded by ghosts wasn't such a bad thing.

Maybe that was what Mrs. Jones had meant when she'd asked how I was going to honor Olivia's memory—maybe she'd been asking if I could handle spending a little time with some ghosts.

We turned onto my driveway, and I let Flavia off his leash. When he started barking like crazy, I raised my head to see what he was barking at, and that's when I saw Calvin sitting on the front steps of my house. His car was parked in my driveway. I'd been so lost in thought I hadn't even noticed it.

I made my way slowly up the steep drive. He didn't get up, just sat there, letting Flavia jump all over him.

"Be careful," I warned Calvin from a few feet away. "He can be pretty vicious."

"I can tell," he said, patting Flavia on the head.

Flavia let out a little whine and sat down on the step next to Calvin. He was wearing a gray T-shirt and a pair of cargo shorts, and he was ever so slightly tan.

He looked great.

"Hi," he said, looking right into my eyes.

"Hi," I said. I couldn't quite look at him, so I studied a spot just past his shoulder.

"How was your walk?" he asked.

I toyed with Flavia's leash, running its rough edge through my fingers. "I was thinking about Olivia," I said. "And about dancing."

"What about it?" Calvin scratched him behind the ears as Flavia barked happily.

"I don't know exactly. I think . . ." I wrapped the leash around my hand a couple of times, still not looking at Calvin. "I think I might not be done with it."

"Yeah," said Calvin. "I could see that."

I forced myself to finally meet his eyes. He was looking at me. I could feel my chin start to quiver. "I just miss her so much, Calvin."

"I know," he said, but when he stood up to come to me, Flavia started barking.

"Jesus, Flavia, enough!" I snapped.

Calvin gently nudged him off the step, keeping his hand on Flavia's head and scratching him. Then he reached his other hand up to mine. After a second, I took it and let him pull me down onto the step. Only our hands were touching, but I could feel the warmth of his body next to mine.

"When do you leave for Middlebury?" I asked, swiping at my nose with the back of my hand.

"Actually . . ." He hesitated. "I decided to defer for a year."

"Seriously?" I turned to look at him.

He met my eyes for a second, then looked away. "Yeah. I'm going to be doing this thing with building houses for about six months. My parents thought it would be good for me to have a year before college. You know." He made a deep, dad voice. "'Get a little life experience.' I don't know. I kind of like the idea. After everything that happened this year." He shrugged. "Jake says he's ready to get away, but . . . I don't know if I could really give a shit about college right now."

I thought of how hard it must have been to be Jake's best friend this year. I remembered that first day in the hospital, how I'd wished it had been Jake instead of Olivia who'd gotten sick. Like death didn't touch you if you were a couple of degrees removed from it.

I'd been such an idiot.

"Yeah," I said slowly. "I think I can see that." I threw the end of the leash out in front of me, as if I were fishing on my driveway. "So where are you going? Africa? Ecuador?" Rich kids from Wamasset were always spending their summers helping people in Latin America and Kenya build schools and houses or start small businesses. It was like the *ultimate* for college applications. *My summer in Quito and how it changed my life . . .*

Eyes on the blacktop, Calvin said, "Ah no. I'll be in Philly." Philadelphia was about an hour from where we lived.

I stared at him. "Oh my God," I said. I said it really quietly.

"What?" he asked, finally turning to face me. Flavia barked with annoyance, but both of us ignored him.

"I . . . when you said that, I was happy. I mean, just for a second. I felt . . ." I could feel my eyes filling with tears. "I felt happy."

"Clearly," said Calvin. He laughed, then reached over and wiped my wet cheeks. I stopped him, taking his hand in both of mine. Touching him—even though it was just holding his hand—felt good. *Really* good. I let my mind search, like when I had a loose tooth and my tongue would seek it out and wiggle it. There it was. Poking through the detritus left by the horrible ice storm of the past year. A tiny green shoot.

A tiny green shoot of happy.

I was still holding Calvin's hand in both of mine. He slipped his other arm around my shoulder and we looked at each other. Then he pulled me to him. He kissed the top of my head, and I squeezed his hand tightly in mine.

We sat like that for a long time, not talking.

Just being together.

❧ acknowledgments ❧

This is a work of fiction. Whenever possible I used accurate medical information, but when I had to make a choice, I chose story over the realities of cancer treatment. Though it is not discussed in the novel, I want readers to know that the vast majority (approximately 70 percent) of pediatric cancer patients survive. As advances in treatment continue, there is every reason not just to hope but to assume that these statistics will only improve.

This book would not have been possible without people who gave above and beyond the call of work, friendship, and love. I am tremendously grateful to Dr. Fein-Levy, Dr. Amy Glaser, Emily Jenkins, Bernie Kaplan, Barbara Kass, Sarah Lutz, Louise Maxwell, Julie Reed, Dr. Blythe Thomson, and Lilah Van Rens.

Rachel Cohn, Rebecca Friedman, Helen Perelman, and JillEllyn Riley were indefatigable champions and gentle critics. Jennifer Klonsky believed in this idea from the first (and with a great deal of hard work made it an idea worth believing in). A shout-out to Cara Petrus, Karen Sherman, Catherine Wallace, and all the other folks at HarperTeen for their amazing work.

Saint Ann's has been my home for almost twenty years, a miracle for which I am so, so eternally grateful.

Finally, let it be known that Ben Gantcher makes everything possible.

In addition to the people thanked above, I would like to express my gratitude to the staff and doctors at the Fred Hutchinson Cancer Research Center for the superb care they took of my father, Dr. Shepard Kantor, when he was undergoing a bone marrow transplant there.

For more information or to find out about how you can help fight leukemia, contact the Leukemia and Lymphoma Society at www.lls.org.

EXTRAS

maybe
one
day

What's in a Name (or, *How There Are No Cheerleaders in Heaven* Became *Maybe One Day*)

Top Ten Best Friend Songs

What's in a Name
(or, *How There Are No Cheerleaders in Heaven* Became *Maybe One Day)*

When I first sold the book about Olivia and Zoe, it was called *There Are No Cheerleaders in Heaven*, and it was about two girls who are cheerleaders and best friends and what happens to them when one of them gets leukemia. I knew a lot about these two girls: I knew that Zoe was the bitter, dark, angry one and Olivia was the sunny, optimistic one. I knew that Olivia had a crush on a boy Zoe thought was a jerk. I knew that Olivia's illness was going to challenge and change Zoe in ways she could not bear. I had an outline of the story, and on a cold February day, I sat down to start it.

And I sat. And I sat. I stared at the screen. I wrote a sentence. I deleted it. I wrote a different sentence. I deleted that one. I got up. I sat down. I wrote a few more sentences. They were terrible. I got up and ate some chips and reread the sentences. Yup. Still terrible.

The problem, I decided, was that I didn't know enough about cheerleading. The problem, I decided, was that I needed to educate myself. And because I had always been a good student, that's what I set out to do. I called people I knew and had them put me in touch with cheerleaders *they* knew. I watched YouTube videos about cheerleading. I rewatched *Bring It On*, and I ordered books about cheerleading and cheers and how to be a cheer squad captain from my local bookstore and the library. I read. I watched. I sat down to write.

And everything I wrote was still really, *really* terrible.

When I conceived of this book, I conceived of a narrator who was bitter and angry, who thought high school was a waste of time and that the people she was surrounded by were idiots. That was Zoe. Her best friend, Olivia, understood how she felt, but she was better at fitting in, and she wasn't nearly so cynical. The problem was, neither of these girls was a cheerleader. It's not because cheerleaders can't be cynical. Or edgy. Or angry. But you can't be a cheerleader and think high school is a waste of time or that anyone who spends his afternoons tackling his friends because they've got a wad of pigskin in their arms is an idiot. To be a cheerleader (even to be a *bad* cheerleader), you've got to have at least a modicum of school spirit.

Zoe did not have a modicum of school spirit. Over the course of the novel, she learns to appreciate what the kids at her school have to offer. And she comes to see that she was too quick to dismiss people who weren't as cynical (she would probably say *worldly*) as she is. But when the book starts, she doesn't think the kids at Wamasset High have anything to teach her and she *certainly* doesn't think the cheerleaders do.

As a writer, I was always suspicious when other writers said their characters had a life of their own, that they—the writer—couldn't make a character do something the character didn't want to do. *Don't be ridiculous,* I'd think. *They're fictional characters. You can make them do anything.*

But it turns out, I was wrong. Try as I might to make her a cheerleader, Zoe refused to be one. February became March and March became April and she *still* wouldn't be a cheerleader. And so, sometime in May, she became a dancer. And she loved dancing, even when she was told she wasn't good enough to be a professional. Dance was in her bones. It defined her. And once it defined Zoe, it defined Olivia, who became a dancer right along with her. Because that's what best friends do for each other.

Top Ten Best Friend Songs

1. "Bridge over Troubled Water," Simon and Garfunkel. Sure, it's older than you are. But that's what makes it a classic. Turn up the volume, call your best friend, and play it for her over the phone. That's the old school way to listen to a song with your BFF.

2. "Right by Your Side," The Eurythmics. Is it a love song or a best friend song? Crank this one up and dance around the room with your best friend while you're getting ready to go out, and you'll realize the real question is, *Is there a difference?*

3. "With a Little Help from My Friends," The Beatles. Try the Joe Cocker variation to put some soul in this one.

4. "Lean on Me," Bill Withers. When it comes right down to it, this is what you and your BFF say to each other every day.

5. "Girls' Room," Liz Phair. The whole song takes less than two minutes, but it's everything you ever wanted to say about sleeping over at your best friend's house (but couldn't quite find the words to say it with).

6. "Count on Me," Bruno Mars. "You'll always have my shoulder when you cry / I'll never let go / never say goodbye." Because best friends really *are* forever.

7. "I Kissed a Girl," Katy Perry. Sometimes best friends kiss and like it. Got a problem with that?

8. "Seasons of Love," Jonathan Larson. Because if you have to measure a year in your life, there's no better way to measure it than in minutes spent with your best friend.

9. "Goodbye Earl," Dixie Chicks. If your best friend married a really bad dude, you'd help her get away from him, right? (Even if the only way to do that involved, well, murder.) Sure you would!

10. "You've Got a Friend," Carole King. Here's how you know she's your best friend: no matter where you are, no matter what time it is, if you need her, she'll be knocking upon your door. Like the song says, all you've gotta do is call.

 1

"I'm going to miss you."

Jason's arms were around me so tightly I could barely breathe, but lack of oxygen wasn't the reason I didn't say anything. If I tried to talk I was definitely going to embarrass myself by bawling, so I just nodded.

He kissed the top of my head. "Don't think of it as being stuck at home. Think of it as a chance to study so you can kick my ass on the SATs."

"Sure, but will my perfect score come between us?" I asked, my cheek still pressed against his chest. Jason had scored a 2380 on his SATs, just shy of a perfect 2400. Those twenty points were a sore spot with him, and if I ever wanted to get him riled up, all I had to do was get a sad look on my face, sigh, and ask what it was like to have gotten *so close* to perfection.

"I'm man enough to handle it," he assured me.

Neither of us said anything about why I'd gotten a crap score on my June SATs, which I'd taken a week after my father broke the news to my mother that he was leaving her, just like neither of us said anything about the reason I wasn't going on a family vacation this year.

Neither of us said anything about how it's hard to go on a family vacation when you don't have a family anymore.

Since there was nothing to say, I stood on tiptoe and kissed him lightly on the lips.

"I'm going to need way more than that to get me through the next two weeks," he said. His hands on my hips were warmer than the August afternoon, and we kissed again, harder. Jason and I had been kissing since eighth grade, when he came up to me at Max Pinto's spin-the-bottle party and asked me if I'd done the English homework.

Which is how nerds fall in love.

I heard the click of the front door, and then Jason's mom called, "Okay, you two. Jason, it's time."

"Hey, Mom. I was just telling Juliet that you changed your mind about the international phone plan and she can text me as much as she wants."

Grace laughed and ran her fingers through her hair, which was dyed the same dirty blond that Jason's hair was naturally. "Try it and spend the rest of the year paying me back," she said. "Remember," Grace added, "absence makes the heart grow fonder." She glanced at the thin gold watch on her wrist. "And . . . we've gotta go. We'll miss you, Juliet." After my dad moved out, Grace had asked me if I wanted her to ask my parents if I could join the Robinsons on their vacation, but I'd told her I couldn't miss the end of my internship at Children United. I'd competed against kids from all over the world

2

to get accepted, and my English teacher who'd written my recommendation for the summer was also writing my recommendation for college. I told Grace that if he found out I'd ditched the program, he might not write my rec in the fall. My reason was a lie, but it was plausible enough that she just smiled and told me how impressed she was by my living up to my responsibilities.

Living up to your responsibilities was a big deal to Jason's mom.

I was embarrassed by how my throat got tight when she said she'd miss me, and I forced myself to give her a cheerful wave and a jaunty "bon voyage."

She waved back. Jason's mother was always beautifully dressed, and today she wore a simple but flattering red linen dress and a pair of red-and-white strappy sandals. The whole ensemble was *tres Français*. "Let's go, Jason," she said again.

As soon as she shut the door, Jason put his arms around me. I leaned against him, trying not to see the next two weeks as a black hole I was getting sucked down into.

"You're gonna be okay," he said quietly.

Lost in my own thoughts, I wasn't quite listening to him, which seemed to happen to me a lot lately. "It's all so weird. Like, who am I now?"

Jason stepped away from me and took my shoulders in his hands. "J, that's crazy. You're still you."

"I don't know, J," I said. My eyes hit Jason right at his

collarbone, and I didn't lift them to his face. I tried to find the words to explain what I was feeling. "You know that thing where you look at your hand and suddenly you're like, 'It's so weird that that's my hand.'"

"Stop." Jason's voice was commanding. Confident. It was his debating voice, the one that had won our team the regional championship last spring. He let go of my shoulders and lifted my chin. His dark gray eyes stared into mine as he enumerated points on his fingers. "One: you're a third-generation legacy. Two: you've got a 4.0 average. Three: you're one of ten Children United interns *in the whole world*. Four: you're going to spend every second while I'm away studying for your SATs, on which you will get a *near*-perfect score." I hip-checked him on that . "Next year, when we're at Harvard, this will all seem like a bad dream." When he said *Harvard*, he tapped me lightly on the nose. That was our plan: to get into Harvard early action.

Jason was our lead debater, but I was no slouch. I thought of countering his points one by one. *First: half the kids applying to Harvard are legacies. Second: there are thousands of applicants with 4.0 averages. Third: my internship has consisted of reading useless reports, summarizing them for no one, and sitting in on endless lectures delivered to nearly empty rooms. Fourth: every time I try to sit down and study for the SATs, the words just swim around on the page.*

But I didn't want our last few seconds together to consist of my whining. Instead, all I said was, "Hey! Don't jinx Harvard." I was superstitious about our acceptance, which

4

was why, while he was wearing a white T-shirt that spelled out *HARVARD* in red letters, I'd made him remove the Harvard bumper sticker that he'd put on my Amazon wish list.

The front door opened again, and Grace stuck her head out. "Jason! In the car! Now!"

You didn't mess with Grace when she said *Now!* like that. Jason opened his arms, and I slipped into them, hugging him back as tightly as he was hugging me, hoping some of his optimism about senior year—which was only two and a half weeks away—would enter my body by osmosis.

The jerk of the garage door rising was followed by the car honking as Mark backed the Lexus into the driveway. Isabella, Jason's little sister, rolled down her window and shouted, "Bye, Juliet! Bye! We'll miss you."

"Bye, Bella," I called back. I'd always wished I had a little sister; Jason and I had been together since Bella was six, so sometimes it felt almost like I had one.

His dad gave me a little salute. "Take care of yourself, Juliet," he said. Mark Robinson was always saying dad things. *Take care of yourself. Drive carefully. Do you kids need any money?* His saying that made me think of my own dad and how my mother said he was having a midlife crisis. My dad, on the other hand, said it was more complicated than that, that they'd both been unhappy for a long time. My older brother said I shouldn't even bother trying to figure out what was going on with them, that I had to focus on school because if my grades dropped first semester senior year, I was screwed with colleges.

Apparently everybody understood and accepted what was going on with my family except me.

Jason gave me one last squeeze, and then he linked his pinky with mine. "J power," he said, gently squeezing.

I smiled and squeezed his pinky back. "J power," I echoed. Then he let go and headed toward the car. I stood on Jason's perfect lawn in front of Jason's perfect house and watched the car carrying his perfect family back down the driveway, and then—with Mark honking the horn good-bye—I watched it drive down the block, turn the corner, and disappear.

Pulling up into my own driveway ten minutes later, I had to admit that my house looked just as perfect as Jason's. The gardeners and the pool guy still showed up right on schedule, so it wasn't like in the movies where you know the family inside is falling apart because the grass is waist high and weeds are growing everywhere.

But as soon as I got out of the car, I could tell my mother was having a Bad Day. Exhibit A: it was a beautiful August afternoon, yet all the shades in the house were drawn. Ever since my dad had moved out, my mother had Good Days and Bad Days. On Good Days, she met friends for tennis, went for lunch, shopped. Maybe had a committee meeting.

On Bad Days, the shades stayed down. And so did she.

Bad Days were the real reason I hadn't gone to France with Jason's family.

"Mom?" I pushed open the front door. My whole life, my house had had the same smell—I'd always assumed it was some combination of my mom's perfume and this lavender-scented powder she had the housekeeper sprinkle on the rugs before she vacuumed. But now the house smelled ever so slightly different, and I'd started to wonder if what it had smelled like before hadn't been plain old happiness.

"Mom?" I called again.

I heard a faint response from the direction of my parents' bedroom. Or I guess I should say my mother's bedroom, since my dad had a new bedroom in his new apartment in Manhattan.

I walked up the stairs, passing the pale squares that lined the walls in place of the family photos that used to hang there. My mother had always been astonishingly organized. The minute there was the hint of a chill in the air, I came home to find my T-shirts replaced with sweaters, my shorts replaced with jeans, my sundresses in plastic bags at the back of my closet. So it wasn't exactly shocking that she spent the weekend after my father left removing evidence of our happy family from the walls. The surprising thing was that she hadn't already had the walls repainted and hung with replacement art.

I walked down the hallway to my mom's bedroom, my eyes on her door, forcing myself not to look at the gallery of blank squares that lined the hall. My mom's room smelled even worse than the rest of the house, as if the air in there were thicker somehow, or maybe just unhappier. The shades were pulled so low there was barely enough light to make out her shape on the bed.

"Mom?" I asked into the darkness. And then I said it again, more sharply this time. "Mom?"

There was a rustling of sheets, and one of my mother's arms stretched up over her head. "Hi, honey," she yawned.

"Mom, I thought you were getting up when I left." I tried to make my voice light, as if I were joking, not mad. Then I crossed the room, snapped up the shade, and opened the window.

"What time is it?" she asked.

I looked at her bedside clock. "Almost four."

"Sorry." She covered her mouth and yawned again. "My back was killing me, so I took a muscle relaxant. It must have really knocked me out. Have you been home long?"

Since June, I'd watched my mom—who used to know my schedule better than I did—try to fudge her way through conversations about my life. I'd first realized what she was doing when I came home after taking my SATs and she asked me how my morning had gone, clearly having no idea where I'd been. Over the summer she'd gotten cagier. She asked open-ended questions or offered up general statements that made it seem as if she was respecting my privacy when really she had

8

no idea how I was spending my time.

"I was at Sofia's. We spent the day shooting smack and hacking into people's bank accounts for cash."

"Ha-ha," said my mom, and then she added, "How could you be a hacker? You can't even remember the alarm code." At least she was trying to be funny. I gave her a smile. A for effort.

She shook her head and sat up against her pillows, reaching for a small bottle of pills on her bedside table. My mom had always taken medication—she had insomnia, so she sometimes took something to help her sleep. And whenever she had to do a presentation for this charity she was on the board of, she took something called a beta blocker so she wouldn't (as she put it) "sweat through my dress and then pass out." And her back bothered her sometimes, so she had a prescription for the muscle relaxant she'd apparently taken earlier.

There had been bottles of pills in her bathroom for as long as I could remember. But now her nightstand sported a veritable pharmacy: She had drugs that were supposed to help her sleep and drugs that were supposed to help her wake up. There were drugs she was supposed to take to not feel anxious and drugs she was supposed to take to not feel sad. But no matter how many pills she took, there were still days like this one, where no matter what time I came home, she was in bed.

"So where were you really?" she asked after swallowing a small blue pill.

"Mom, you know where I was. I was saying good-bye to

9

Jason. They're leaving for France."

My mom rubbed her forehead. "I'm sorry, honey. I'm just so . . . fuzzy." And then she squeezed her eyes tightly as her voice broke. "I'm sorry we're not going on vacation this year." A tear slid out from between her lids, and she bit her lip. "I'm so sorry about everything."

This happened on Bad Days. On Good Days, I'd come home and my mother would be full of plans for the future: She was going to go back to work. She was going to redo the house. We were going to go on a cruise at Christmas. Some of the things she talked about doing really sounded fun, and I'd eat dinner imagining my mother returning to her job as a consultant, which she'd done before I was born, or picturing her and Oliver and me on a flight to Seattle, where we'd board a ship bound for Alaska. Other times, her ideas were tedious, like when she'd show me a dozen swatches of blue fabric and ask which one I thought would be best for the couch.

Still, anything was better than this. Bad Days just sucked.

"Mom, it's okay." I crossed over to the bed, sat down, and put my arm over her shoulders. She patted my hand and sniffled while I looked around the room. Even with the shades and the window up, it felt like a prison. I pictured Oliver, who'd stayed up at Yale for the summer and who'd texted me yesterday that he was going camping with friends for the week. I wondered if my dad had canceled the reservation we'd made for the house in Maine that we rented every

10

summer or if he was planning to go without us, to walk the familiar floors of the house by himself. I imagined Jason getting out of the car in the airport's long-term parking lot, the sound of jet engines revving, assured he'd be thirty thousand feet up in the air soon.

How come everyone had a get-out-of-jail-free card except me?

I got to my feet. "Why don't I make us a salad?" I said. "I'll put lots of fruit in the way you like it."

"I don't know if there's much in the fridge," said my mom. She looked at me apologetically, and I noticed how much gray there was in the roots of her hair. My parents had been a very good-looking couple. I'm not just saying that because they're my parents. My mom's hair was long and blond. (It had been naturally blond when she was younger, and as she got older and it got darker, she highlighted it.) She and my dad were in great shape, and they both wore expensive, designer clothes. My mom always liked it when I told her that one of my friends had said she was well-dressed or beautiful, which happened pretty regularly.

Right now, though, with her strangely bisected hair and her wrinkled T-shirt and yoga pants, my mom wasn't going to be getting compliments from my friends anytime soon. She just looked tired. Tired and a little bit old.

"If there's nothing in the fridge, we can order." I didn't want to look at her thinking about how old and tired she seemed, so I turned and went to the door. "I think you should take a shower and get dressed."

Because on Bad Days, I sounded like the mom.

"You're right, honey," she said. I heard her pull a tissue from the box on her bedside table and blow her nose.

"Mom, it's gonna be okay," I promised her. I could hear the irritation in my voice, and I wondered if she heard it too.

"I know," she squeaked. "I know, honey." She took some tissues out of the dispenser, one after the other in rapid succession, then blew her nose. "I'll be okay. Just let me shower and I'll come down."

"I'll see what we have to eat," I said. I waited to close the door behind me until she flipped the covers off her legs and got out of bed.

There was a blank rectangle on the wall immediately to the right of my parents' bedroom door; I didn't need to see the photo that had hung there to remember it. It was of my father, taken the day he and Oliver came home from their first father-son camping trip. My dad had a three-day growth of beard, and he was standing by the door of our old Subaru, a backpack in one hand, a fishing rod in the other. He looked like a man who could handle anything. He looked like a man who could *fix* anything.

I want my dad, I thought to myself. *I want my dad to fix this.*

But I knew he wasn't going to be able to. After all, his leaving was the reason everything was broken in the first place.

JOIN THE
Epic Reads
COMMUNITY

THE ULTIMATE YA DESTINATION

◀ **DISCOVER** ▶
your next favorite read

◀ **FIND** ▶
new authors to love

◀ **WIN** ▶
free books

◀ **SHARE** ▶
infographics, playlists, quizzes, and more

◀ **WATCH** ▶
the latest videos

◀ **TUNE IN** ▶
to Tea Time with Team Epic Reads